D0956983

**MARVEL UNIVERSE ULTIMATE SPIDER-MAN: WEB WARRIORS VOL. 2.** Contains material originally published in magazine form as MARVEL UNIVERSE ULTIMATE SPIDER-MAN: WEB WARRIORS #5-8. First printing 2015. ISBN# 978-0-7851-9384-5. Published by MARVEL WORLDWIDE, INC., a subsidiary of MARVEL ENTERTAINMENT, LLC. OFFICE OF PUBLICATION: 135 West 50th Street, New York, NY 10020. Copyright © 2015 MARVEL No similarity between any of the names, characters, persons, and/or institutions in this magazine with those of any living or dead person or institution is intended, and any such similarity which may exist is purely coincidental. **Printed in the U.S.A.** ALAN FINE, President, Marvel Entertainment; DAN BUCKLEY, President, TV, Publishing and Brand Management; JOE QUESADA, Chief Creative Officer; TOM BREVOORT, SVP of Publishing; DAVID BOGART, SVP of Operations & Procurement, Publishing; C.B. CEBULSKI, VP of International Development & Brand Management; DAVID GABRIEL, SVP Print, Sales & Marketing; JIM O'KEEFE, VP of Operations & Logistics; DAN CARR, Executive Director of Publishing Technology; SUSAN CRESPI, Editorial Operations Manager; ALEX MORALES, Publishing Operations Manager; STAN LEE, Chairman Emeritus. For information regarding advertising in Marvel Comics or on Marvel.com, please contact Jonathan Rheingold, VP of Custom Solutions & Ad Sales, at jrheingold@ marvel.com. For Marvel subscription inquiries, please call 800-217-9158. **Manufactured between 6/19/2015 and 7/27/2015 by SHERIDAN BOOKS, INC., CHELSEA, MI, USA.**

10 9 8 7 6 5 4 3 2 1

# MARVEL
# ULTIMATE SPIDER-MAN
# WEB-WARRIORS

**BASED ON THE TV SERIES WRITTEN BY**
*MAN OF ACTION, JACOB SEMAHN, BRIAN MICHAEL BENDIS, JOE FALLON & ED VALENTINE*

**DIRECTED BY**
*ROY BURDINE, PHIL PIGNOTTI & TIM MALTBY*

**ADAPTED BY**
*JOE CARAMAGNA*

**EDITOR**
*SEBASTIAN GIRNER*

**CONSULTING EDITORS**
*JON MOISAN & MARK BASSO*

**SENIOR EDITOR**
*MARK PANICCIA*

**SPIDER-MAN CREATED BY STAN LEE & STEVE DITKO**

Collection Editor: **Alex Starbuck**
Assistant Editor: **Sarah Brunstad**
Editors, Special Projects: **Jennifer Grünwald & Mark D. Beazley**
Senior Editor, Special Projects: **Jeff Youngquist**
SVP Print, Sales & Marketing: **David Gabriel**
Head of Marvel Television: **Jeph Loeb**

Editor In Chief: **Axel Alonso**
Chief Creative Officer: **Joe Quesada**
Publisher: **Dan Buckley**
Executive Producer: **Alan Fine**

**SPECIAL THANKS TO PRODUCT FACTORY**

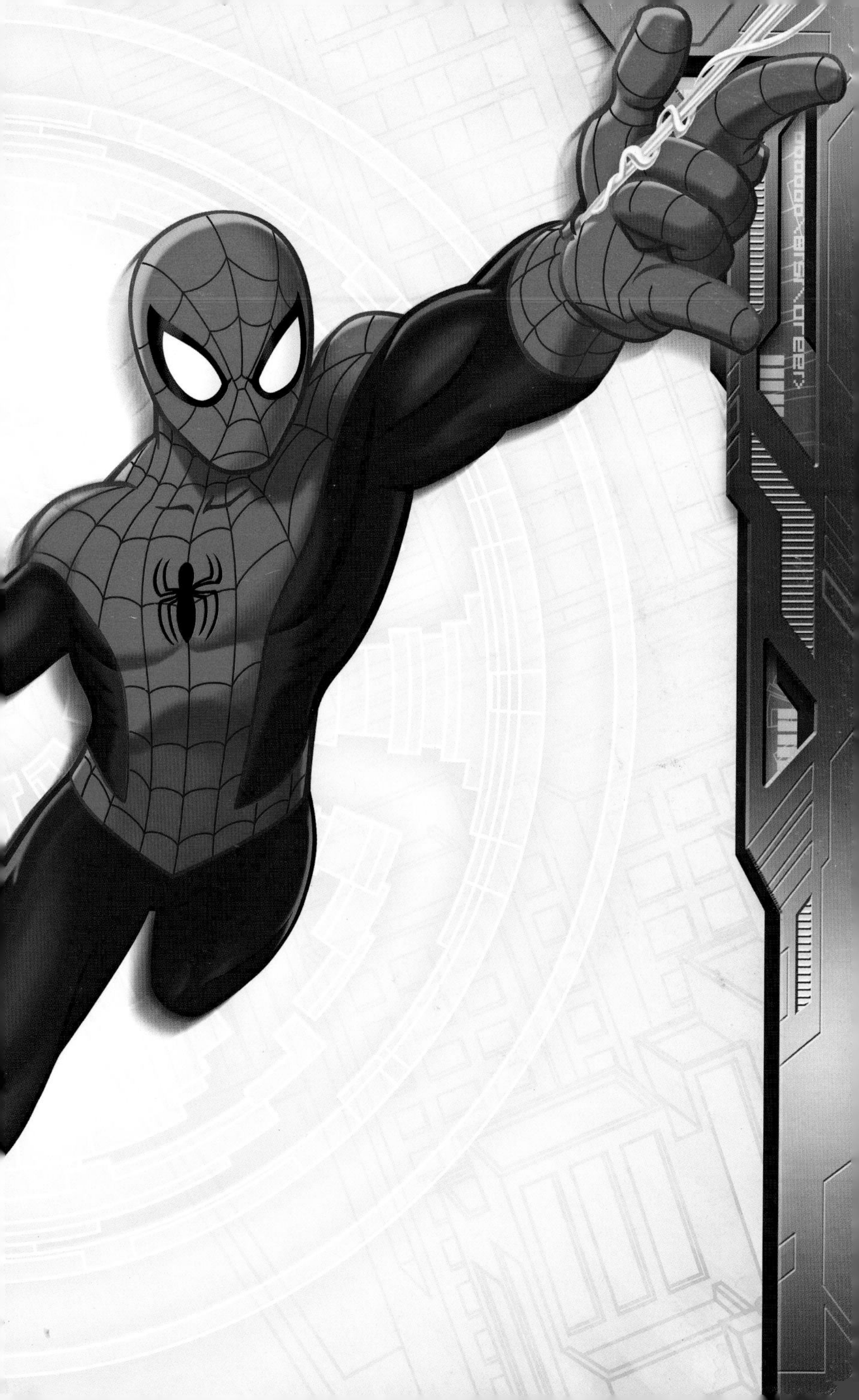

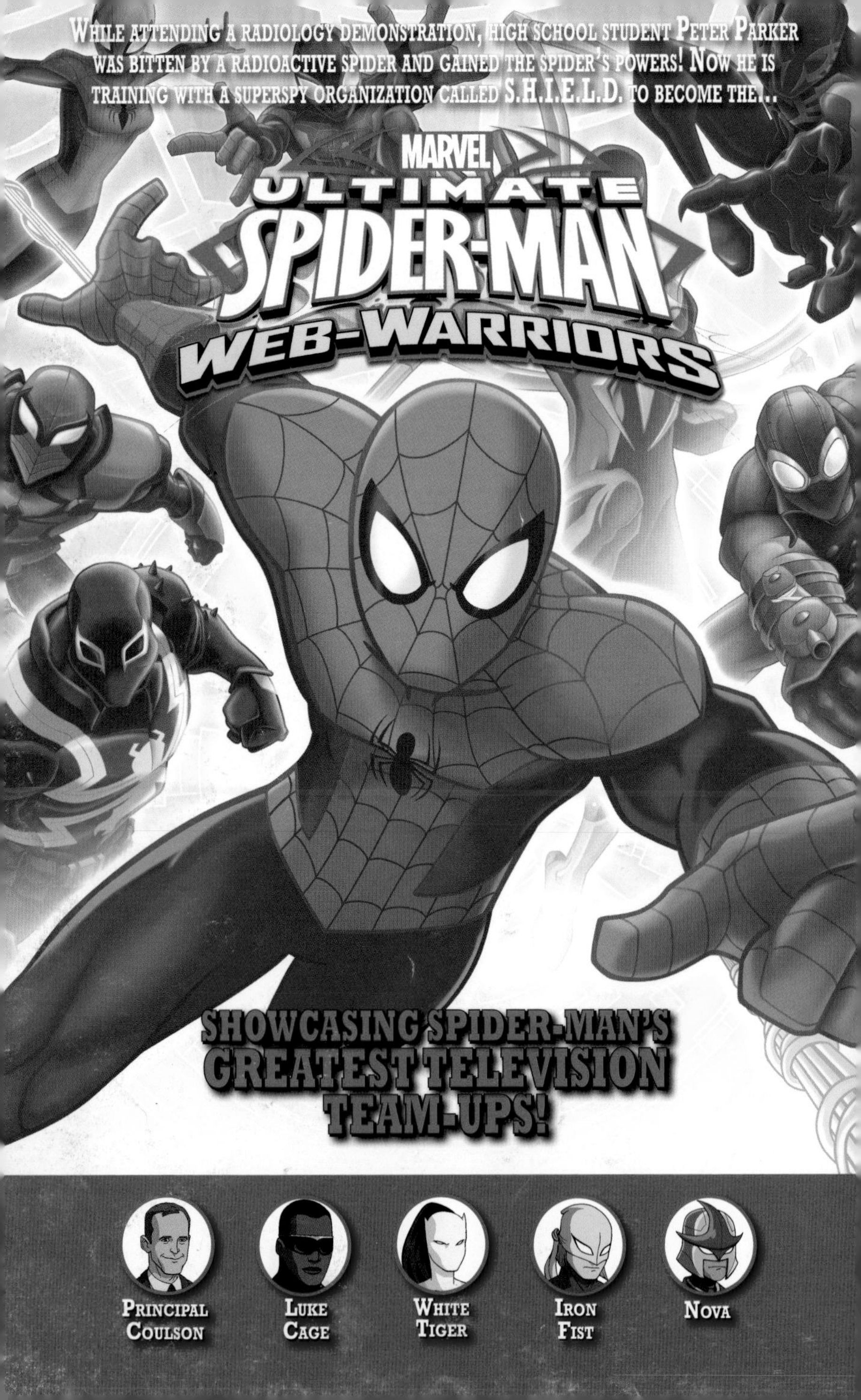

WHILE ATTENDING A RADIOLOGY DEMONSTRATION, HIGH SCHOOL STUDENT PETER PARKER WAS BITTEN BY A RADIOACTIVE SPIDER AND GAINED THE SPIDER'S POWERS! NOW HE IS TRAINING WITH A SUPERSPY ORGANIZATION CALLED S.H.I.E.L.D. TO BECOME THE...
MARVEL
ULTIMATE SPIDER-MAN
WEB-WARRIORS
SHOWCASING SPIDER-MAN'S GREATEST TELEVISION TEAM-UPS!
PRINCIPAL COULSON
LUKE CAGE
WHITE TIGER
IRON FIST
NOVA

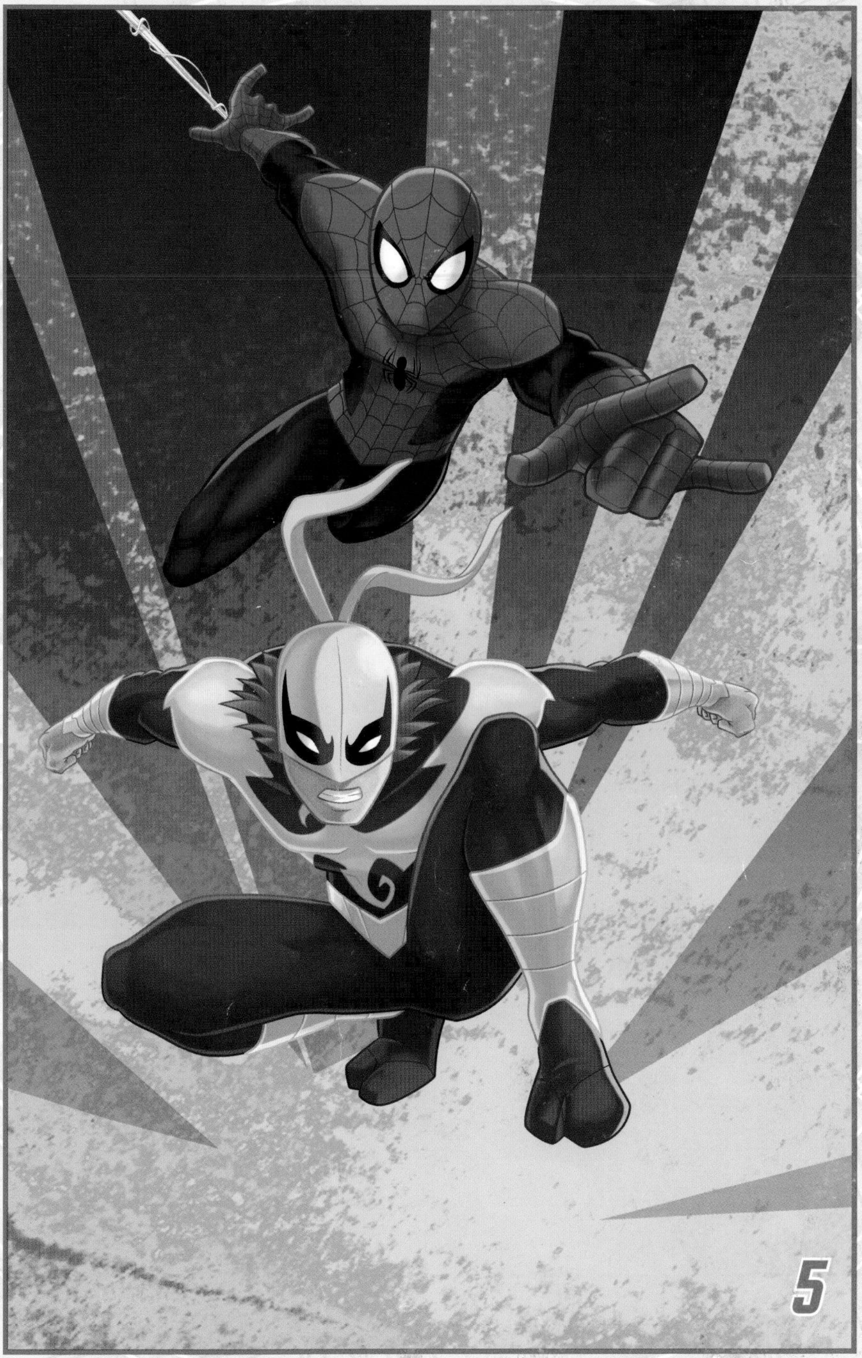
5

Based on "Journey of the Iron Fist"

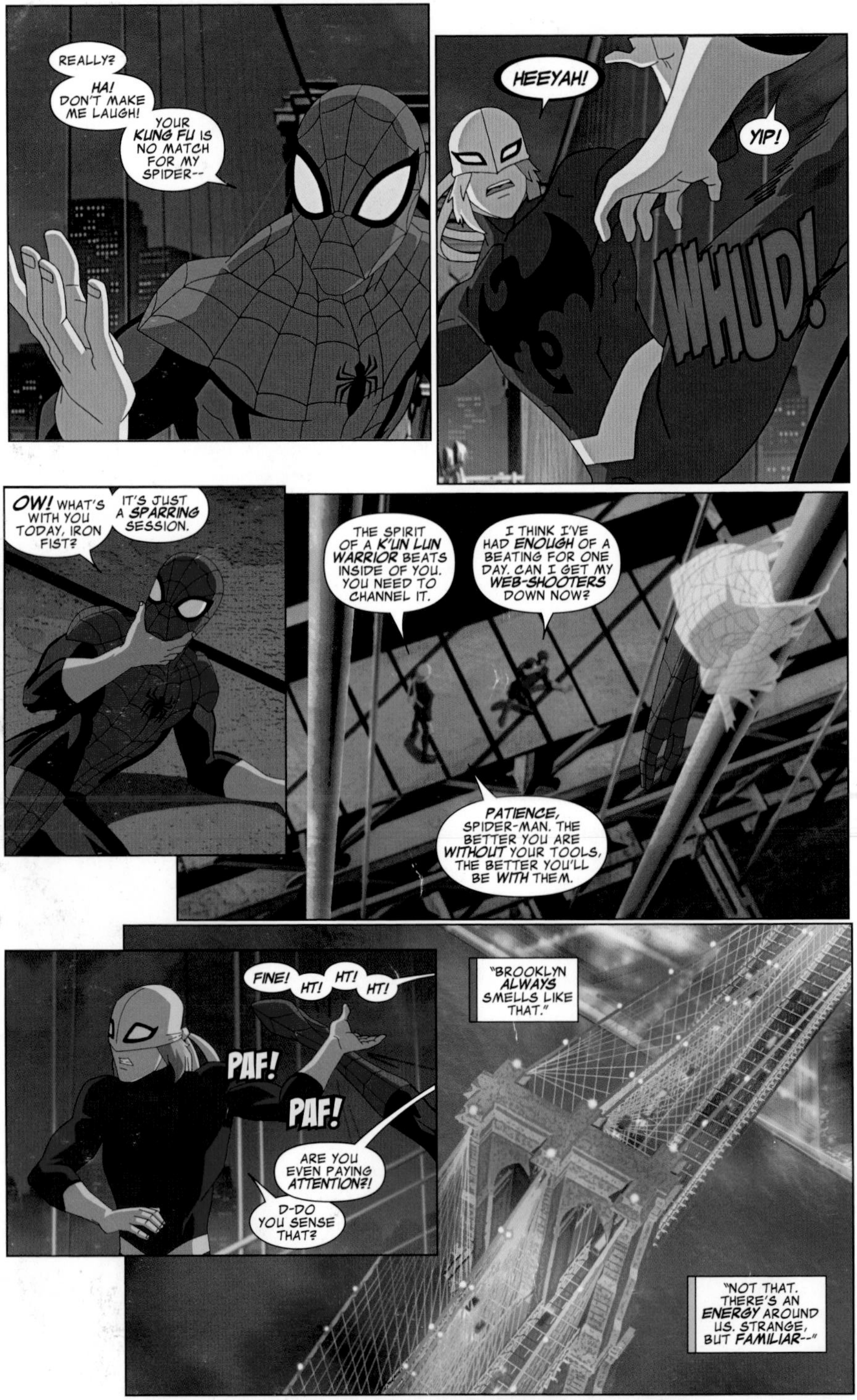

REALLY?
HA! DON'T MAKE ME LAUGH!
YOUR KUNG FU IS NO MATCH FOR MY SPIDER--
HEEYAH!
YIP!
WHUD!
OW! WHAT'S WITH YOU TODAY, IRON FIST?
IT'S JUST A SPARRING SESSION.
THE SPIRIT OF A K'UN LUN WARRIOR BEATS INSIDE OF YOU. YOU NEED TO CHANNEL IT.
I THINK I'VE HAD ENOUGH OF A BEATING FOR ONE DAY. CAN I GET MY WEB-SHOOTERS DOWN NOW?
PATIENCE, SPIDER-MAN. THE BETTER YOU ARE WITHOUT YOUR TOOLS, THE BETTER YOU'LL BE WITH THEM.
FINE! HT! HT! HT!
PAF!
PAF!
ARE YOU EVEN PAYING ATTENTION?!
D-DO YOU SENSE THAT?
"BROOKLYN ALWAYS SMELLS LIKE THAT."
"NOT THAT. THERE'S AN ENERGY AROUND US. STRANGE, BUT FAMILIAR--"

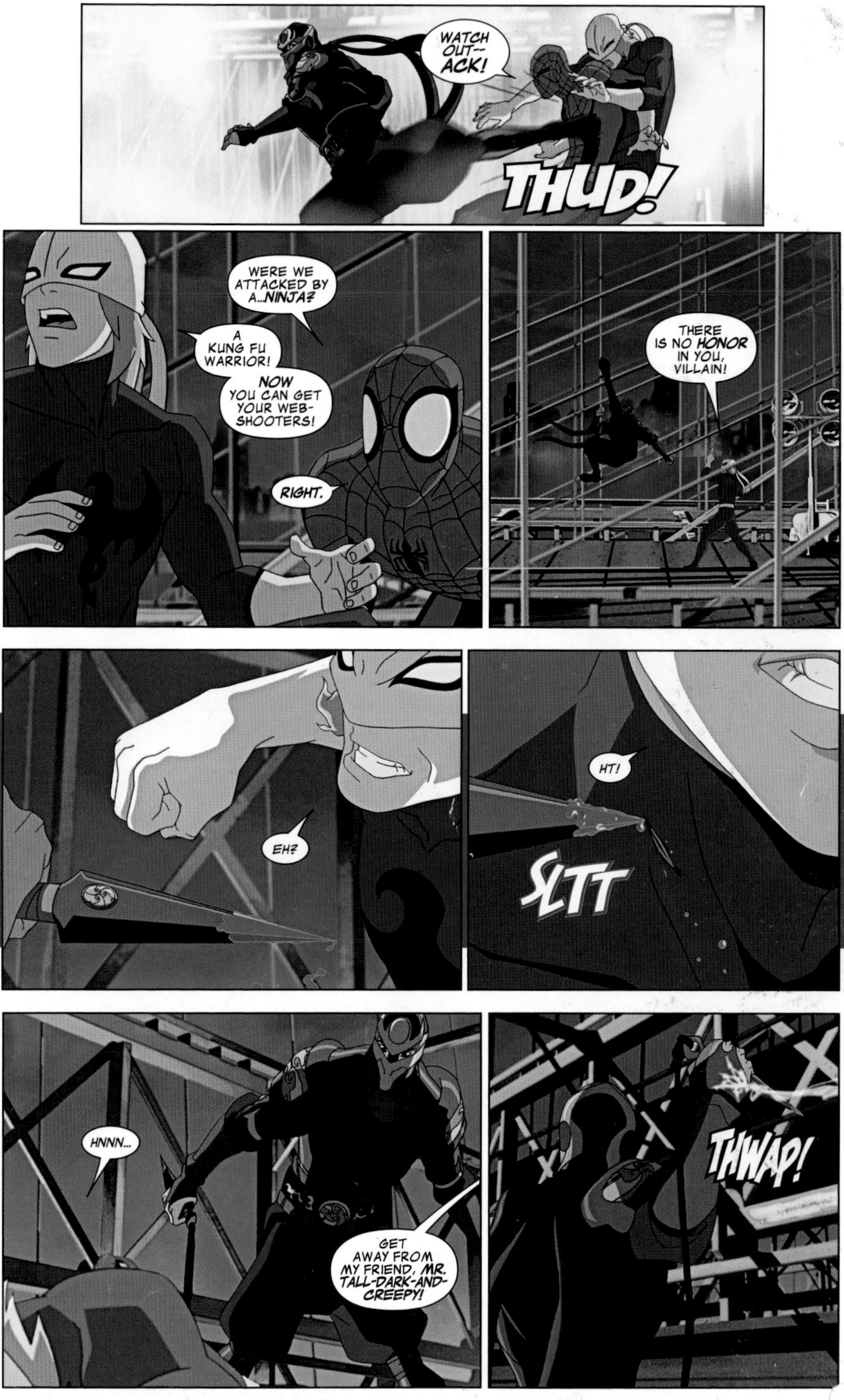
WATCH OUT-- ACK!
THUD!
WERE WE ATTACKED BY A...NINJA?
A KUNG FU WARRIOR!
NOW YOU CAN GET YOUR WEB-SHOOTERS!
RIGHT.
THERE IS NO HONOR IN YOU, VILLAIN!
EH?
HT!
SLTT
HNNN...
GET AWAY FROM MY FRIEND, MR. TALL-DARK-AND-CREEPY!
THWAP!

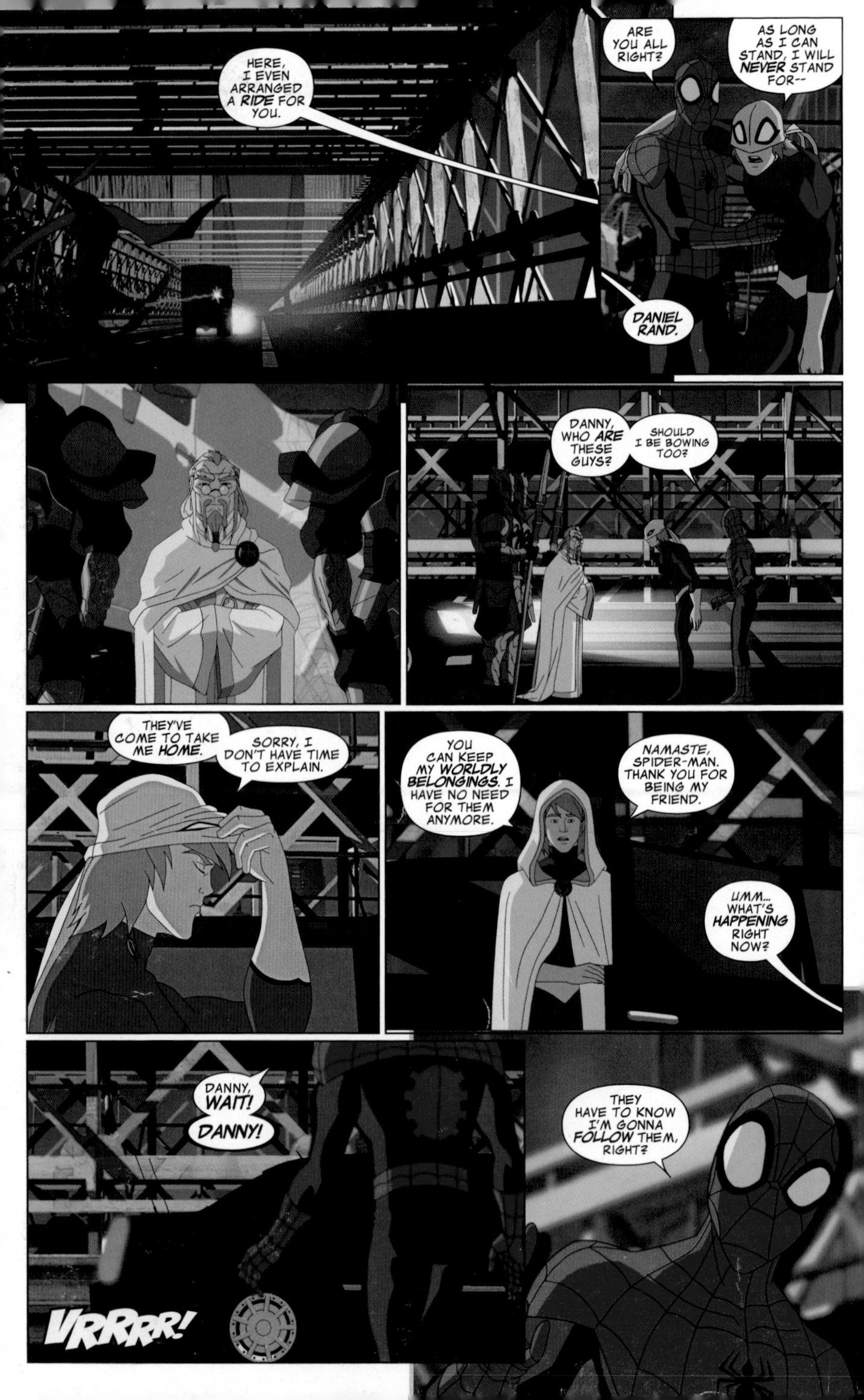

HERE, I EVEN ARRANGED A RIDE FOR YOU.
ARE YOU ALL RIGHT?
AS LONG AS I CAN STAND, I WILL NEVER STAND FOR--
DANIEL RAND.
DANNY, WHO ARE THESE GUYS?
SHOULD I BE BOWING TOO?
THEY'VE COME TO TAKE ME HOME.
SORRY, I DON'T HAVE TIME TO EXPLAIN.
YOU CAN KEEP MY WORLDLY BELONGINGS. I HAVE NO NEED FOR THEM ANYMORE.
NAMASTE, SPIDER-MAN. THANK YOU FOR BEING MY FRIEND.
UMM... WHAT'S HAPPENING RIGHT NOW?
DANNY, WAIT!
DANNY!
VRRRR!
THEY HAVE TO KNOW I'M GONNA FOLLOW THEM, RIGHT?

MOMENTS LATER...

WHERE ARE THEY TAKING HIM? AND WHY ON A *RAND INDUSTRIES* PRIVATE JET?

WAITASEC! *DANNY'S* LAST NAME IS RAND.

DANNY IS *THAT* RAND? THE HEIR TO THE *RAND INDUSTRIES* FORTUNE?!

HE LEFT ALL OF HIS WORLDLY POSSESSIONS TO ME.

I'M *RICH!*

I'M *WEALTHY!*

I'M--

I'M DANNY'S *FRIEND.*

AND HE DOESN'T LOOK TOO HAPPY ABOUT LEAVING.

I CAN'T LET HIM GO WITHOUT GETTING TO THE BOTTOM OF THIS.

AFTER ALL, THIS IS...

# "...THAT TIME I TEAMED UP WITH IRON FIST!"

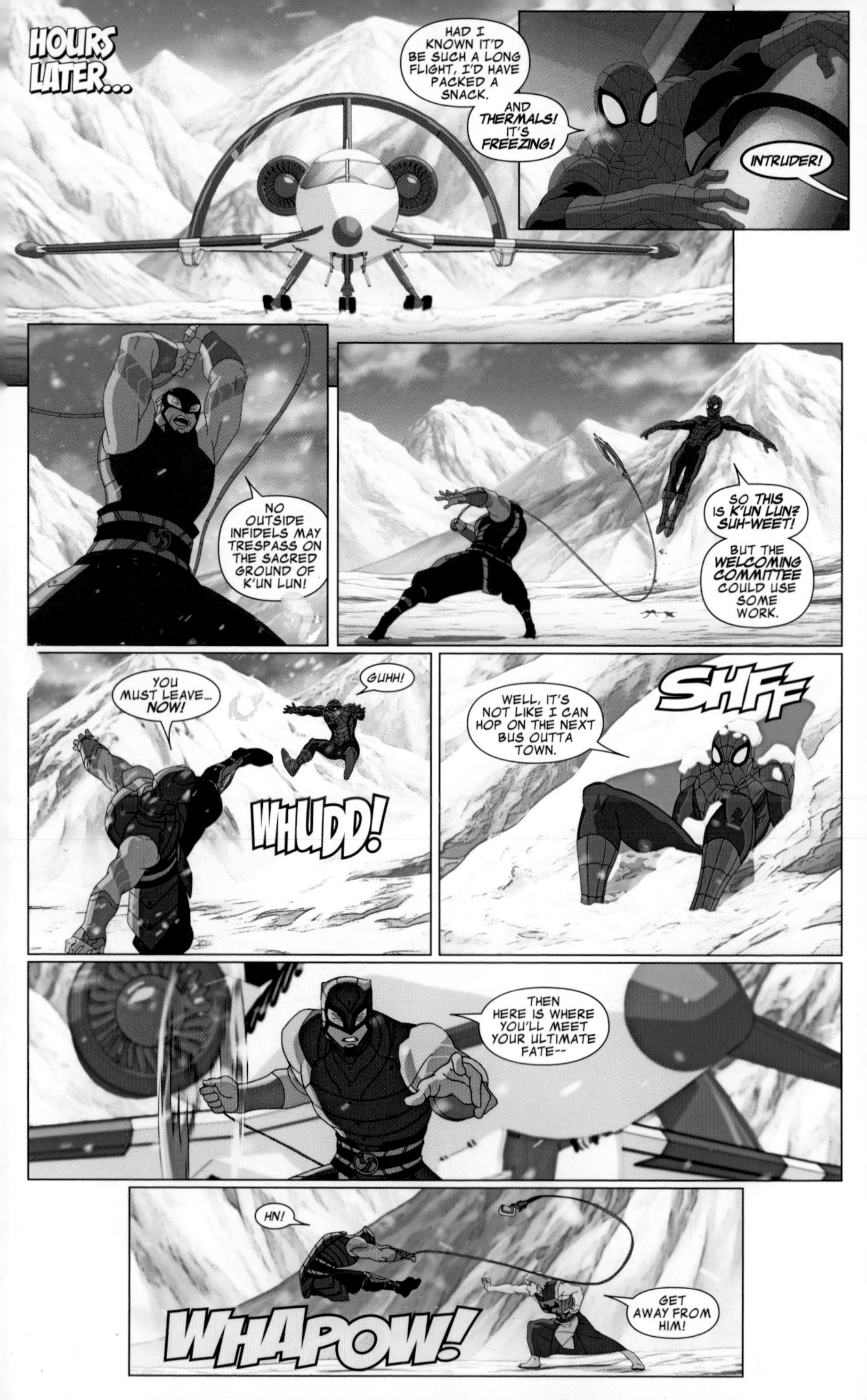
HOURS LATER...
HAD I KNOWN IT'D BE SUCH A LONG FLIGHT, I'D HAVE PACKED A SNACK.
AND THERMALS! IT'S FREEZING!
INTRUDER!
NO OUTSIDE INFIDELS MAY TRESPASS ON THE SACRED GROUND OF K'UN LUN!
SO THIS IS K'UN LUN? SUH-WEET!
BUT THE WELCOMING COMMITTEE COULD USE SOME WORK.
YOU MUST LEAVE... NOW!
GUHH!
WHUDD!
SHFF
WELL, IT'S NOT LIKE I CAN HOP ON THE NEXT BUS OUTTA TOWN.
THEN HERE IS WHERE YOU'LL MEET YOUR ULTIMATE FATE--
HN!
GET AWAY FROM HIM!
WHAPOW!

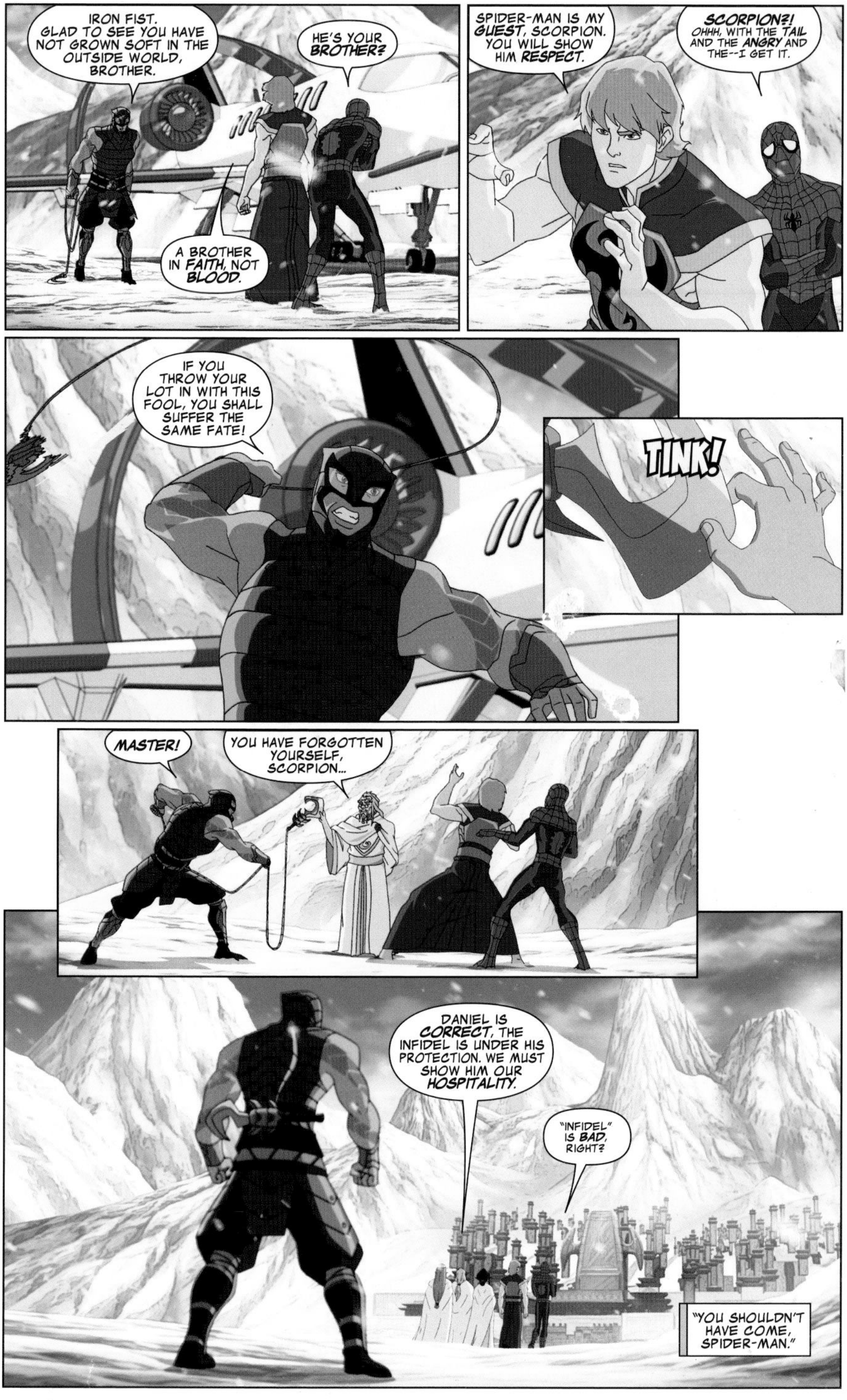
IRON FIST. GLAD TO SEE YOU HAVE NOT GROWN SOFT IN THE OUTSIDE WORLD, BROTHER.
HE'S YOUR BROTHER?
A BROTHER IN FAITH, NOT BLOOD.
SPIDER-MAN IS MY GUEST, SCORPION. YOU WILL SHOW HIM RESPECT.
SCORPION?! OHHH, WITH THE TAIL AND THE ANGRY AND THE--I GET IT.
IF YOU THROW YOUR LOT IN WITH THIS FOOL, YOU SHALL SUFFER THE SAME FATE!
TINK!
MASTER!
YOU HAVE FORGOTTEN YOURSELF, SCORPION...
DANIEL IS CORRECT, THE INFIDEL IS UNDER HIS PROTECTION. WE MUST SHOW HIM OUR HOSPITALITY.
"INFIDEL" IS BAD, RIGHT?
"YOU SHOULDN'T HAVE COME, SPIDER-MAN."

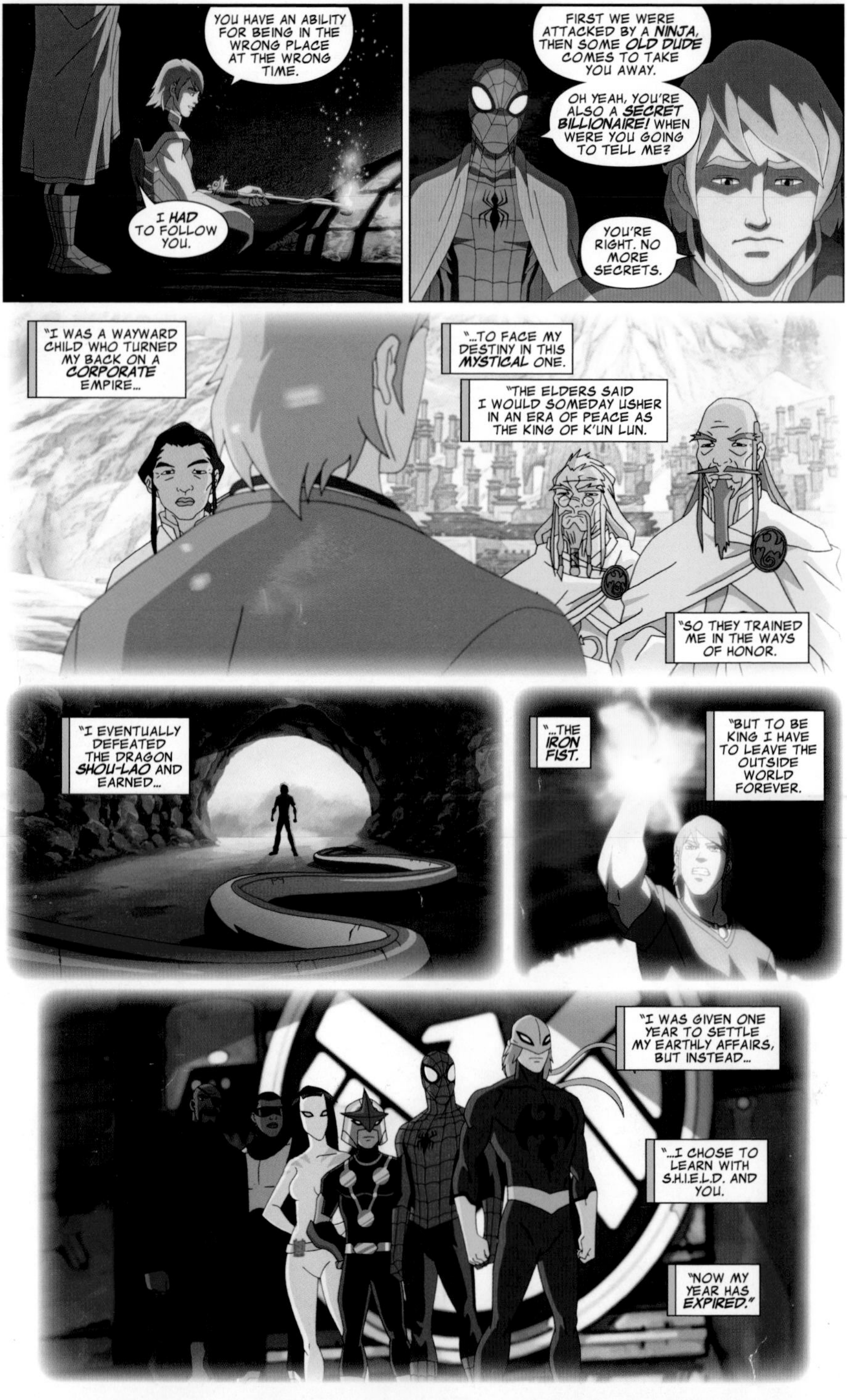
YOU HAVE AN ABILITY FOR BEING IN THE WRONG PLACE AT THE WRONG TIME.
I HAD TO FOLLOW YOU.
FIRST WE WERE ATTACKED BY A NINJA, THEN SOME OLD DUDE COMES TO TAKE YOU AWAY.
OH YEAH, YOU'RE ALSO A SECRET BILLIONAIRE! WHEN WERE YOU GOING TO TELL ME?
YOU'RE RIGHT. NO MORE SECRETS.
"I WAS A WAYWARD CHILD WHO TURNED MY BACK ON A CORPORATE EMPIRE...
"...TO FACE MY DESTINY IN THIS MYSTICAL ONE.
"THE ELDERS SAID I WOULD SOMEDAY USHER IN AN ERA OF PEACE AS THE KING OF K'UN LUN.
"SO THEY TRAINED ME IN THE WAYS OF HONOR.
"I EVENTUALLY DEFEATED THE DRAGON SHOU-LAO AND EARNED...
"...THE IRON FIST.
"BUT TO BE KING I HAVE TO LEAVE THE OUTSIDE WORLD FOREVER.
"I WAS GIVEN ONE YEAR TO SETTLE MY EARTHLY AFFAIRS, BUT INSTEAD...
"...I CHOSE TO LEARN WITH S.H.I.E.L.D. AND YOU.
"NOW MY YEAR HAS EXPIRED."

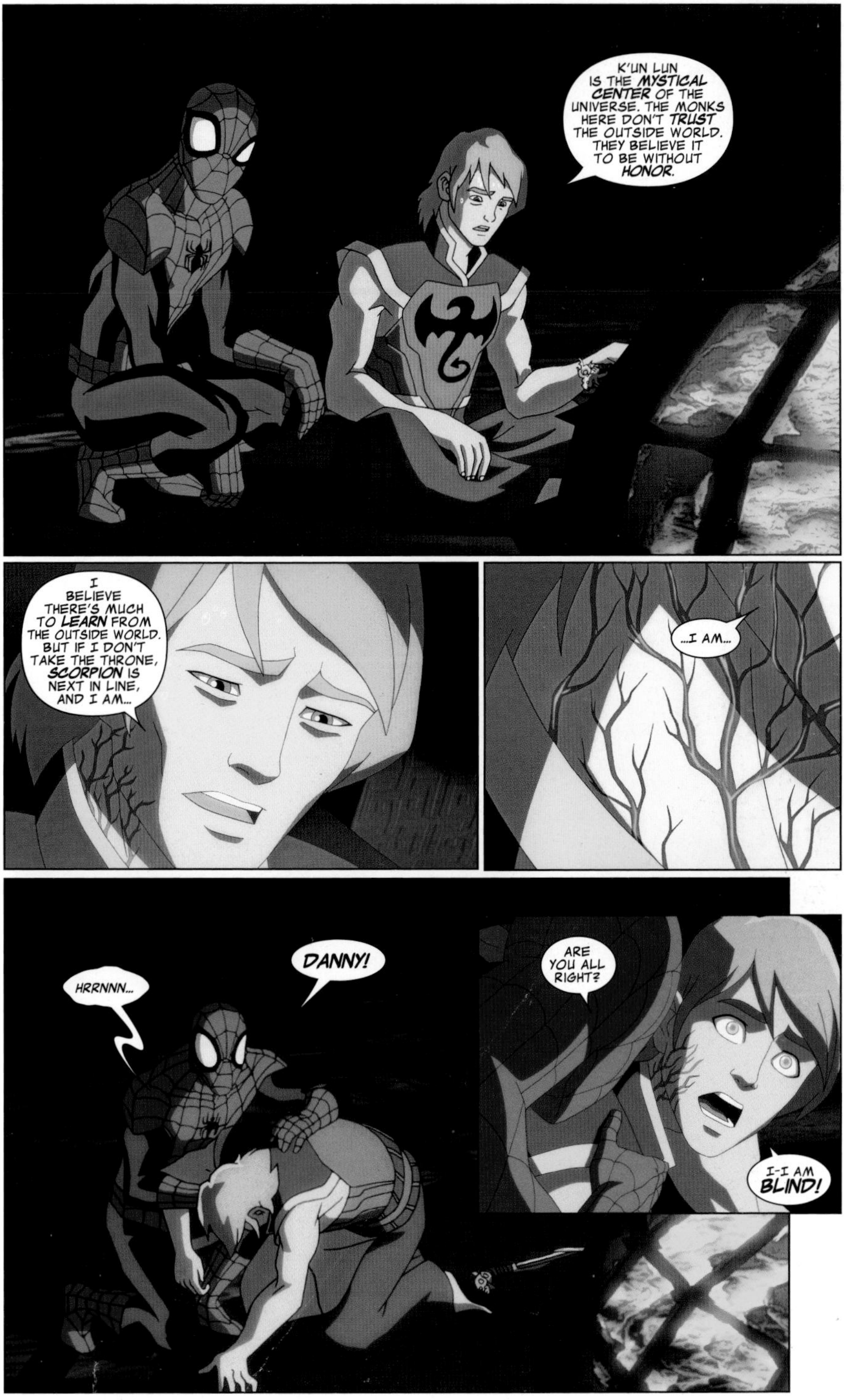
K'UN LUN IS THE MYSTICAL CENTER OF THE UNIVERSE. THE MONKS HERE DON'T TRUST THE OUTSIDE WORLD. THEY BELIEVE IT TO BE WITHOUT HONOR.
I BELIEVE THERE'S MUCH TO LEARN FROM THE OUTSIDE WORLD. BUT IF I DON'T TAKE THE THRONE, SCORPION IS NEXT IN LINE, AND I AM...
...I AM...
HRRNNN...
DANNY!
ARE YOU ALL RIGHT?
I-I AM BLIND!

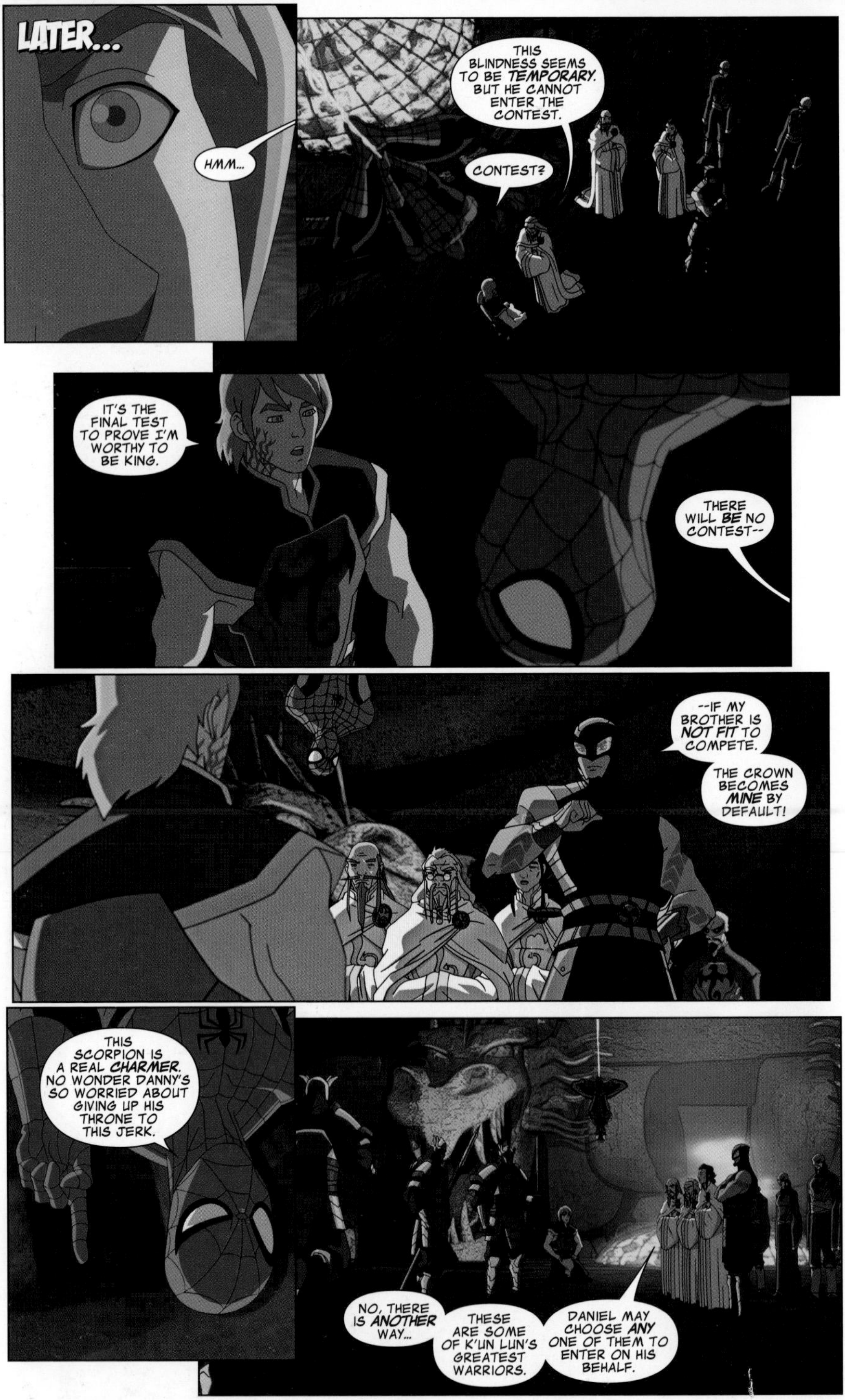
LATER...
HMM...
THIS BLINDNESS SEEMS TO BE TEMPORARY. BUT HE CANNOT ENTER THE CONTEST.
CONTEST?
IT'S THE FINAL TEST TO PROVE I'M WORTHY TO BE KING.
THERE WILL BE NO CONTEST--
--IF MY BROTHER IS NOT FIT TO COMPETE.
THE CROWN BECOMES MINE BY DEFAULT!
THIS SCORPION IS A REAL CHARMER. NO WONDER DANNY'S SO WORRIED ABOUT GIVING UP HIS THRONE TO THIS JERK.
NO, THERE IS ANOTHER WAY...
THESE ARE SOME OF K'UN LUN'S GREATEST WARRIORS.
DANIEL MAY CHOOSE ANY ONE OF THEM TO ENTER ON HIS BEHALF.

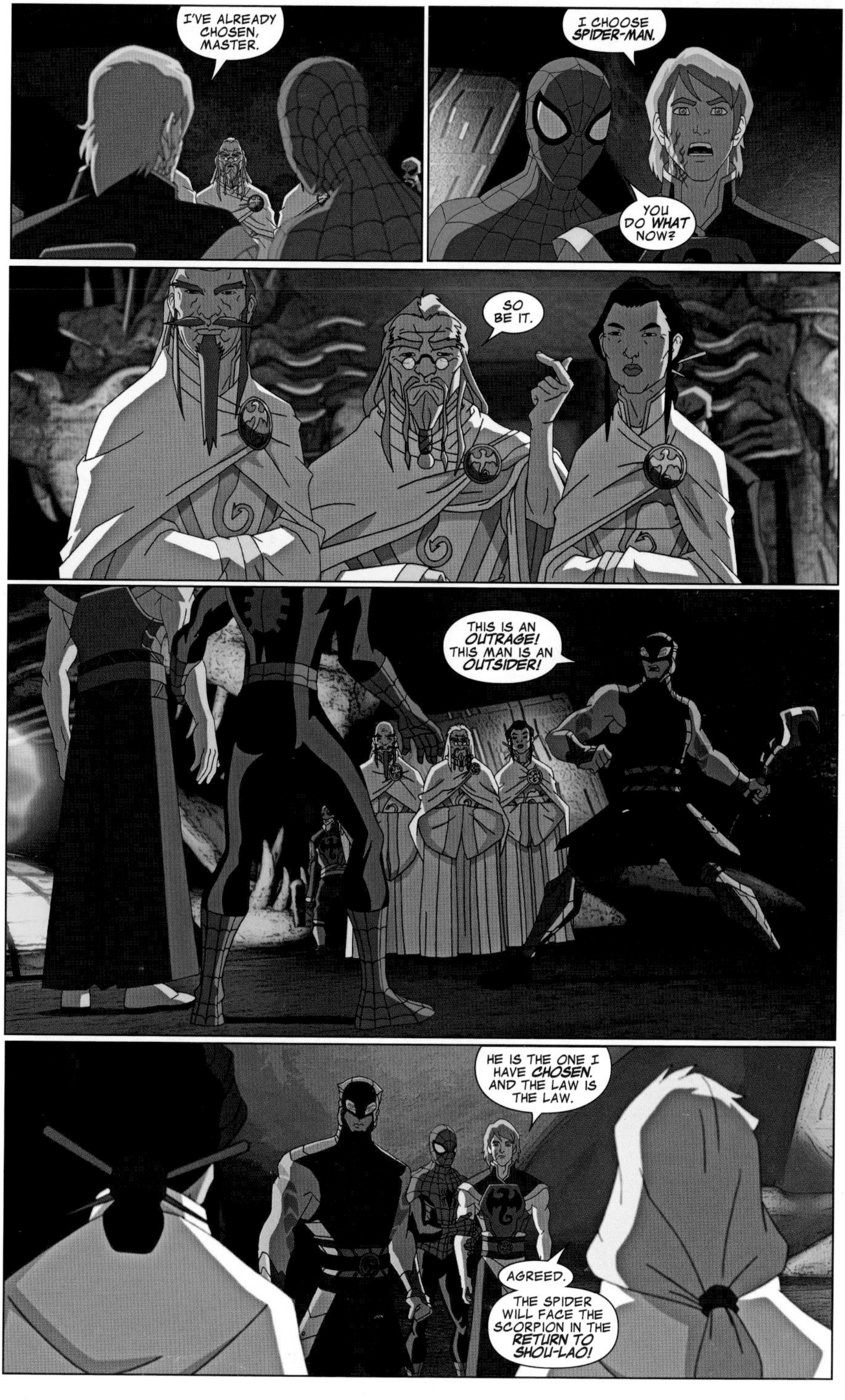
I'VE ALREADY CHOSEN, MASTER.
I CHOOSE SPIDER-MAN.
YOU DO WHAT NOW?
SO BE IT.
THIS IS AN OUTRAGE! THIS MAN IS AN OUTSIDER!
HE IS THE ONE I HAVE CHOSEN. AND THE LAW IS THE LAW.
AGREED.
THE SPIDER WILL FACE THE SCORPION IN THE RETURN TO SHOU-LAO!

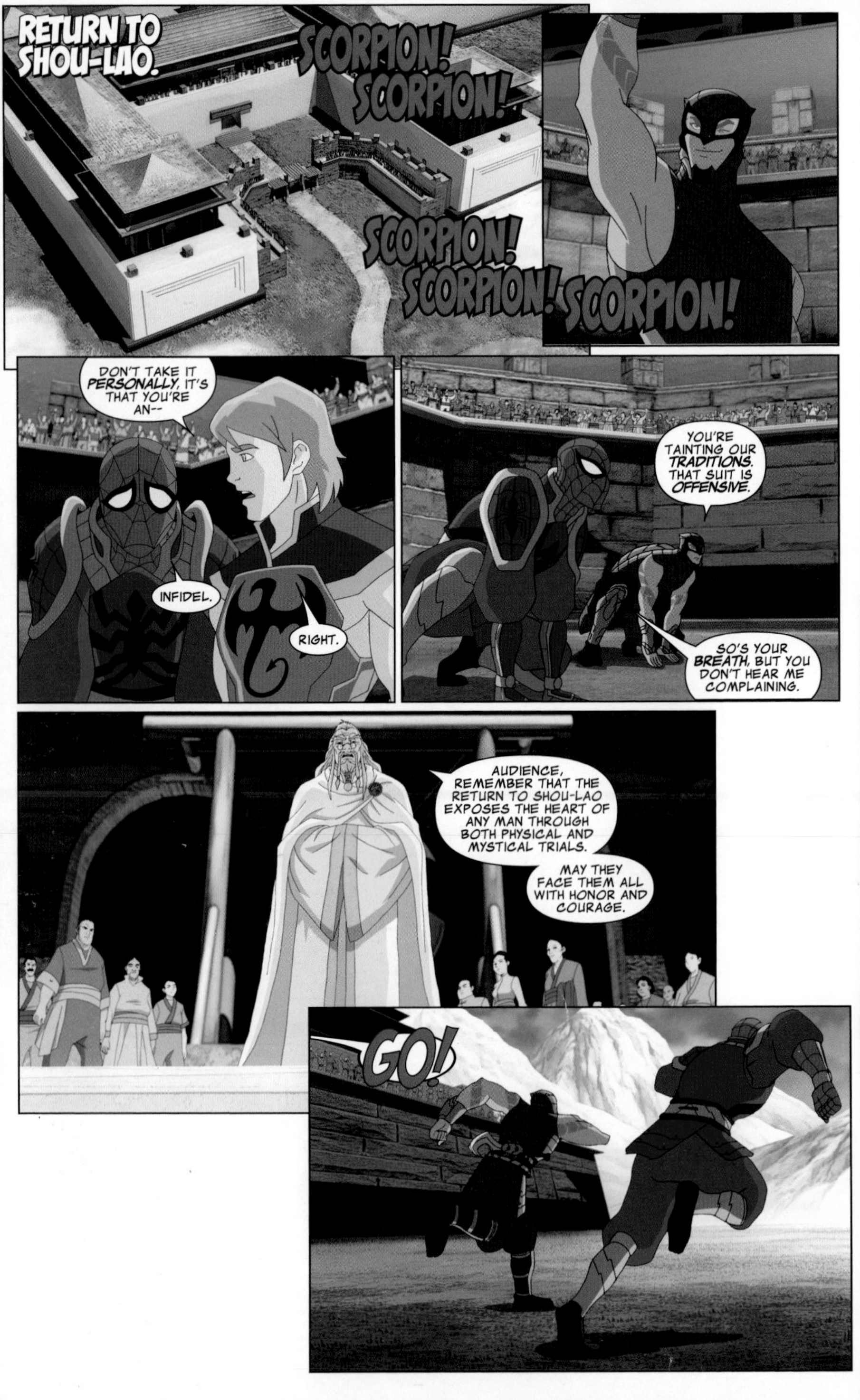
RETURN TO SHOU-LAO.
SCORPION! SCORPION!
SCORPION! SCORPION! SCORPION!
DON'T TAKE IT PERSONALLY, IT'S THAT YOU'RE AN--
INFIDEL.
RIGHT.
YOU'RE TAINTING OUR TRADITIONS. THAT SUIT IS OFFENSIVE.
SO'S YOUR BREATH, BUT YOU DON'T HEAR ME COMPLAINING.
AUDIENCE, REMEMBER THAT THE RETURN TO SHOU-LAO EXPOSES THE HEART OF ANY MAN THROUGH BOTH PHYSICAL AND MYSTICAL TRIALS.
MAY THEY FACE THEM ALL WITH HONOR AND COURAGE.
GO!

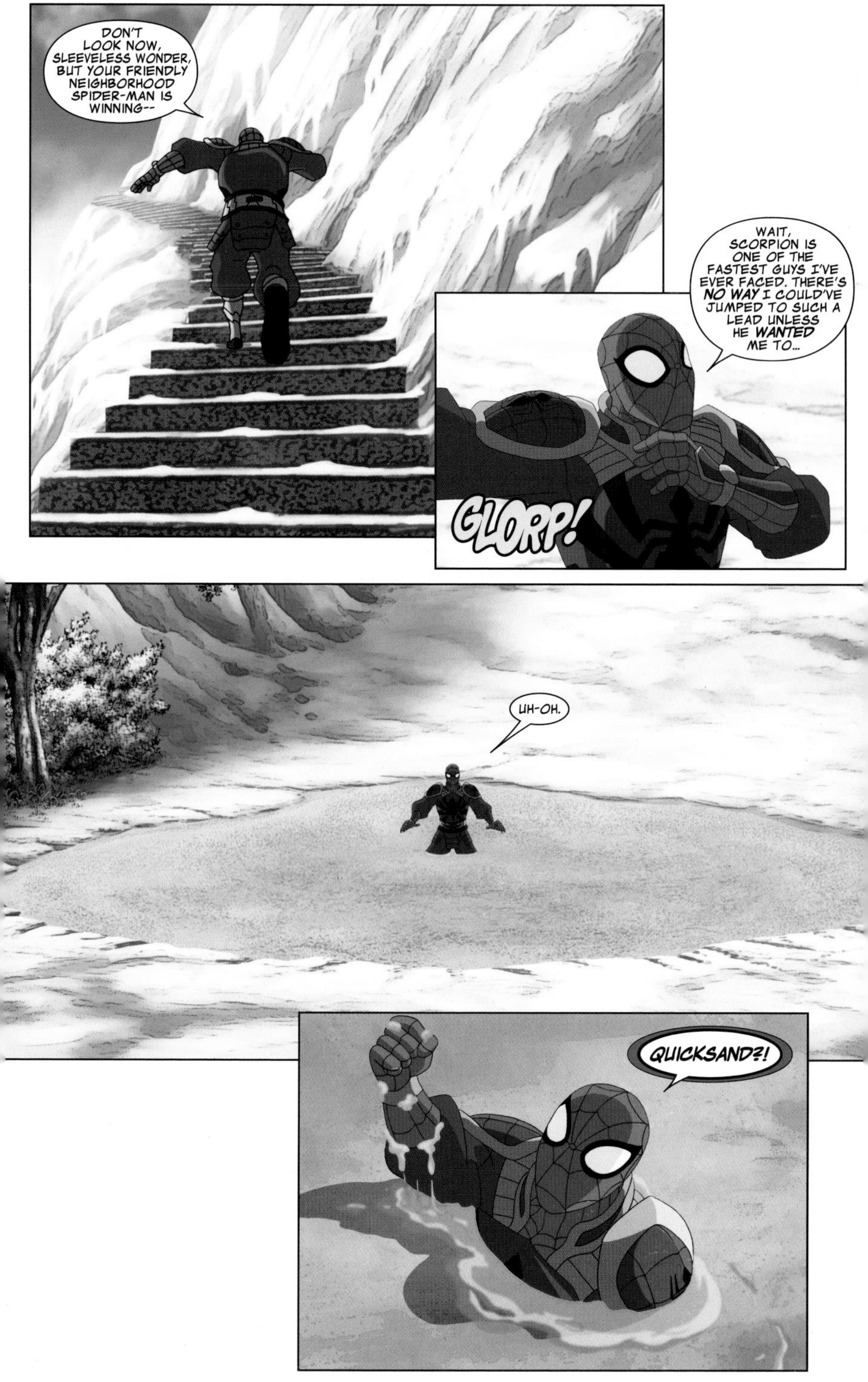
DON'T LOOK NOW, SLEEVELESS WONDER, BUT YOUR FRIENDLY NEIGHBORHOOD SPIDER-MAN IS WINNING--
WAIT, SCORPION IS ONE OF THE FASTEST GUYS I'VE EVER FACED. THERE'S NO WAY I COULD'VE JUMPED TO SUCH A LEAD UNLESS HE WANTED ME TO...
GLORP!
UH-OH.
QUICKSAND?!

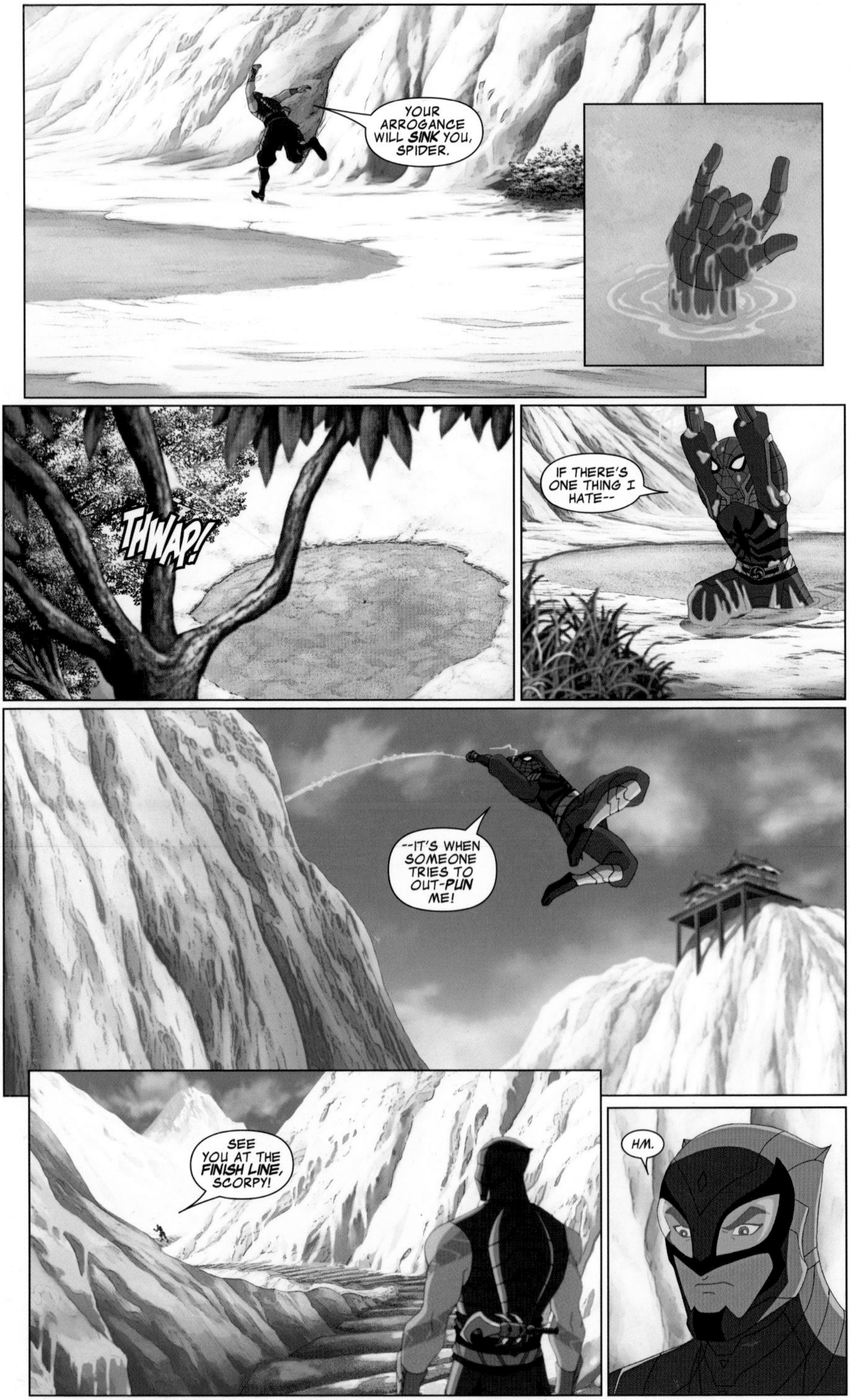
YOUR ARROGANCE WILL SINK YOU, SPIDER.
THWAP!
IF THERE'S ONE THING I HATE--
--IT'S WHEN SOMEONE TRIES TO OUT-PUN ME!
SEE YOU AT THE FINISH LINE, SCORPY!
HM.

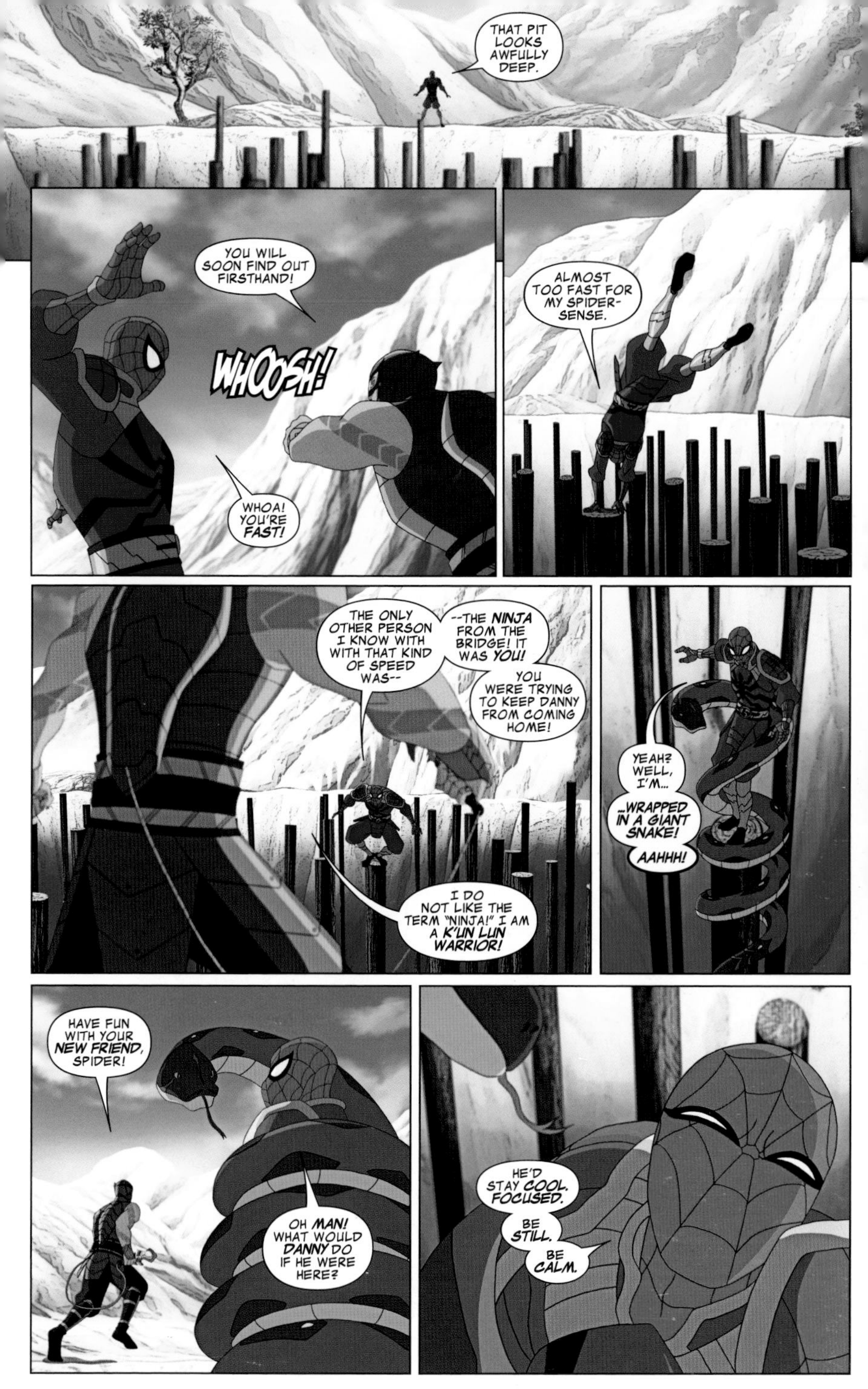
THAT PIT LOOKS AWFULLY DEEP.
YOU WILL SOON FIND OUT FIRSTHAND!
WHOOSH!
WHOA! YOU'RE FAST!
ALMOST TOO FAST FOR MY SPIDER-SENSE.
THE ONLY OTHER PERSON I KNOW WITH WITH THAT KIND OF SPEED WAS--
--THE NINJA FROM THE BRIDGE! IT WAS YOU!
YOU WERE TRYING TO KEEP DANNY FROM COMING HOME!
I DO NOT LIKE THE TERM "NINJA!" I AM A K'UN LUN WARRIOR!
YEAH? WELL, I'M...
...WRAPPED IN A GIANT SNAKE!
AAHHH!
HAVE FUN WITH YOUR NEW FRIEND, SPIDER!
OH MAN! WHAT WOULD DANNY DO IF HE WERE HERE?
HE'D STAY COOL. FOCUSED.
BE STILL.
BE CALM.

...
THAT ACTUALLY WORKED!
LET'S HOPE I'M NOT TOO LATE!
HA! THE SPIDER IS TOO LATE!
THE FINISH LINE IS IN SIGHT!
I AM THE NEW KING OF K'UN LUN!
SO WHAT DO YOU GET FOR THE K'UN LUN-ATIC WHO HAS EVERYTHING?
A K'UN-UCKLE SANDWICH!
WHAM!
OUT-PUN ME?! I THINK NOT!

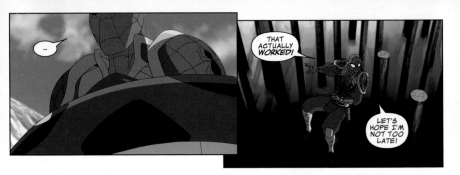

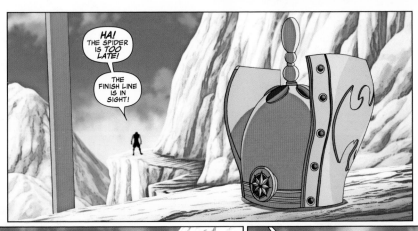

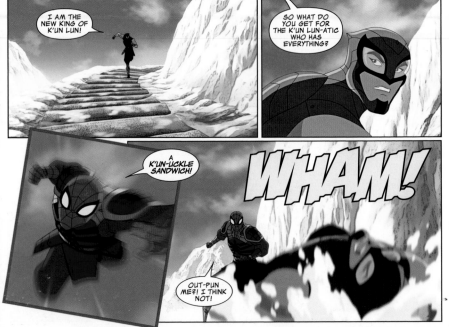

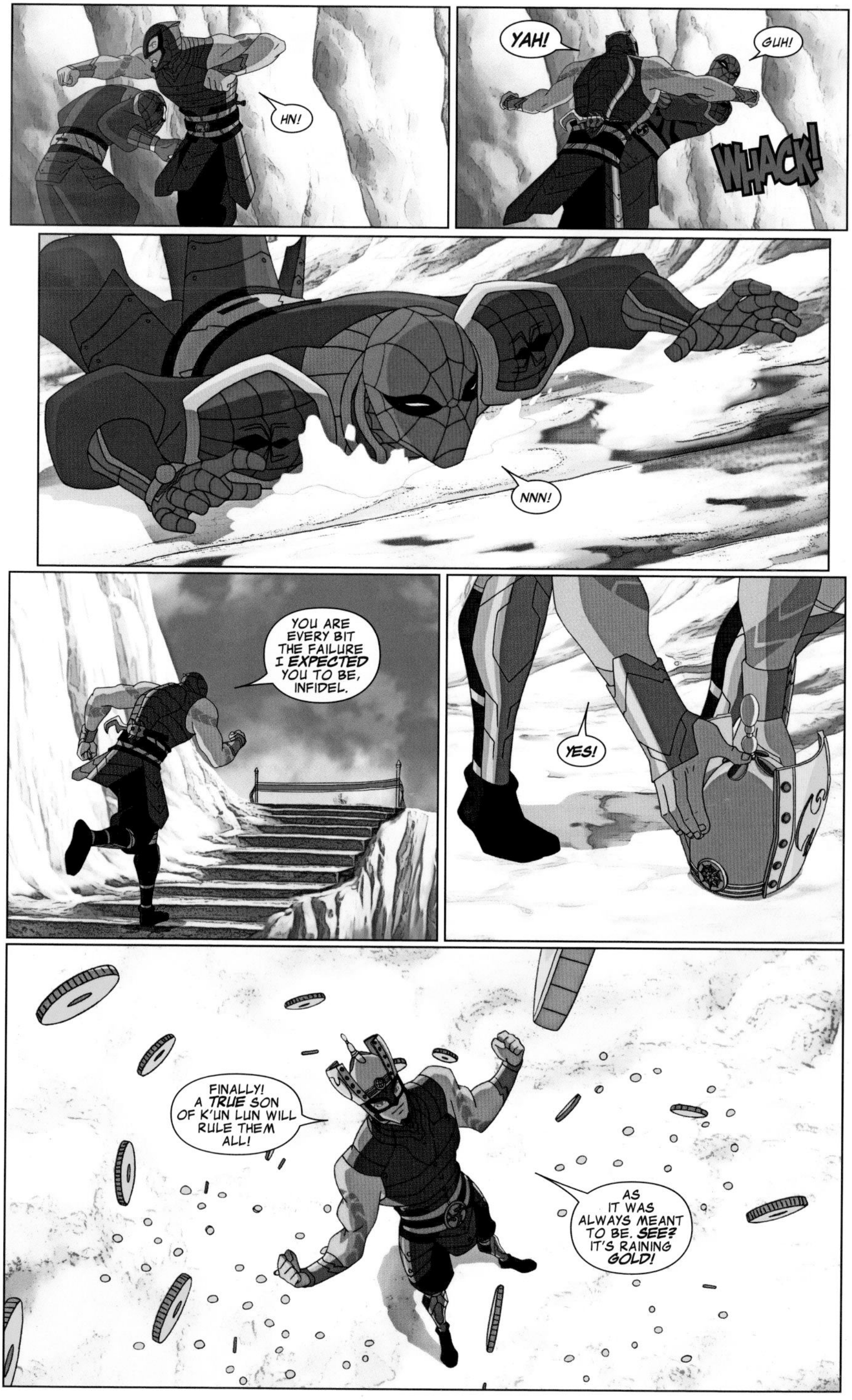
HN!
YAH!
GUH!
WHACK!
NNN!
YOU ARE EVERY BIT THE FAILURE I EXPECTED YOU TO BE, INFIDEL.
YES!
FINALLY! A TRUE SON OF K'UN LUN WILL RULE THEM ALL!
AS IT WAS ALWAYS MEANT TO BE. SEE? IT'S RAINING GOLD!

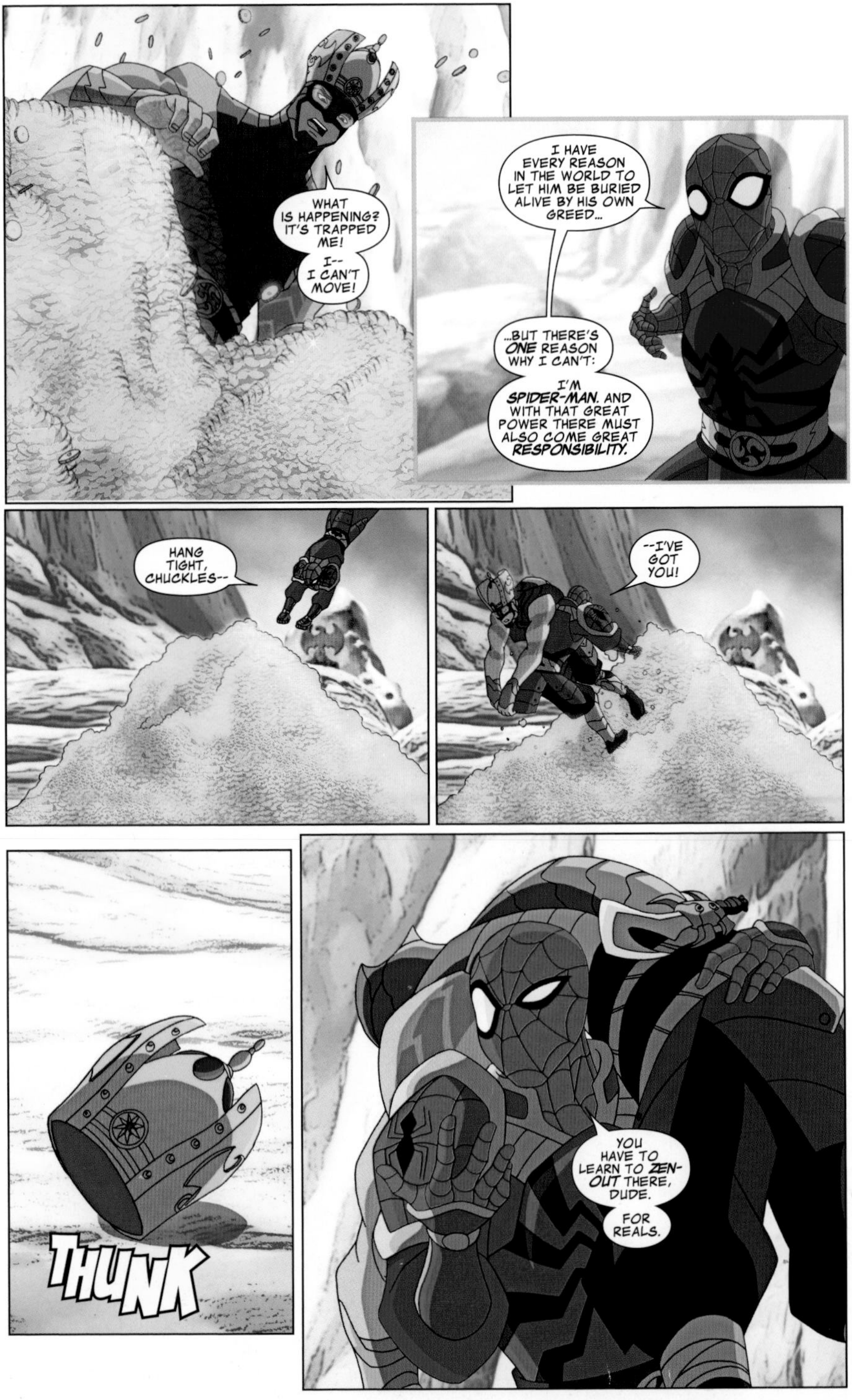
WHAT IS HAPPENING? IT'S TRAPPED ME!
I-- I CAN'T MOVE!
I HAVE EVERY REASON IN THE WORLD TO LET HIM BE BURIED ALIVE BY HIS OWN GREED...
...BUT THERE'S ONE REASON WHY I CAN'T:
I'M SPIDER-MAN. AND WITH THAT GREAT POWER THERE MUST ALSO COME GREAT RESPONSIBILITY.
HANG TIGHT, CHUCKLES--
--I'VE GOT YOU!
THUNK
YOU HAVE TO LEARN TO ZEN-OUT THERE, DUDE.
FOR REALS.

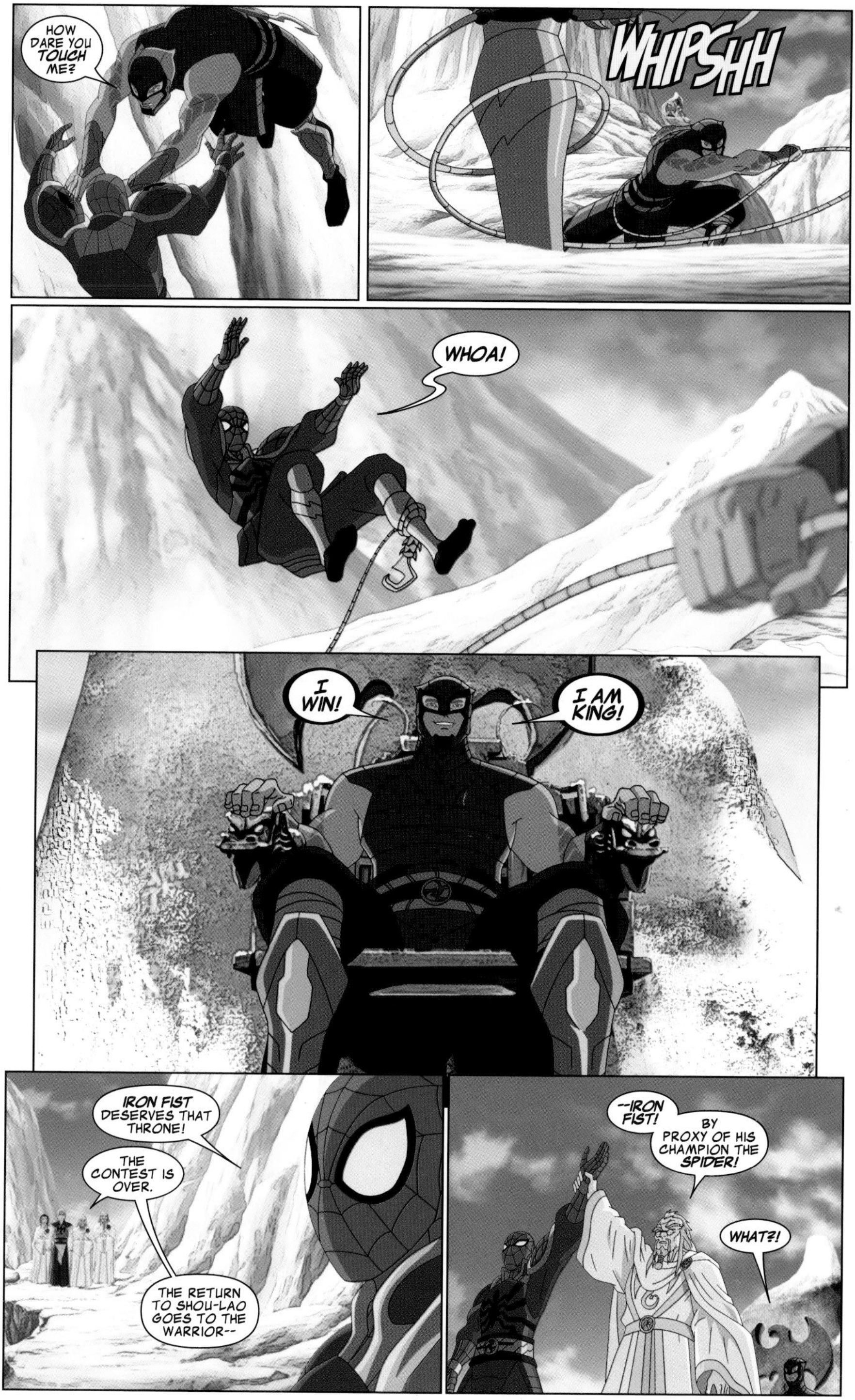
HOW DARE YOU TOUCH ME?
WHIPSHH
WHOA!
I WIN!
I AM KING!
IRON FIST DESERVES THAT THRONE!
THE CONTEST IS OVER.
THE RETURN TO SHOU-LAO GOES TO THE WARRIOR--
--IRON FIST!
BY PROXY OF HIS CHAMPION THE SPIDER!
WHAT?!

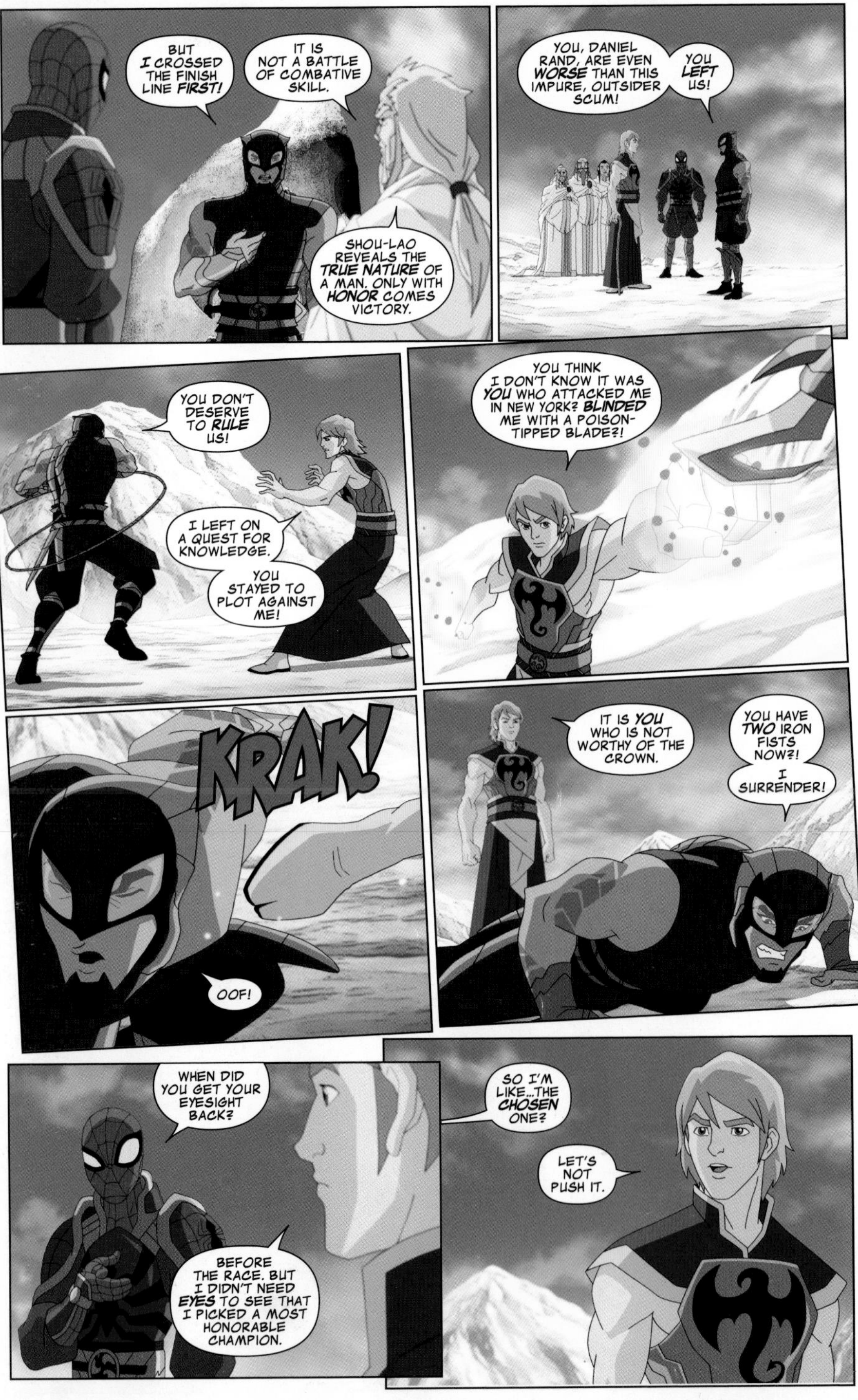

BUT I CROSSED THE FINISH LINE FIRST!
IT IS NOT A BATTLE OF COMBATIVE SKILL.
SHOU-LAO REVEALS THE TRUE NATURE OF A MAN. ONLY WITH HONOR COMES VICTORY.
YOU, DANIEL RAND, ARE EVEN WORSE THAN THIS IMPURE, OUTSIDER SCUM!
YOU LEFT US!
YOU DON'T DESERVE TO RULE US!
I LEFT ON A QUEST FOR KNOWLEDGE.
YOU STAYED TO PLOT AGAINST ME!
YOU THINK I DON'T KNOW IT WAS YOU WHO ATTACKED ME IN NEW YORK? BLINDED ME WITH A POISON-TIPPED BLADE?!
KRAK!
OOF!
IT IS YOU WHO IS NOT WORTHY OF THE CROWN.
YOU HAVE TWO IRON FISTS NOW?!
I SURRENDER!
WHEN DID YOU GET YOUR EYESIGHT BACK?
BEFORE THE RACE. BUT I DIDN'T NEED EYES TO SEE THAT I PICKED A MOST HONORABLE CHAMPION.
SO I'M LIKE...THE CHOSEN ONE?
LET'S NOT PUSH IT.

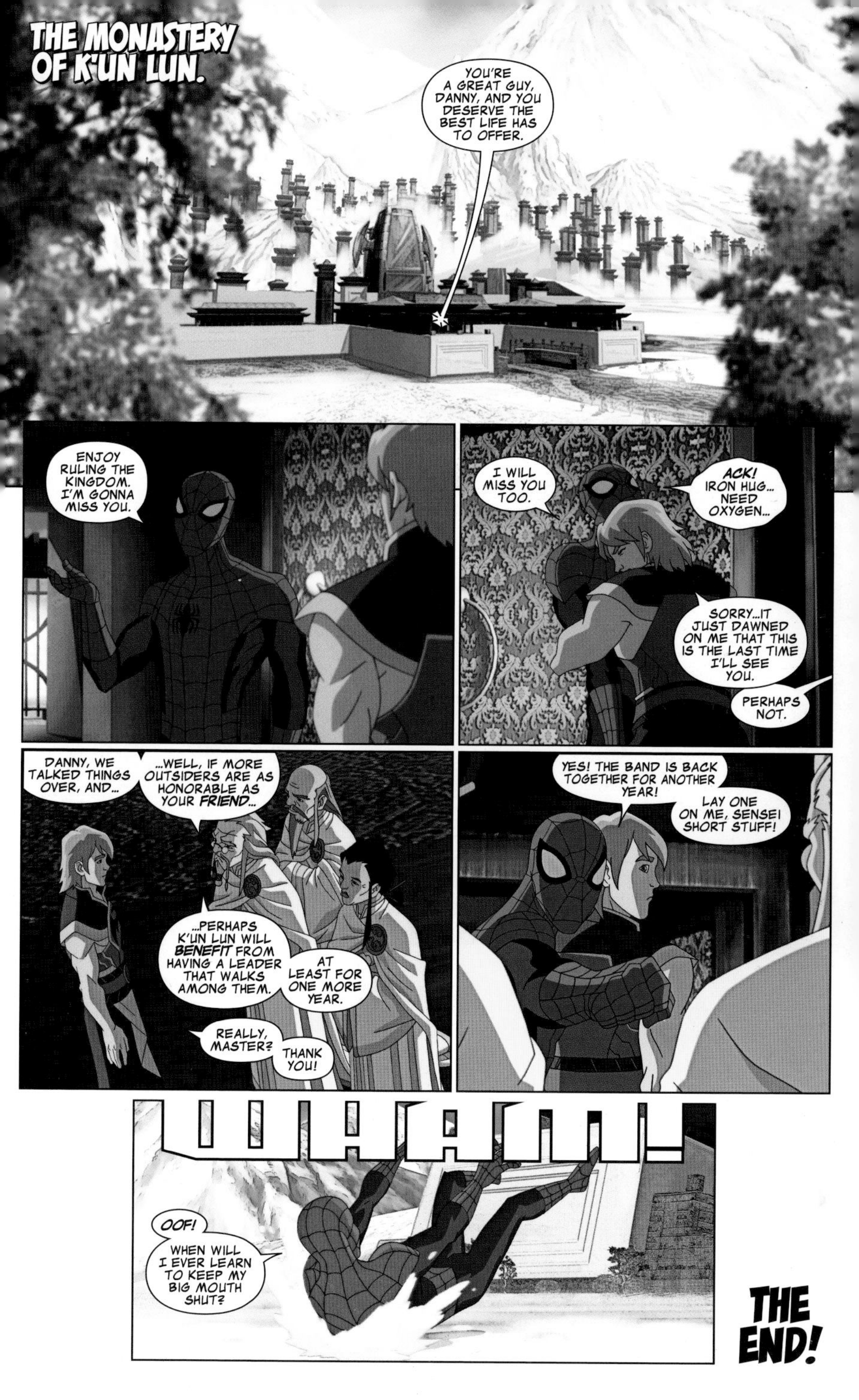
THE MONASTERY OF K'UN LUN.
YOU'RE A GREAT GUY, DANNY, AND YOU DESERVE THE BEST LIFE HAS TO OFFER.
ENJOY RULING THE KINGDOM. I'M GONNA MISS YOU.
I WILL MISS YOU TOO.
ACK! IRON HUG... NEED OXYGEN...
SORRY...IT JUST DAWNED ON ME THAT THIS IS THE LAST TIME I'LL SEE YOU.
PERHAPS NOT.
DANNY, WE TALKED THINGS OVER, AND...
...WELL, IF MORE OUTSIDERS ARE AS HONORABLE AS YOUR FRIEND...
...PERHAPS K'UN LUN WILL BENEFIT FROM HAVING A LEADER THAT WALKS AMONG THEM.
AT LEAST FOR ONE MORE YEAR.
REALLY, MASTER?
THANK YOU!
YES! THE BAND IS BACK TOGETHER FOR ANOTHER YEAR!
LAY ONE ON ME, SENSEI SHORT STUFF!
WHAM!
OOF!
WHEN WILL I EVER LEARN TO KEEP MY BIG MOUTH SHUT?
THE END!

# MIND SWAP?!

Based on "The Incredible Spider-Hulk"

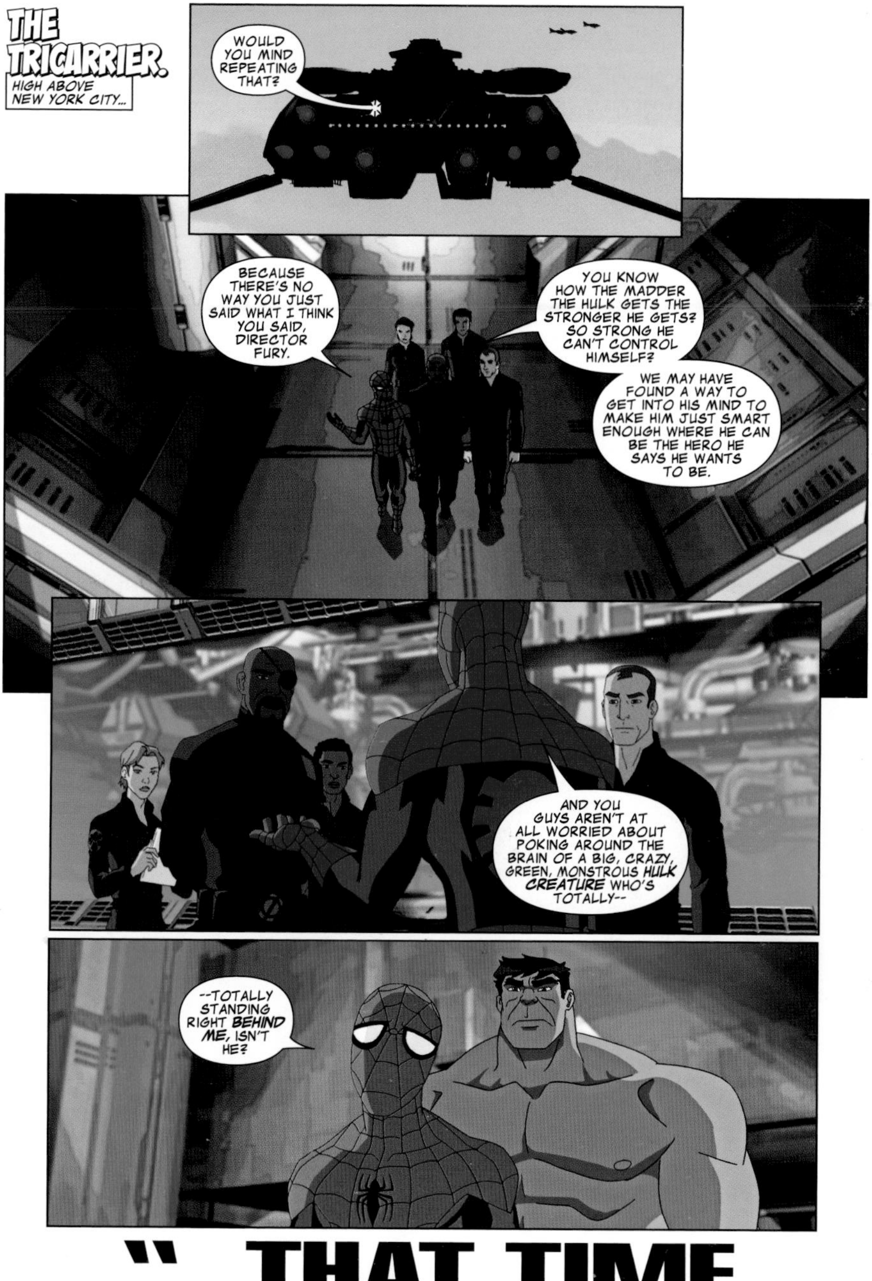
THE TRICARRIER.
HIGH ABOVE NEW YORK CITY...
WOULD YOU MIND REPEATING THAT?
BECAUSE THERE'S NO WAY YOU JUST SAID WHAT I THINK YOU SAID, DIRECTOR FURY.
YOU KNOW HOW THE MADDER THE HULK GETS THE STRONGER HE GETS? SO STRONG HE CAN'T CONTROL HIMSELF?
WE MAY HAVE FOUND A WAY TO GET INTO HIS MIND TO MAKE HIM JUST SMART ENOUGH WHERE HE CAN BE THE HERO HE SAYS HE WANTS TO BE.
AND YOU GUYS AREN'T AT ALL WORRIED ABOUT POKING AROUND THE BRAIN OF A BIG, CRAZY, GREEN, MONSTROUS HULK CREATURE WHO'S TOTALLY--
--TOTALLY STANDING RIGHT BEHIND ME, ISN'T HE?

# "...THAT TIME I TEAMED UP WITH THE HULK!"

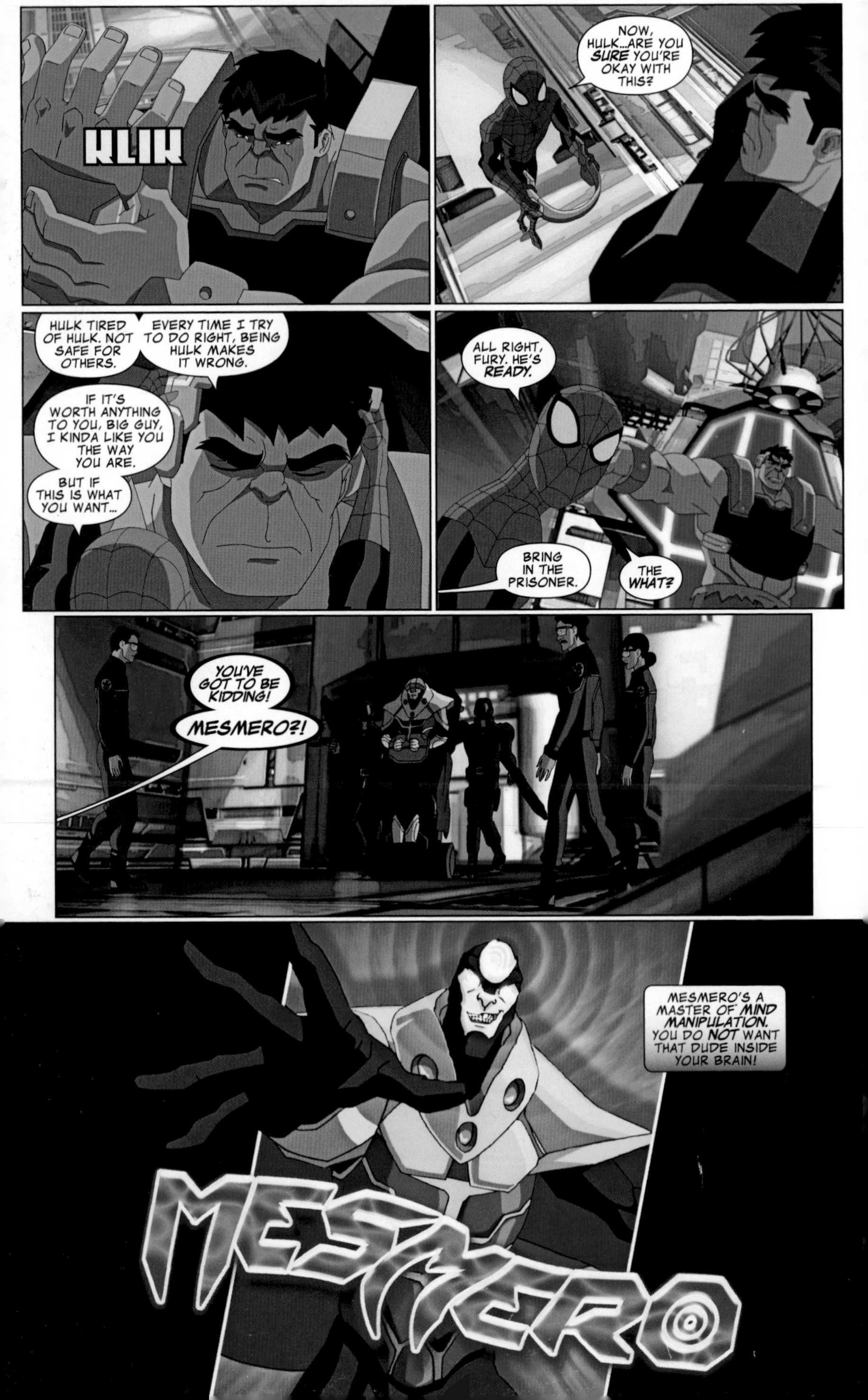
KLIK
NOW, HULK...ARE YOU SURE YOU'RE OKAY WITH THIS?
HULK TIRED OF HULK. NOT SAFE FOR OTHERS.
EVERY TIME I TRY TO DO RIGHT, BEING HULK MAKES IT WRONG.
IF IT'S WORTH ANYTHING TO YOU, BIG GUY, I KINDA LIKE YOU THE WAY YOU ARE.
BUT IF THIS IS WHAT YOU WANT...
ALL RIGHT, FURY. HE'S READY.
BRING IN THE PRISONER.
THE WHAT?
YOU'VE GOT TO BE KIDDING!
MESMERO?!
MESMERO'S A MASTER OF MIND MANIPULATION. YOU DO NOT WANT THAT DUDE INSIDE YOUR BRAIN!
MESMERO

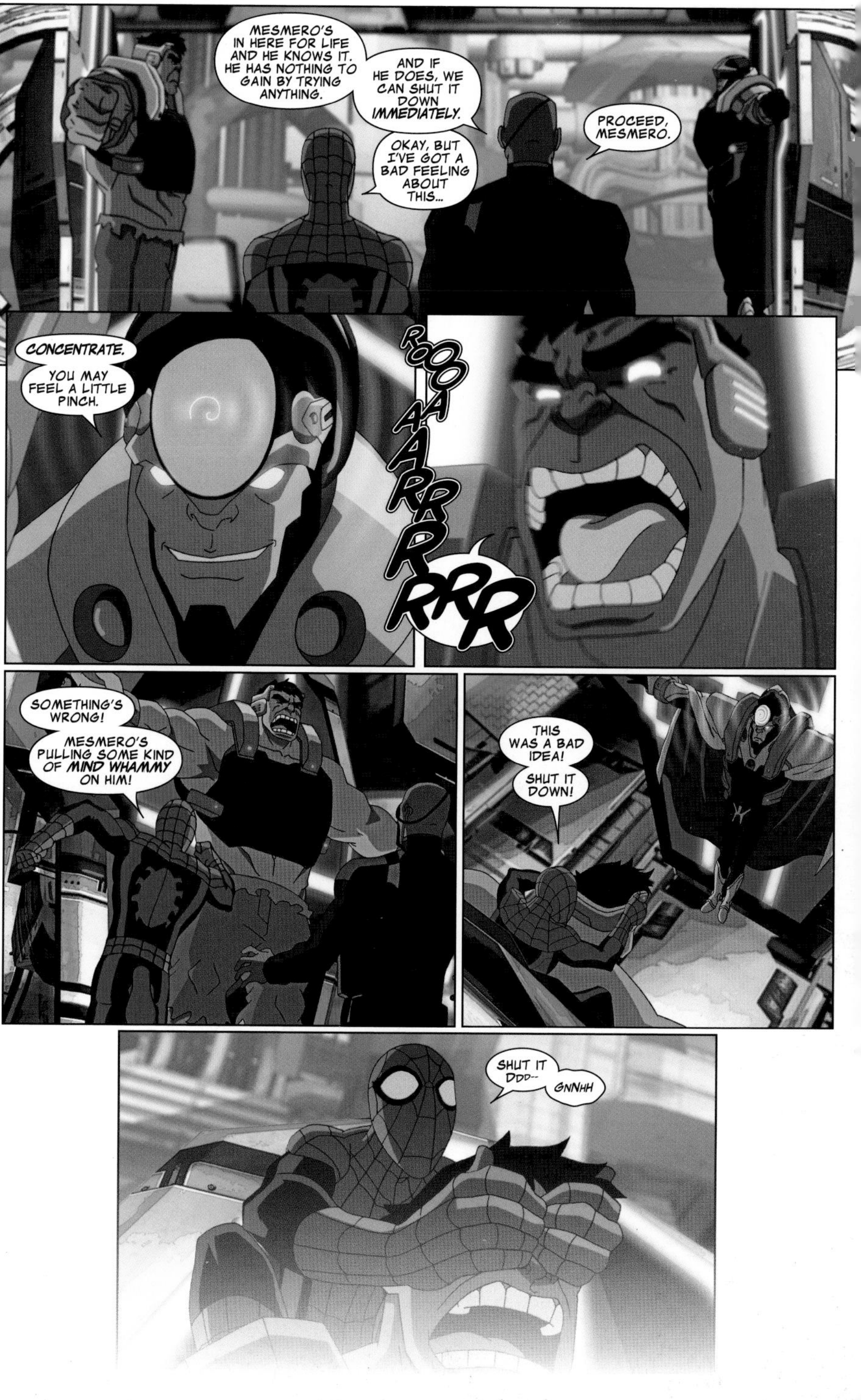
MESMERO'S IN HERE FOR LIFE AND HE KNOWS IT. HE HAS NOTHING TO GAIN BY TRYING ANYTHING.
AND IF HE DOES, WE CAN SHUT IT DOWN IMMEDIATELY.
OKAY, BUT I'VE GOT A BAD FEELING ABOUT THIS...
PROCEED, MESMERO.
CONCENTRATE.
YOU MAY FEEL A LITTLE PINCH.
ROOOAAARRRRRR
SOMETHING'S WRONG!
MESMERO'S PULLING SOME KIND OF MIND WHAMMY ON HIM!
THIS WAS A BAD IDEA!
SHUT IT DOWN!
SHUT IT DDD--
GNNHH

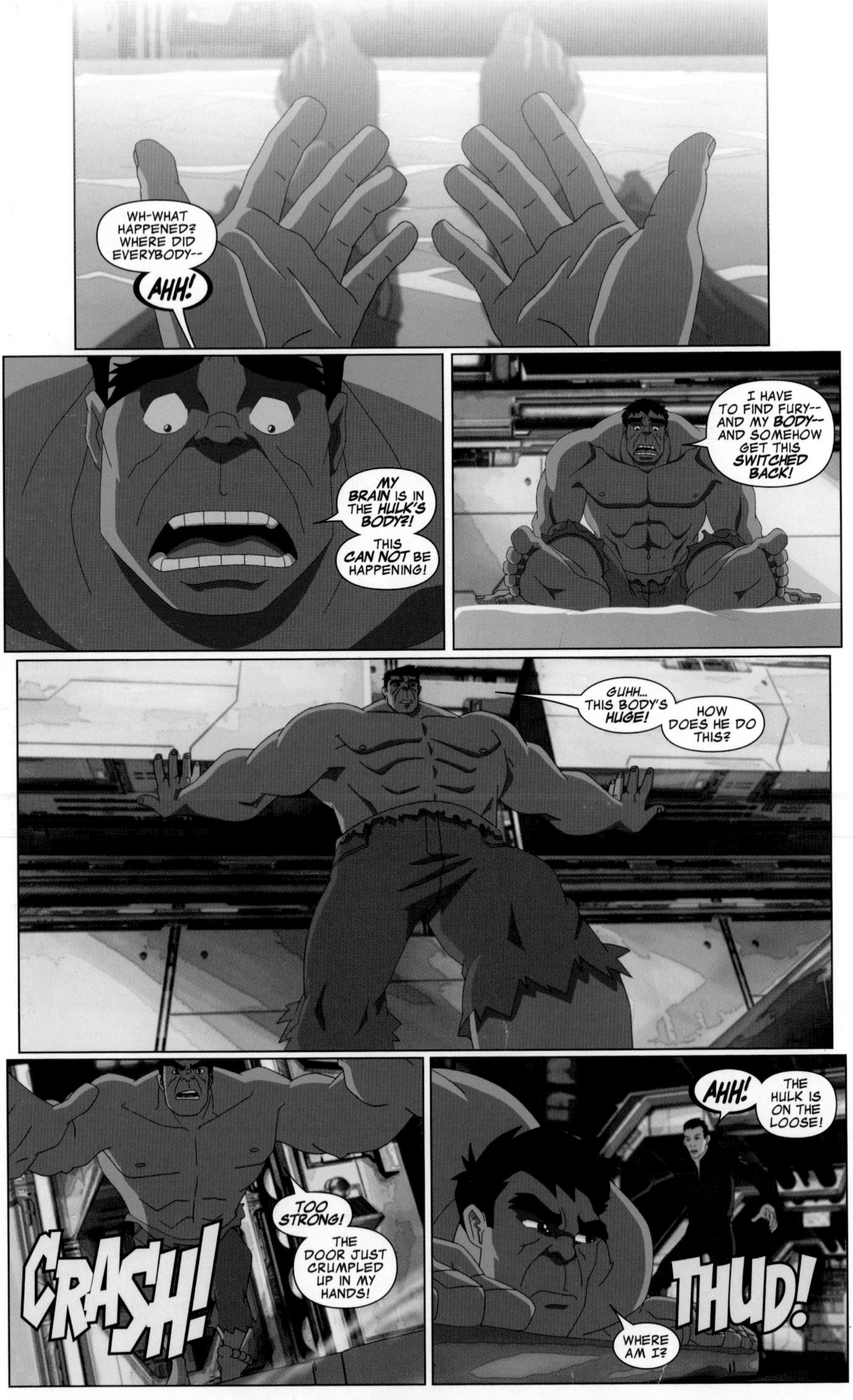
WH-WHAT HAPPENED? WHERE DID EVERYBODY--
AHH!
MY BRAIN IS IN THE HULK'S BODY?!
THIS CAN NOT BE HAPPENING!
I HAVE TO FIND FURY-- AND MY BODY-- AND SOMEHOW GET THIS SWITCHED BACK!
GUHH... THIS BODY'S HUGE!
HOW DOES HE DO THIS?
TOO STRONG!
THE DOOR JUST CRUMPLED UP IN MY HANDS!
CRASH!
AHH!
THE HULK IS ON THE LOOSE!
THUD!
WHERE AM I?

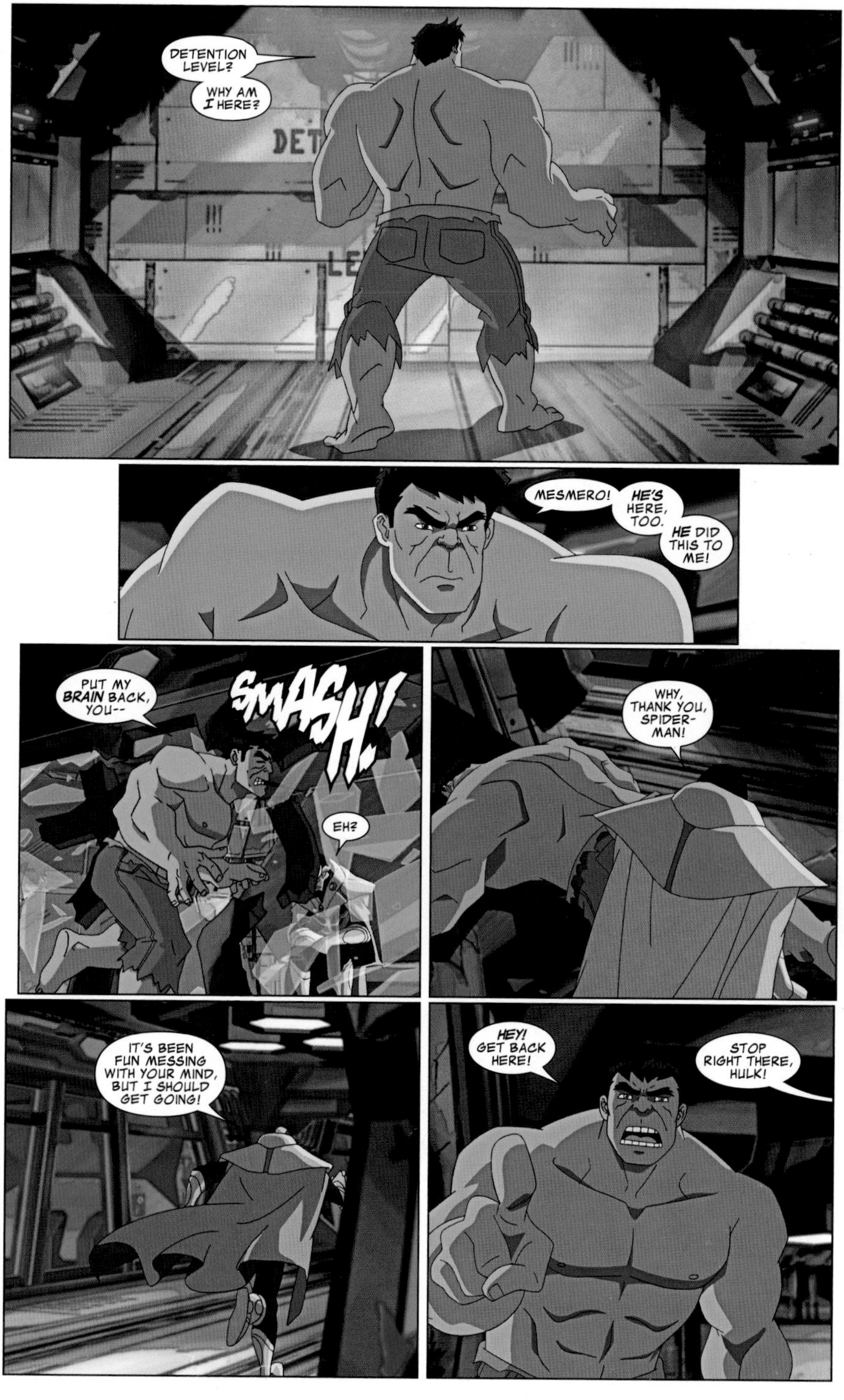
DETENTION LEVEL?
WHY AM I HERE?
DET
LE
MESMERO! HE'S HERE, TOO.
HE DID THIS TO ME!
PUT MY BRAIN BACK, YOU--
SMASH!
EH?
WHY, THANK YOU, SPIDER-MAN!
IT'S BEEN FUN MESSING WITH YOUR MIND, BUT I SHOULD GET GOING!
HEY! GET BACK HERE!
STOP RIGHT THERE, HULK!

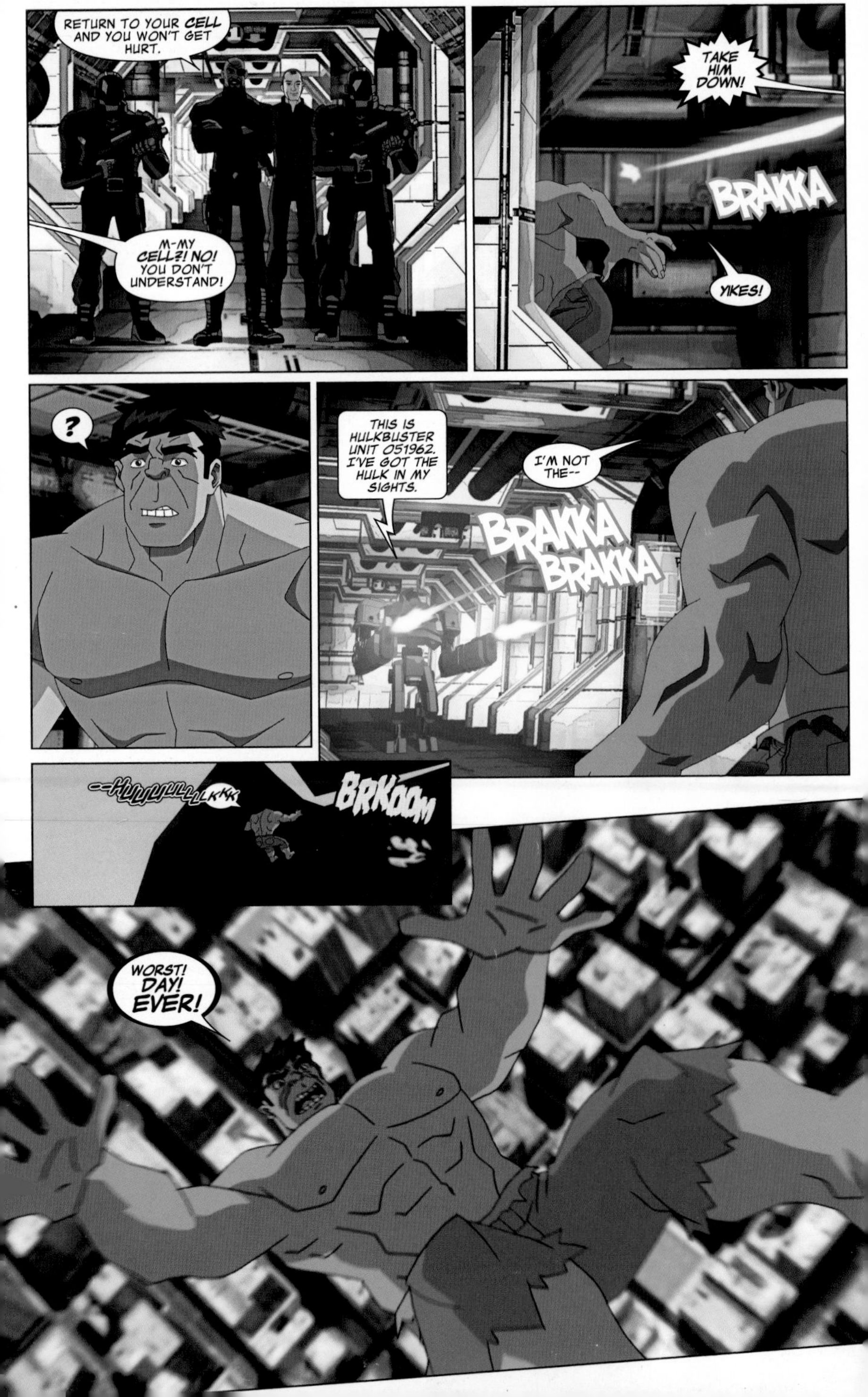
RETURN TO YOUR CELL AND YOU WON'T GET HURT.
M-MY CELLZ?! NO! YOU DON'T UNDERSTAND!
TAKE HIM DOWN!
BRAKKA
YIKES!
?
THIS IS HULKBUSTER UNIT 051962. I'VE GOT THE HULK IN MY SIGHTS.
I'M NOT THE--
BRAKKA
BRAKKA
--HUUUUULLLKKK
BRKOOM
WORST! DAY! EVER!

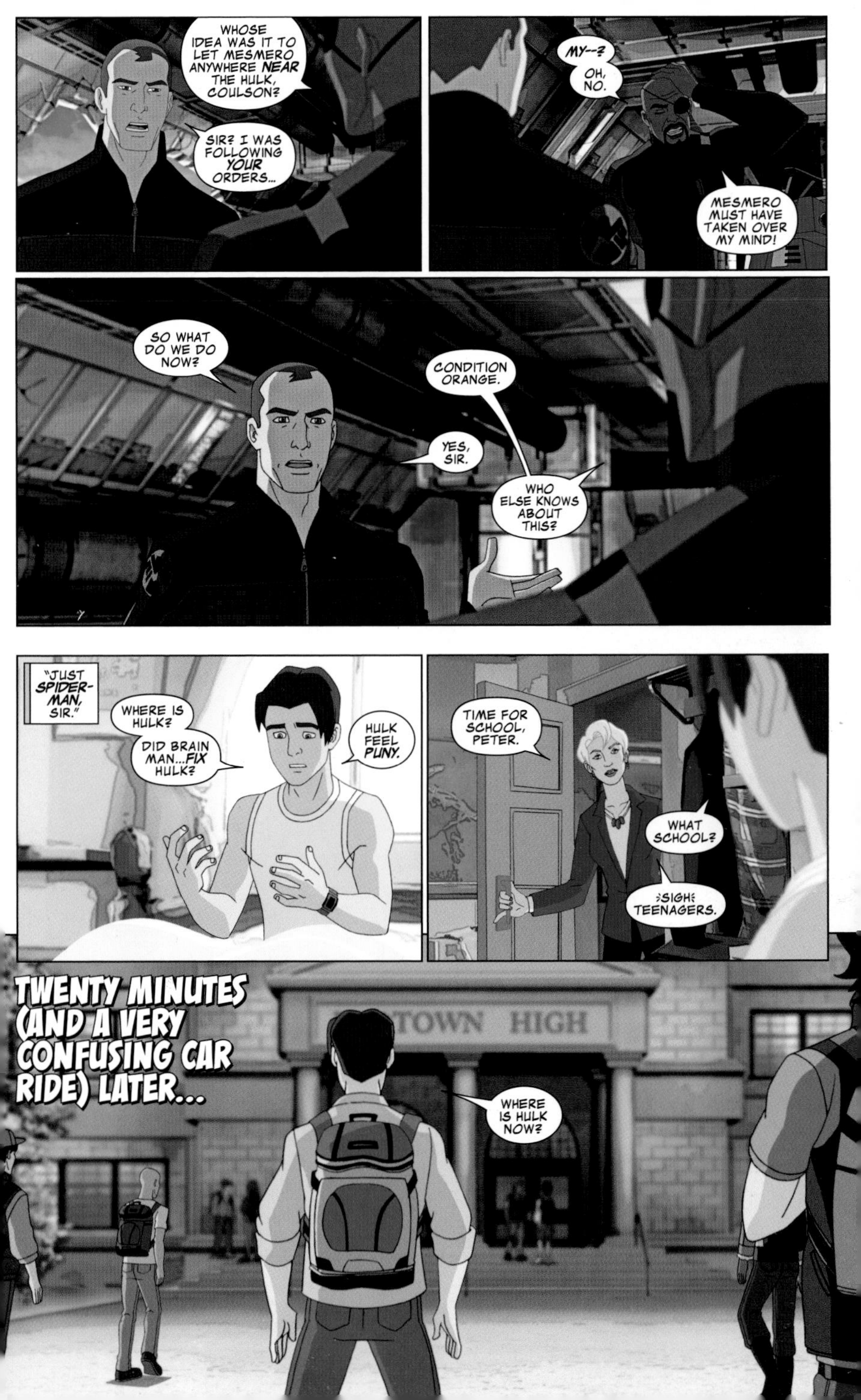
WHOSE IDEA WAS IT TO LET MESMERO ANYWHERE NEAR THE HULK, COULSON?
SIR? I WAS FOLLOWING YOUR ORDERS...
MY--?
OH, NO.
MESMERO MUST HAVE TAKEN OVER MY MIND!
SO WHAT DO WE DO NOW?
CONDITION ORANGE.
YES, SIR.
WHO ELSE KNOWS ABOUT THIS?
"JUST SPIDER-MAN, SIR."
WHERE IS HULK?
DID BRAIN MAN...FIX HULK?
HULK FEEL PUNY.
TIME FOR SCHOOL, PETER.
WHAT SCHOOL?
SIGH TEENAGERS.
TWENTY MINUTES (AND A VERY CONFUSING CAR RIDE) LATER...
TOWN HIGH
WHERE IS HULK NOW?

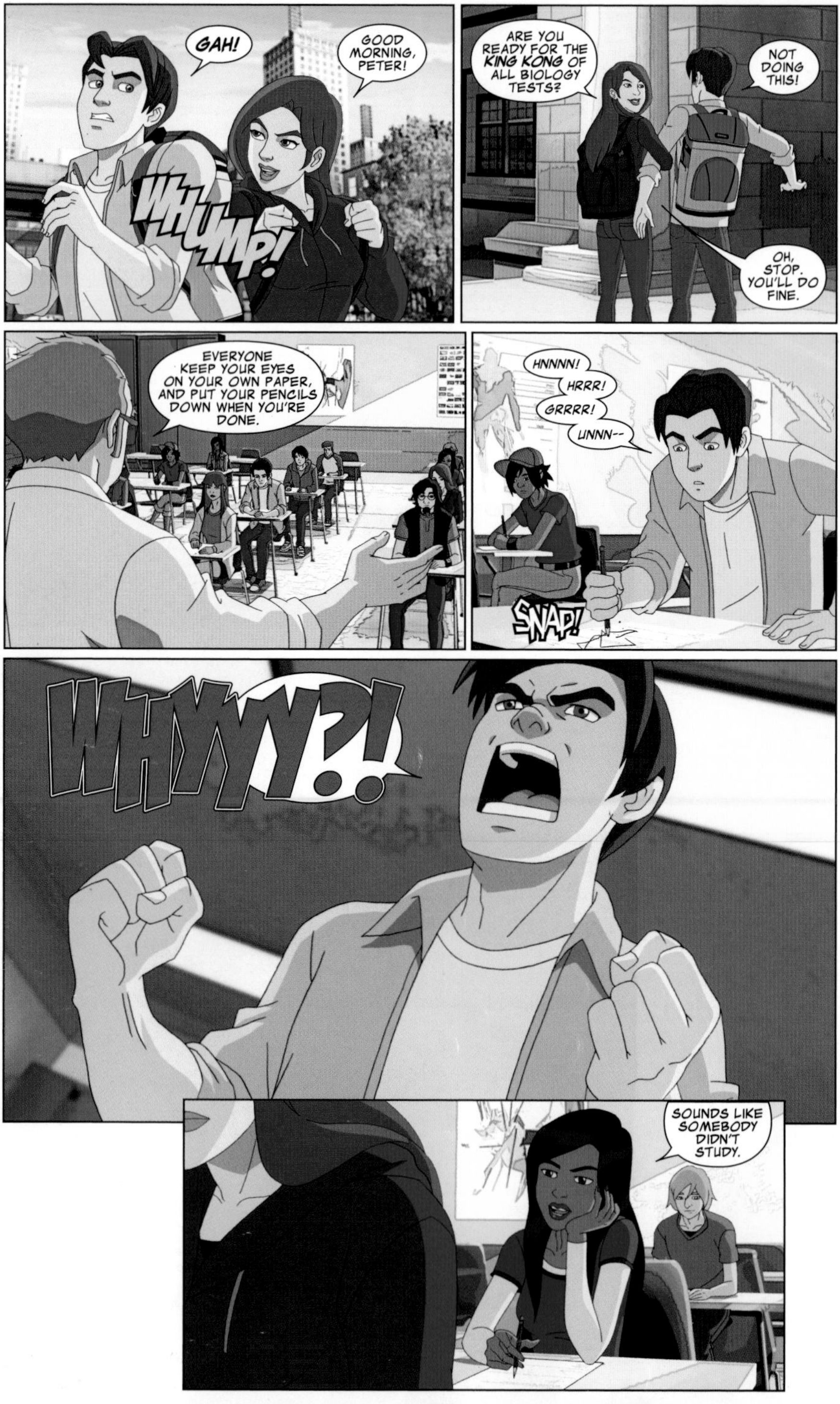
GAH!
GOOD MORNING, PETER!
WHUMP!
ARE YOU READY FOR THE KING KONG OF ALL BIOLOGY TESTS?
NOT DOING THIS!
OH, STOP. YOU'LL DO FINE.
EVERYONE KEEP YOUR EYES ON YOUR OWN PAPER, AND PUT YOUR PENCILS DOWN WHEN YOU'RE DONE.
HNNNN!
HRRR!
GRRRR!
UNNN--
SNAP!
WHYYY?!
SOUNDS LIKE SOMEBODY DIDN'T STUDY.

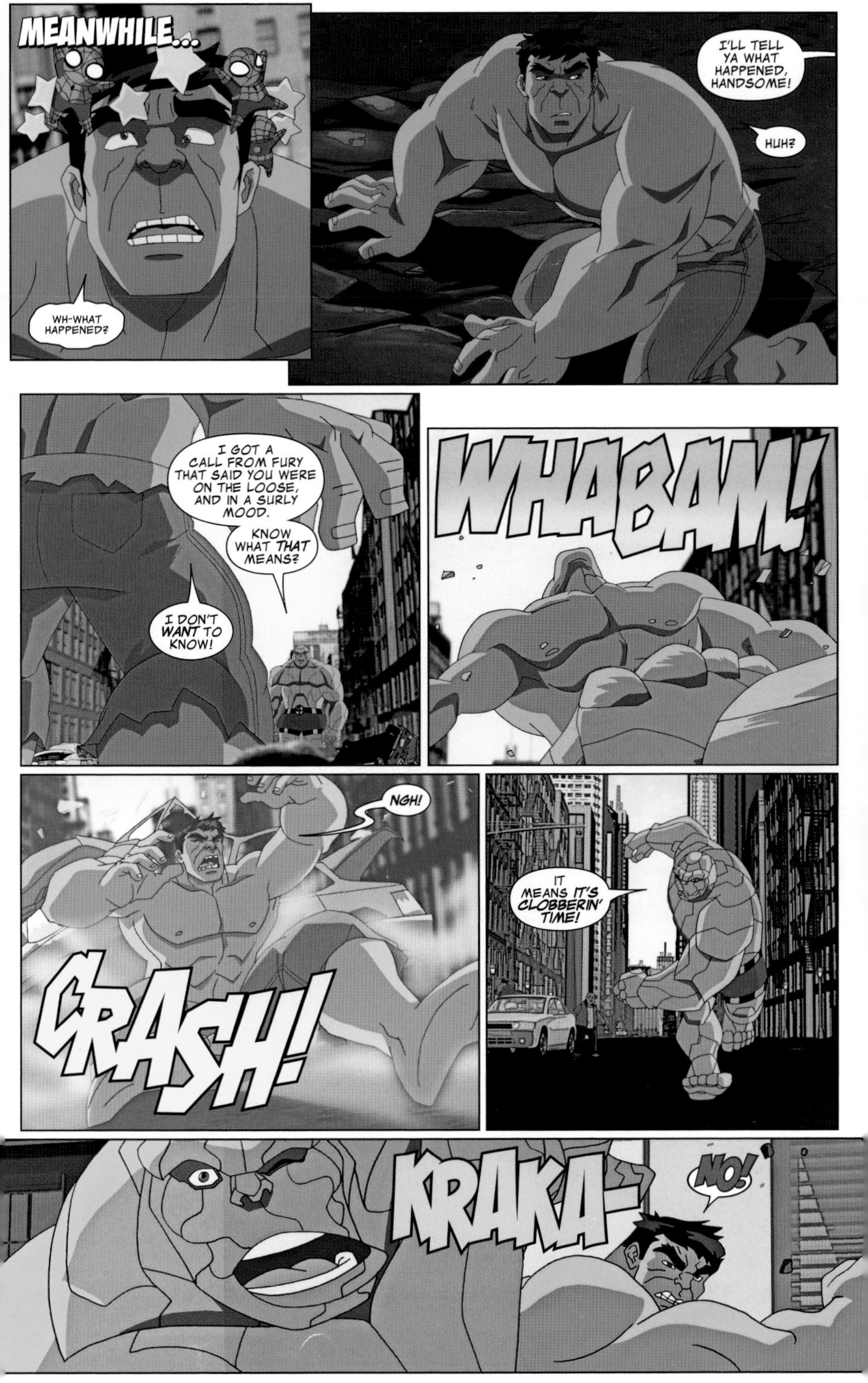
MEANWHILE...
WH-WHAT HAPPENED?
I'LL TELL YA WHAT HAPPENED, HANDSOME!
HUH?
I GOT A CALL FROM FURY THAT SAID YOU WERE ON THE LOOSE, AND IN A SURLY MOOD.
KNOW WHAT THAT MEANS?
I DON'T WANT TO KNOW!
WHABAM!
NGH!
CRASH!
IT MEANS IT'S CLOBBERIN' TIME!
KRAKA-
NO!

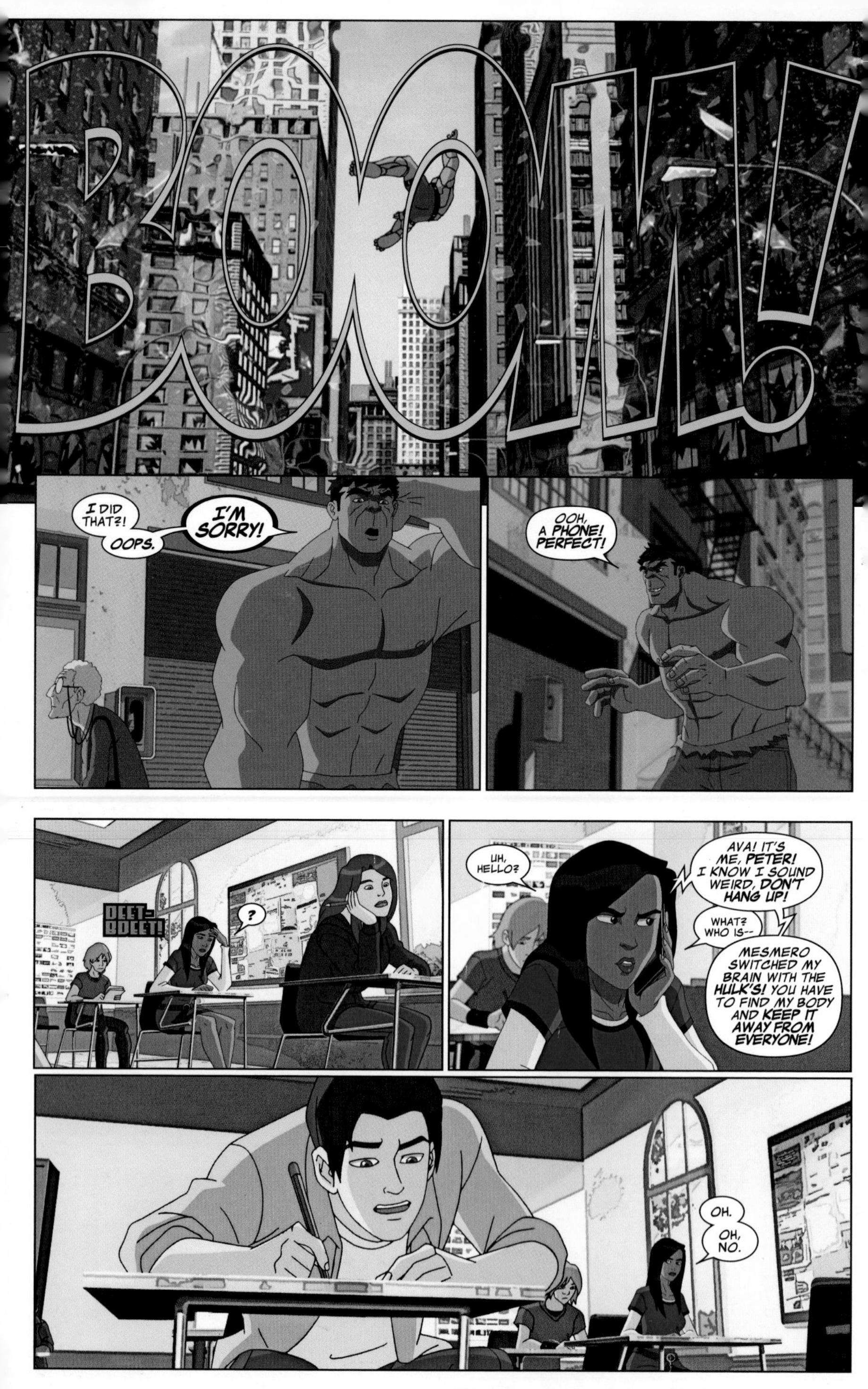

BOOOM!
I DID THAT?!
OOPS.
I'M SORRY!
OOH, A PHONE! PERFECT!
DEET-DEET!
?
UH, HELLO?
AVA! IT'S ME, PETER! I KNOW I SOUND WEIRD, DON'T HANG UP!
WHAT? WHO IS--
MESMERO SWITCHED MY BRAIN WITH THE HULK'S! YOU HAVE TO FIND MY BODY AND KEEP IT AWAY FROM EVERYONE!
OH.
OH, NO.

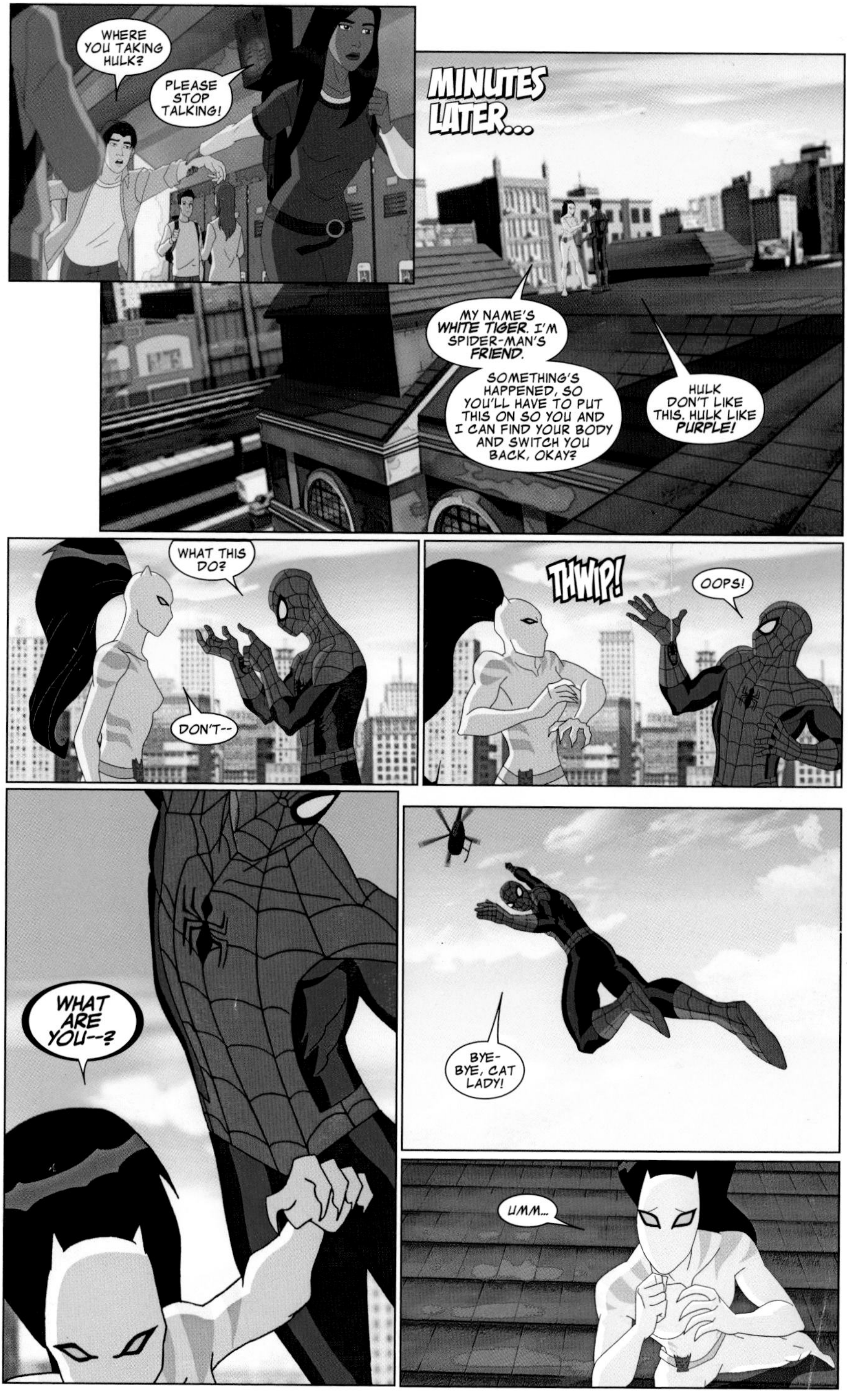
WHERE YOU TAKING HULK?
PLEASE STOP TALKING!
MINUTES LATER...
MY NAME'S WHITE TIGER. I'M SPIDER-MAN'S FRIEND.
SOMETHING'S HAPPENED, SO YOU'LL HAVE TO PUT THIS ON SO YOU AND I CAN FIND YOUR BODY AND SWITCH YOU BACK, OKAY?
HULK DON'T LIKE THIS. HULK LIKE PURPLE!
WHAT THIS DO?
DON'T--
THWIP!
OOPS!
WHAT ARE YOU--?
BYE-BYE, CAT LADY!
UMM...

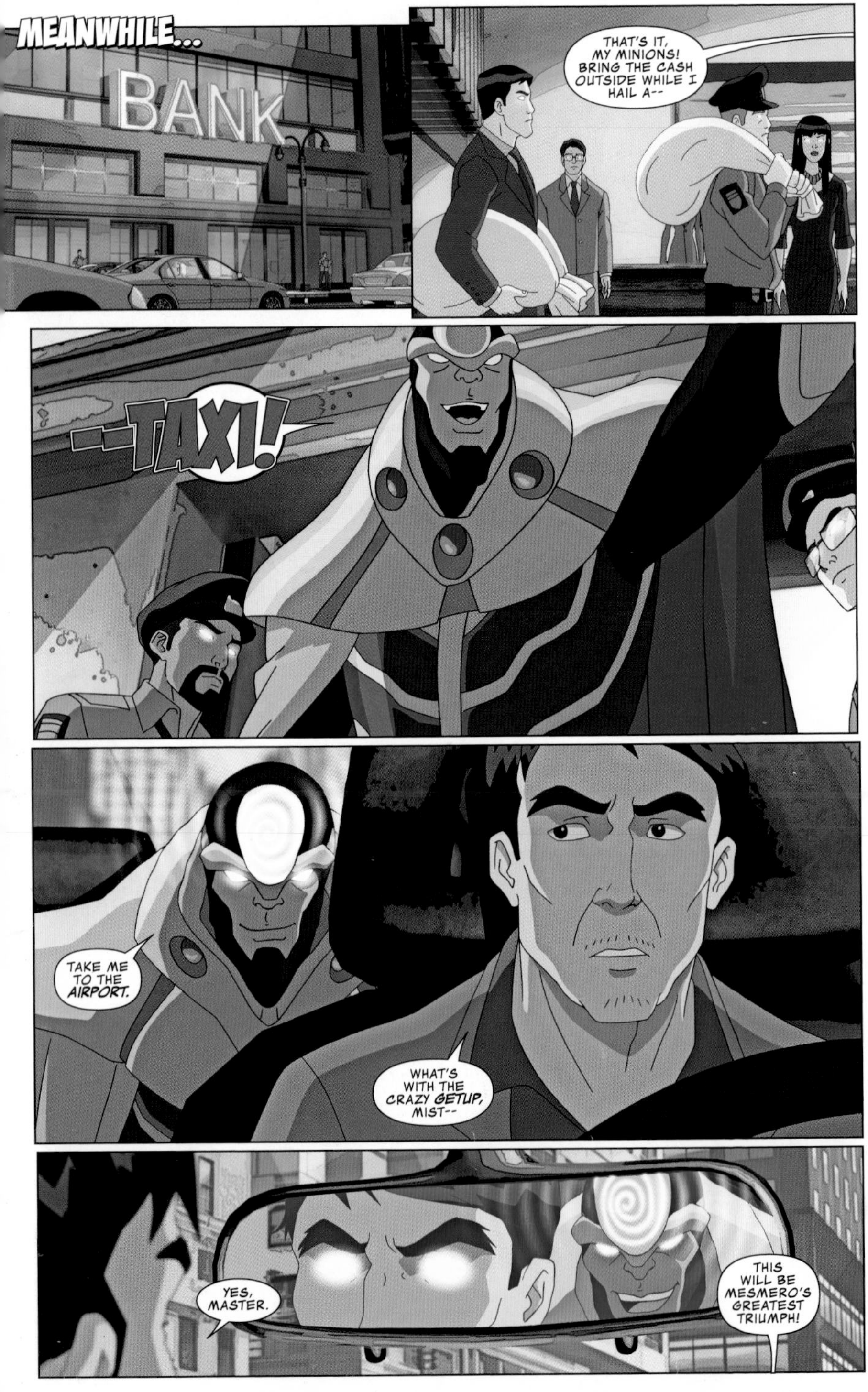
MEANWHILE...
BANK
THAT'S IT, MY MINIONS! BRING THE CASH OUTSIDE WHILE I HAIL A--
--TAXI!
TAKE ME TO THE AIRPORT.
WHAT'S WITH THE CRAZY GETUP, MIST--
YES, MASTER.
THIS WILL BE MESMERO'S GREATEST TRIUMPH!

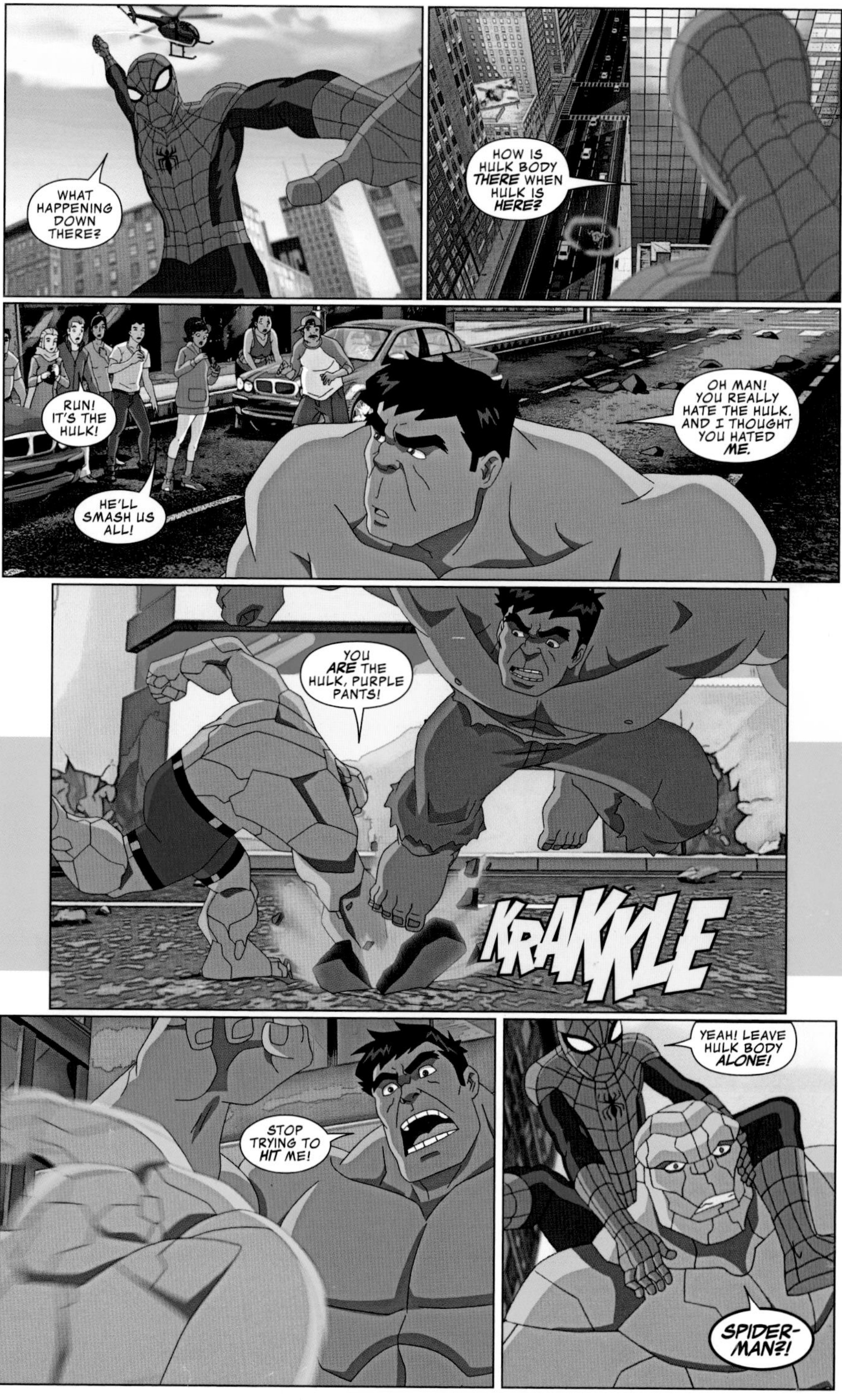
WHAT HAPPENING DOWN THERE?
HOW IS HULK BODY *THERE* WHEN HULK IS *HERE?*
RUN! IT'S THE HULK!
HE'LL SMASH US ALL!
OH MAN! YOU REALLY HATE THE HULK. AND I THOUGHT YOU HATED *ME.*
YOU *ARE* THE HULK, PURPLE PANTS!
KRAKKLE
STOP TRYING TO *HIT* ME!
YEAH! LEAVE HULK BODY *ALONE!*
SPIDER-MAN?!

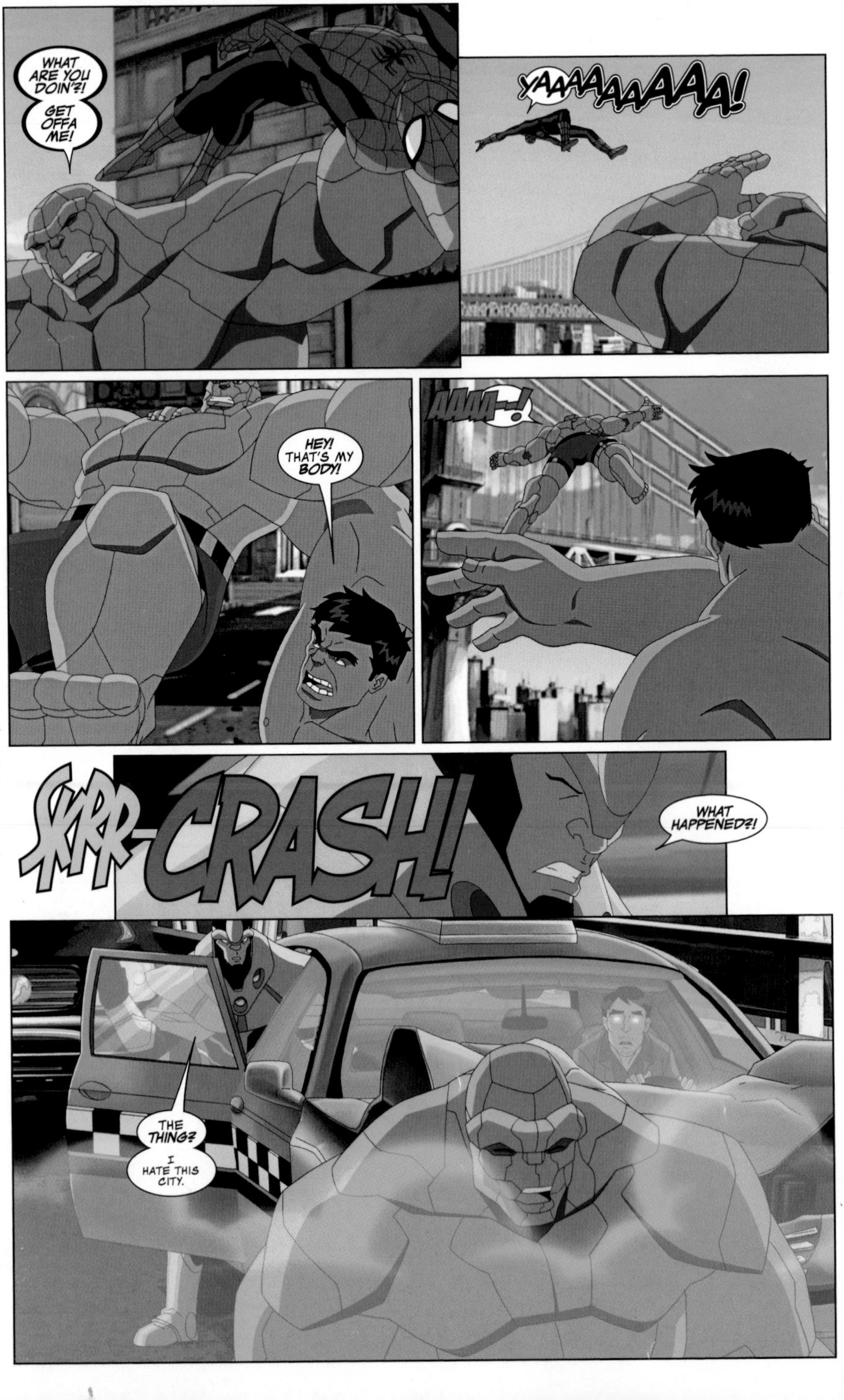
WHAT ARE YOU DOIN'?!
GET OFFA ME!
YAAAAAAAAAA!
HEY! THAT'S MY BODY!
AAAA--!
SKRR-CRASH!
WHAT HAPPENED?!
THE THING?
I HATE THIS CITY.

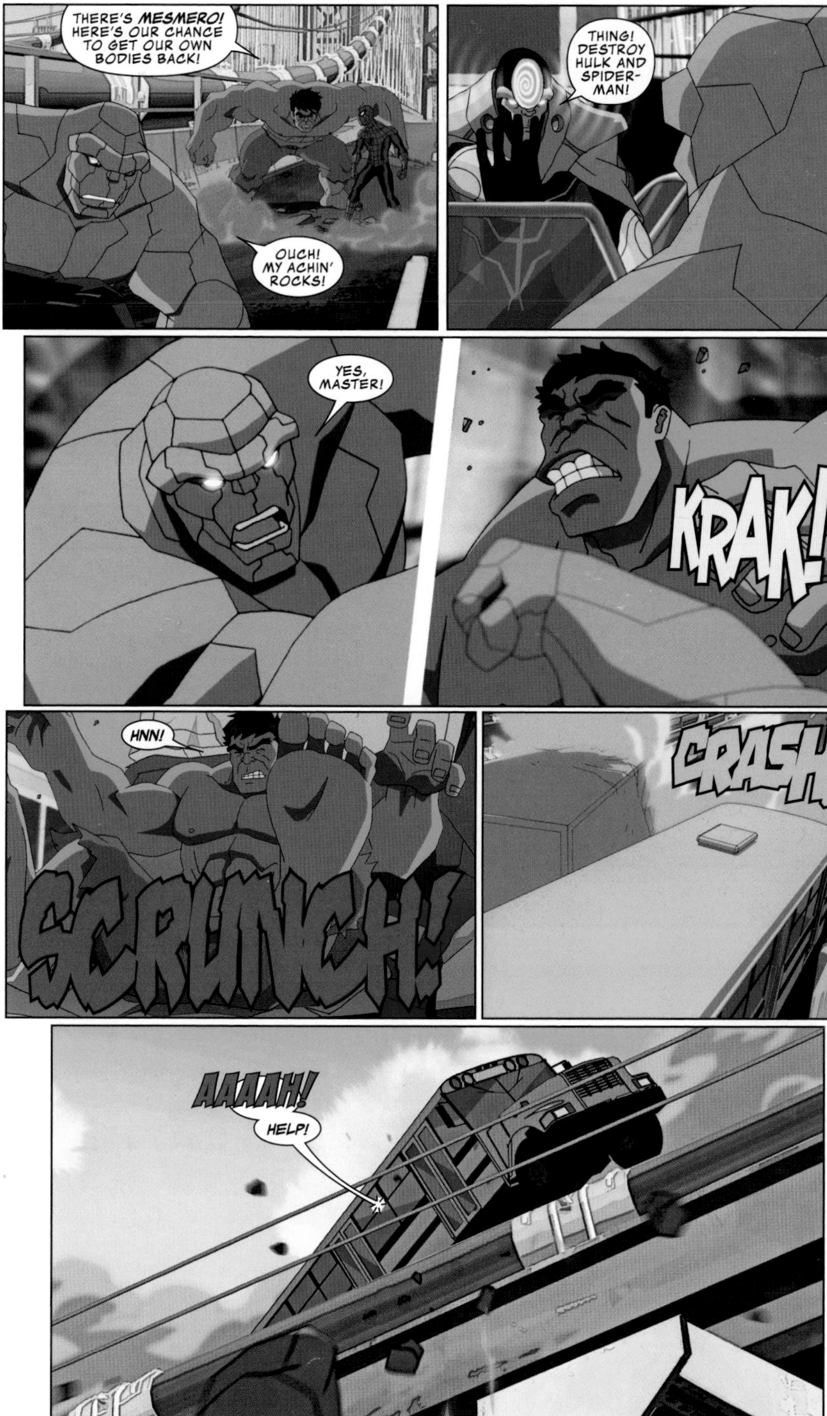
THERE'S MESMERO! HERE'S OUR CHANCE TO GET OUR OWN BODIES BACK!
OUCH! MY ACHIN' ROCKS!
THING! DESTROY HULK AND SPIDER-MAN!
YES, MASTER!
KRAK!
HNN!
SCRUNCH!
CRASH!
AAAAH!
HELP!

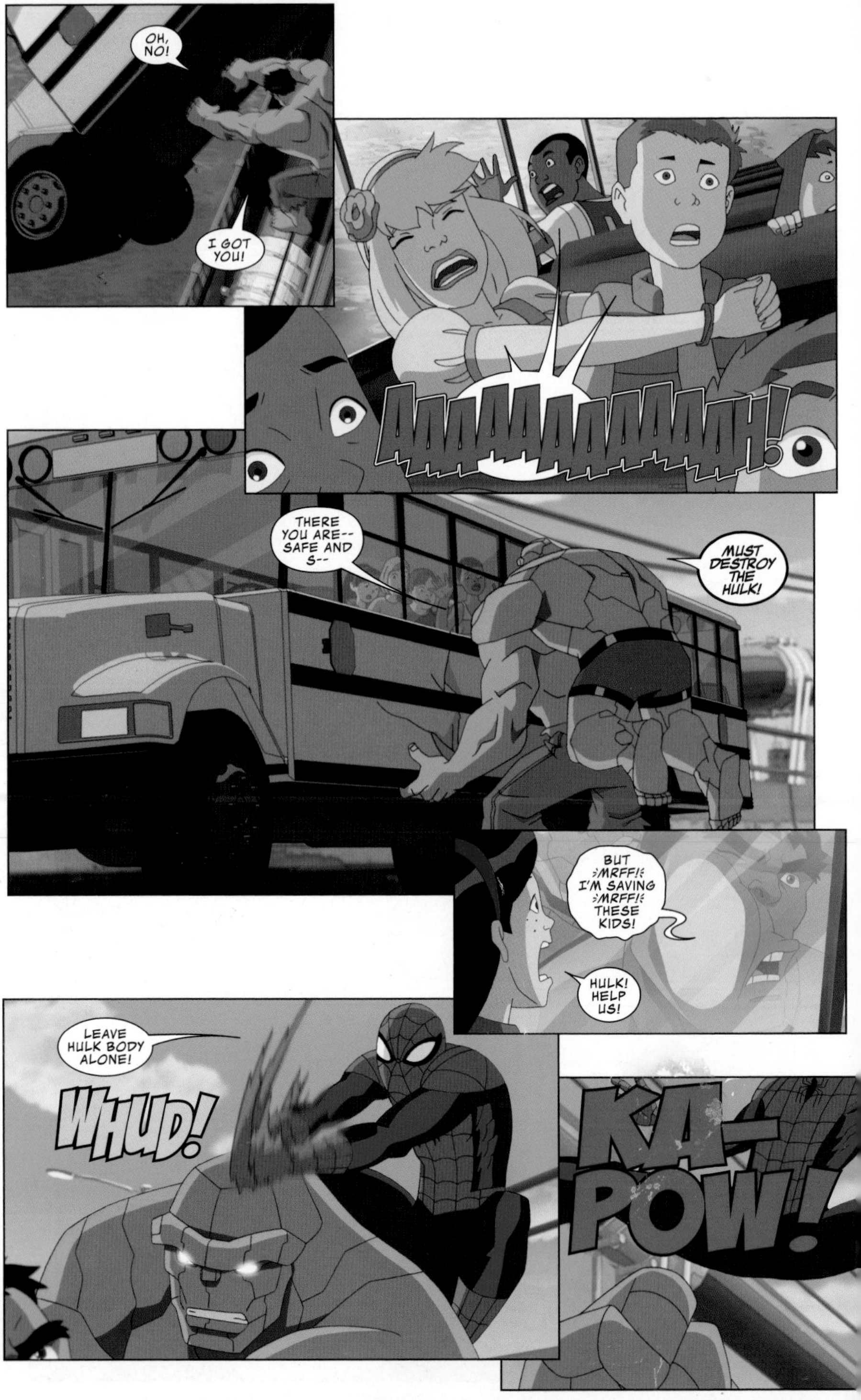
OH, NO!
I GOT YOU!
AAAAAAAAAAAAH!
THERE YOU ARE-- SAFE AND S--
MUST DESTROY THE HULK!
BUT *MRFF!* I'M SAVING *MRFF!* THESE KIDS!
HULK! HELP US!
LEAVE HULK BODY ALONE!
WHUD!
KA-POW!

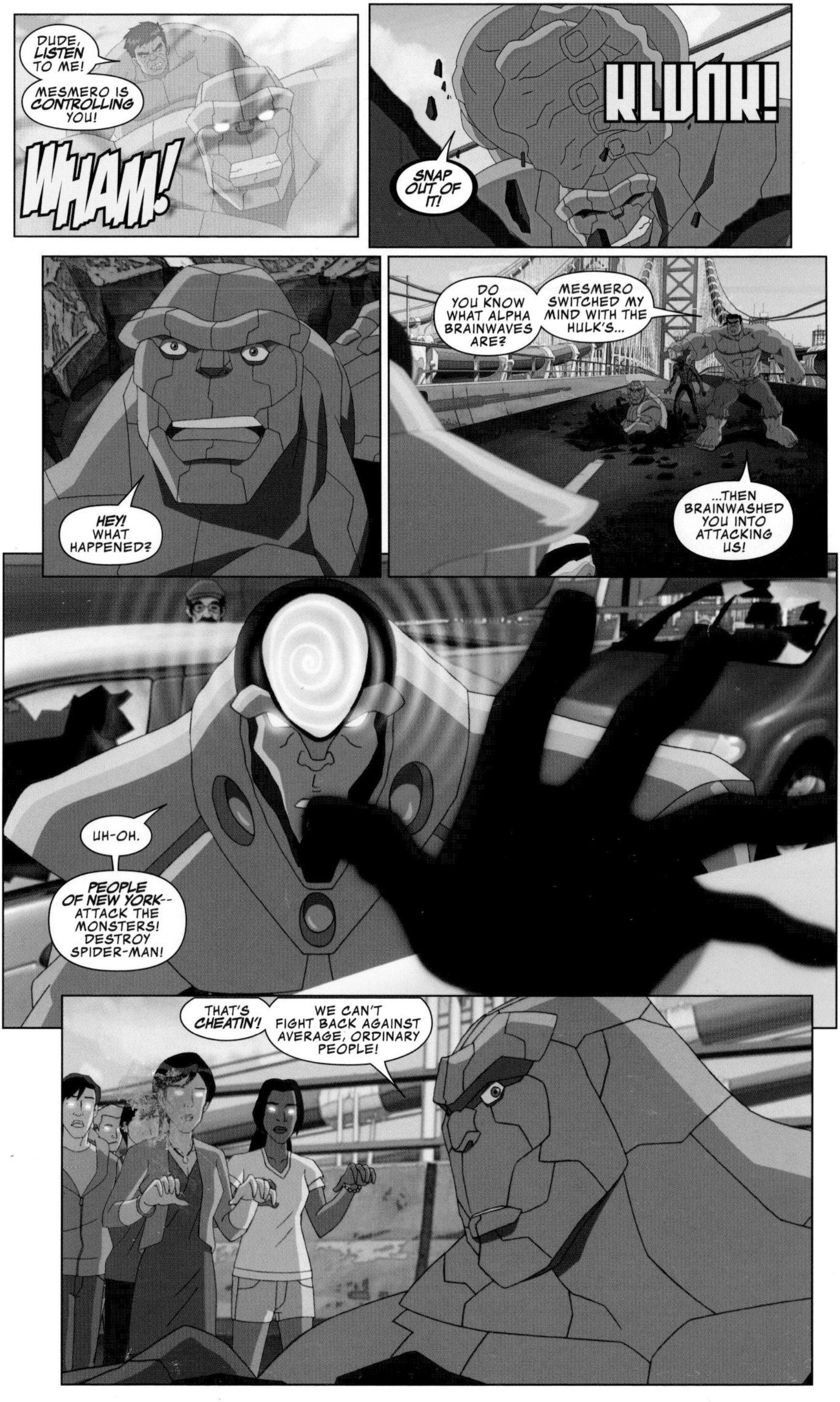
DUDE, LISTEN TO ME!
MESMERO IS CONTROLLING YOU!
WHAM!
KLUNK!
SNAP OUT OF IT!
HEY! WHAT HAPPENED?
DO YOU KNOW WHAT ALPHA BRAINWAVES ARE?
MESMERO SWITCHED MY MIND WITH THE HULK'S...
...THEN BRAINWASHED YOU INTO ATTACKING US!
UH-OH.
PEOPLE OF NEW YORK--ATTACK THE MONSTERS! DESTROY SPIDER-MAN!
THAT'S CHEATIN'!
WE CAN'T FIGHT BACK AGAINST AVERAGE, ORDINARY PEOPLE!

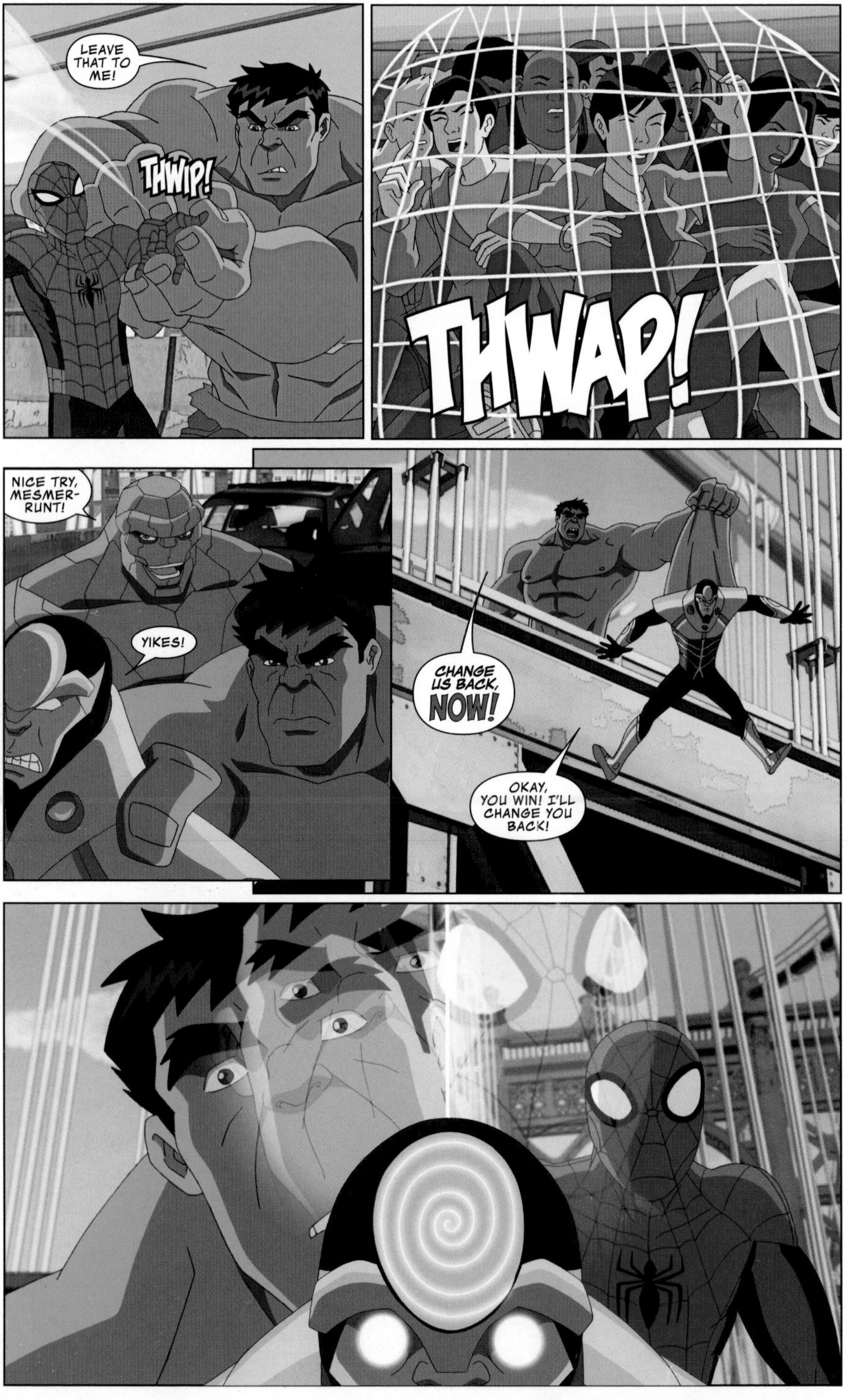
LEAVE THAT TO ME!
THWIP!
THWAP!
NICE TRY, MESMER-RUNT!
YIKES!
CHANGE US BACK, NOW!
OKAY, YOU WIN! I'LL CHANGE YOU BACK!

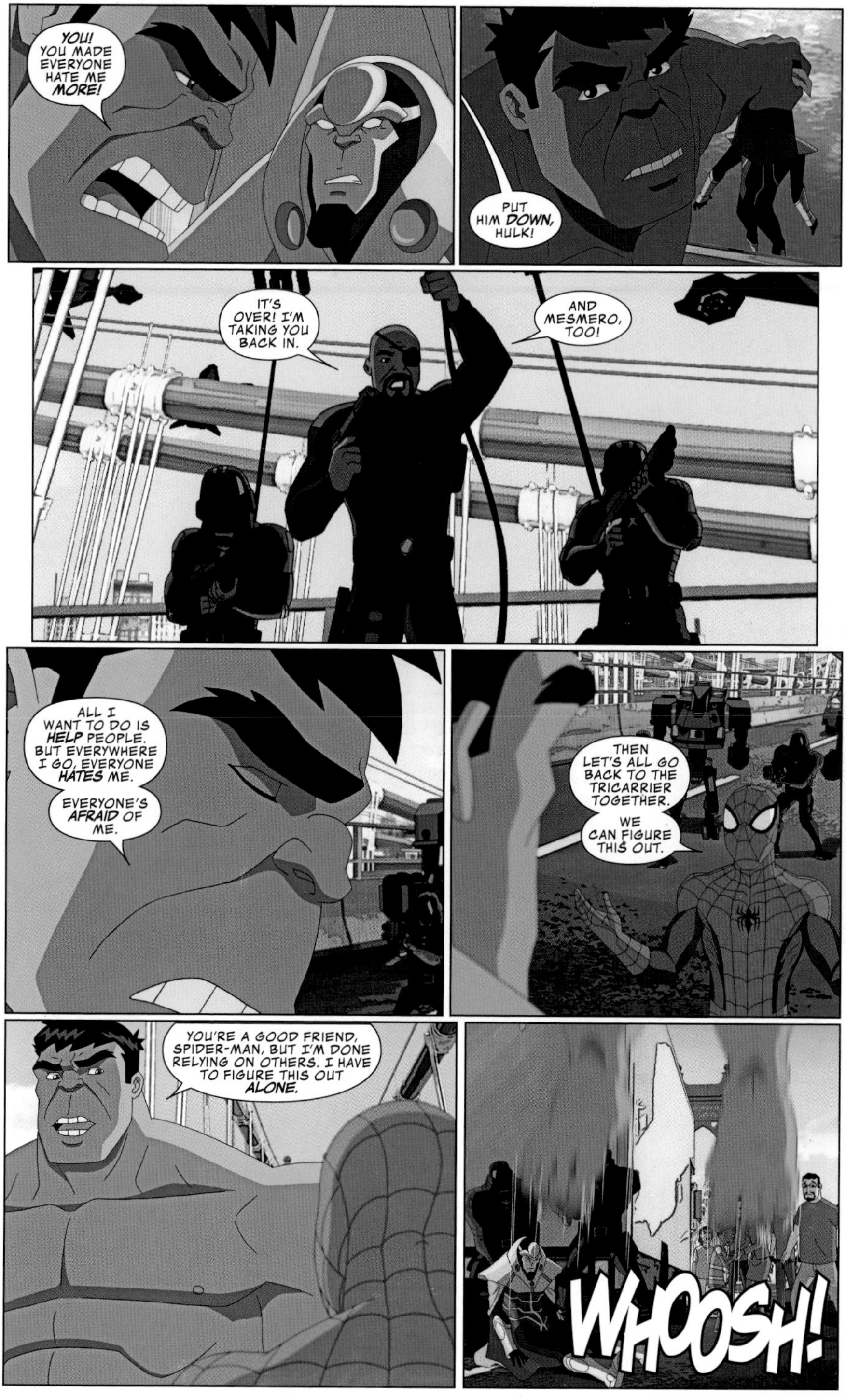
YOU! YOU MADE EVERYONE HATE ME MORE!
PUT HIM DOWN, HULK!
IT'S OVER! I'M TAKING YOU BACK IN.
AND MESMERO, TOO!
ALL I WANT TO DO IS HELP PEOPLE. BUT EVERYWHERE I GO, EVERYONE HATES ME.
EVERYONE'S AFRAID OF ME.
THEN LET'S ALL GO BACK TO THE TRICARRIER TOGETHER.
WE CAN FIGURE THIS OUT.
YOU'RE A GOOD FRIEND, SPIDER-MAN, BUT I'M DONE RELYING ON OTHERS. I HAVE TO FIGURE THIS OUT ALONE.
WHOOSH!

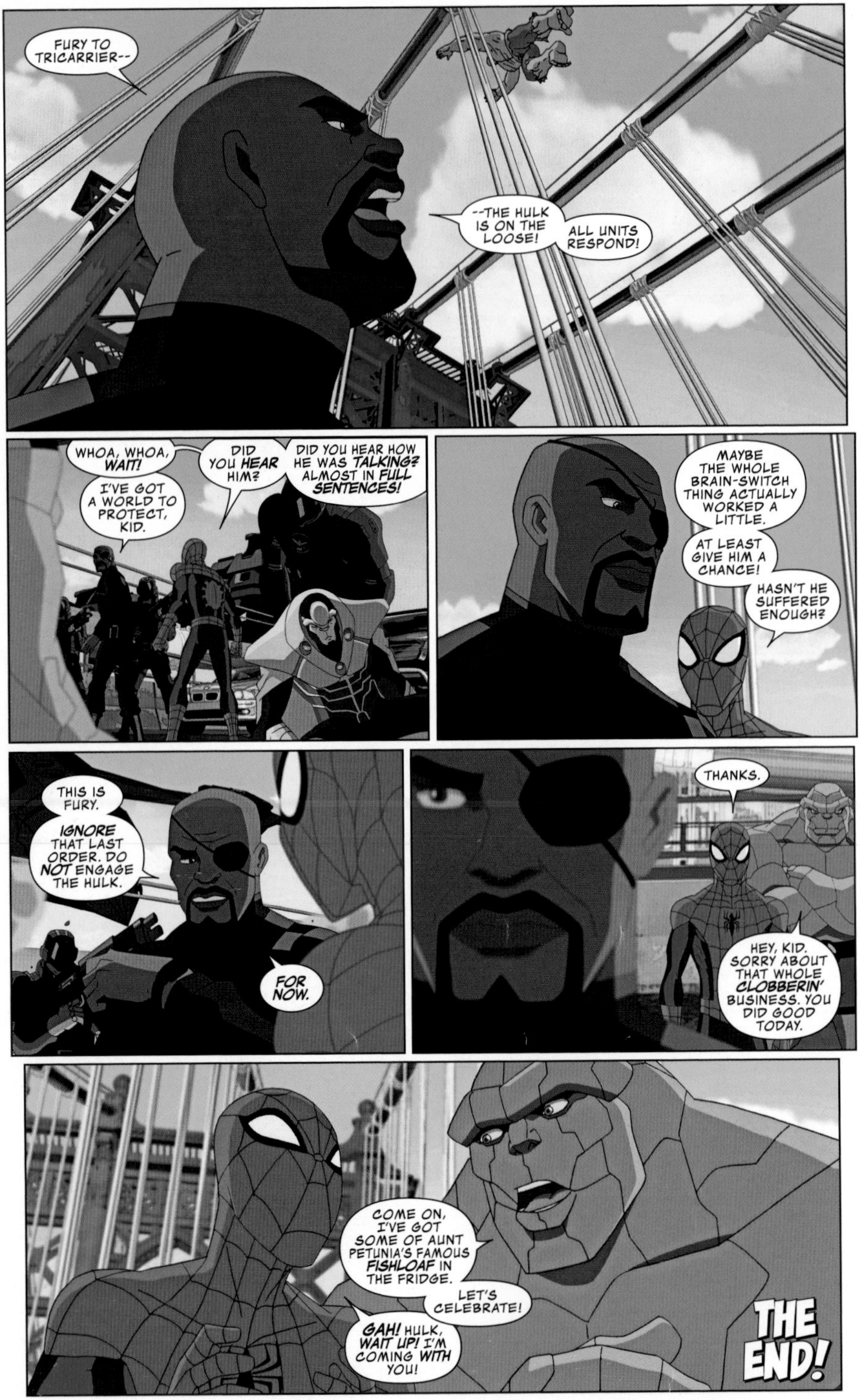
FURY TO TRICARRIER--
--THE HULK IS ON THE LOOSE!
ALL UNITS RESPOND!
WHOA, WHOA, WAIT!
I'VE GOT A WORLD TO PROTECT, KID.
DID YOU HEAR HIM?
DID YOU HEAR HOW HE WAS TALKING? ALMOST IN FULL SENTENCES!
MAYBE THE WHOLE BRAIN-SWITCH THING ACTUALLY WORKED A LITTLE.
AT LEAST GIVE HIM A CHANCE!
HASN'T HE SUFFERED ENOUGH?
THIS IS FURY.
IGNORE THAT LAST ORDER. DO NOT ENGAGE THE HULK.
FOR NOW.
THANKS.
HEY, KID. SORRY ABOUT THAT WHOLE CLOBBERIN' BUSINESS. YOU DID GOOD TODAY.
COME ON, I'VE GOT SOME OF AUNT PETUNIA'S FAMOUS FISHLOAF IN THE FRIDGE.
LET'S CELEBRATE!
GAH! HULK, WAIT UP! I'M COMING WITH YOU!
THE END!

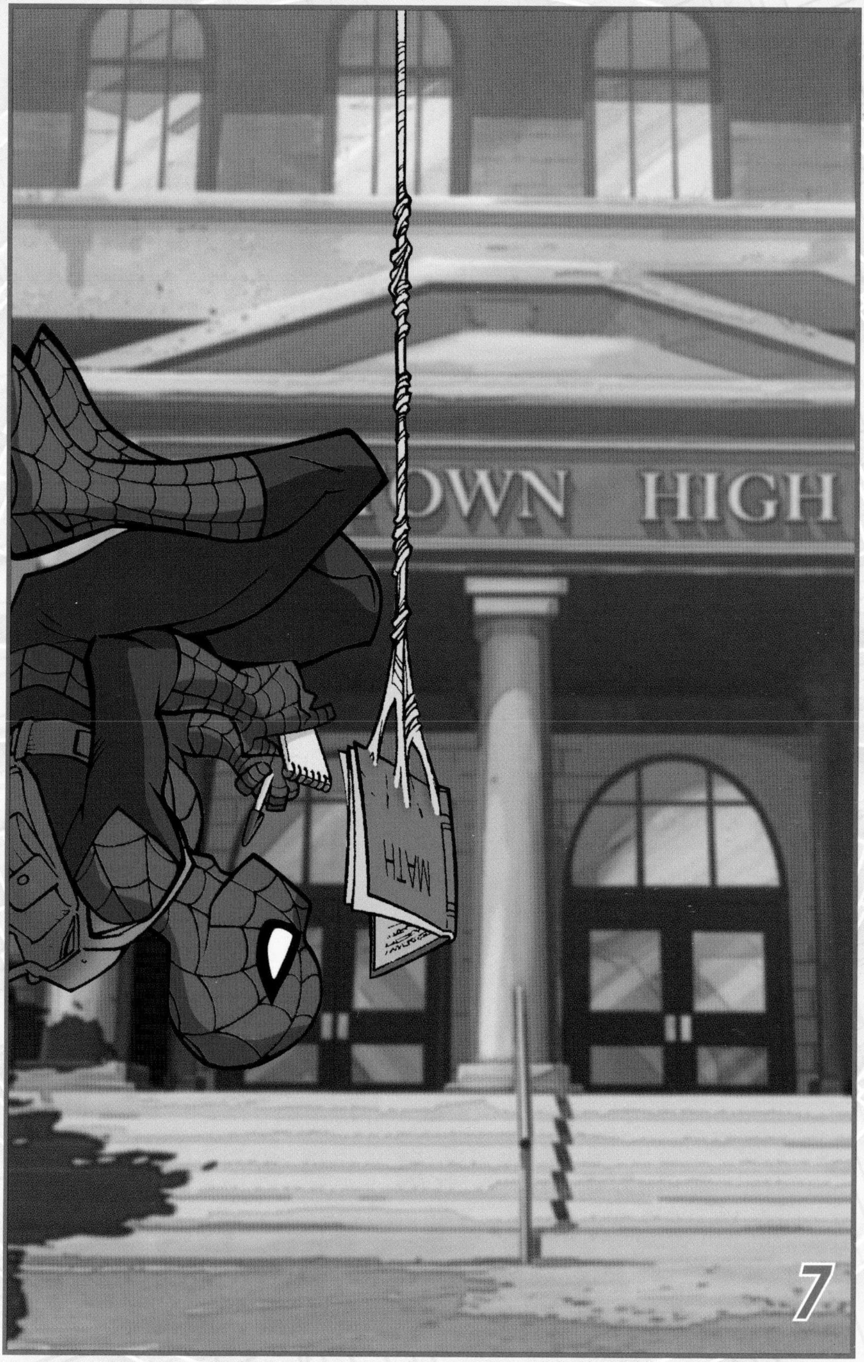
HIGH
MATH

# 7

Based on “Stan by Me”

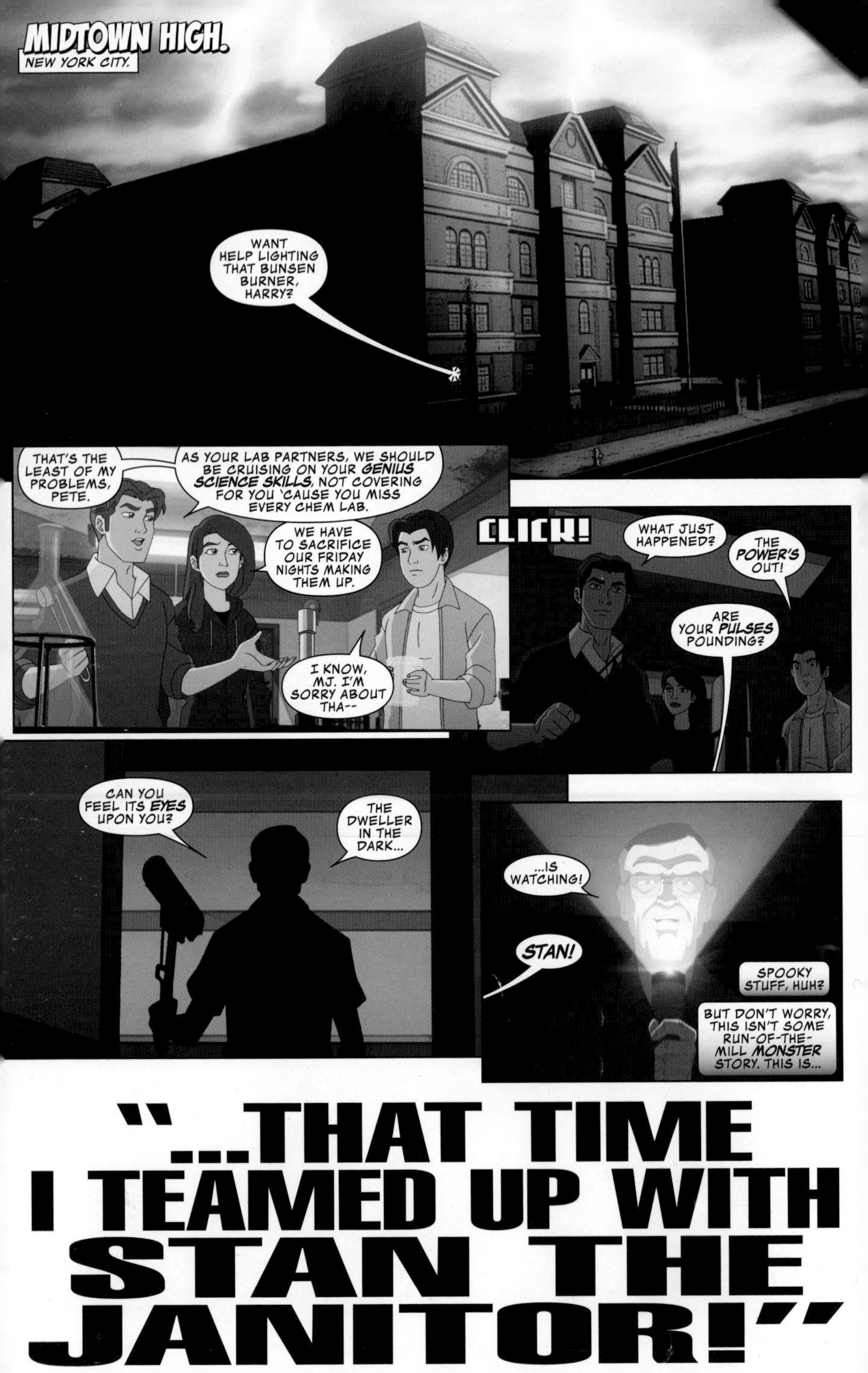
MIDTOWN HIGH.
NEW YORK CITY.
WANT HELP LIGHTING THAT BUNSEN BURNER, HARRY?
THAT'S THE LEAST OF MY PROBLEMS, PETE.
AS YOUR LAB PARTNERS, WE SHOULD BE CRUISING ON YOUR GENIUS SCIENCE SKILLS, NOT COVERING FOR YOU 'CAUSE YOU MISS EVERY CHEM LAB.
WE HAVE TO SACRIFICE OUR FRIDAY NIGHTS MAKING THEM UP.
I KNOW, MJ. I'M SORRY ABOUT THA--
CLICK!
WHAT JUST HAPPENED?
THE POWER'S OUT!
ARE YOUR PULSES POUNDING?
CAN YOU FEEL ITS EYES UPON YOU?
THE DWELLER IN THE DARK...
...IS WATCHING!
STAN!
SPOOKY STUFF, HUH?
BUT DON'T WORRY, THIS ISN'T SOME RUN-OF-THE-MILL MONSTER STORY. THIS IS...

# "...THAT TIME I TEAMED UP WITH STAN THE JANITOR!"

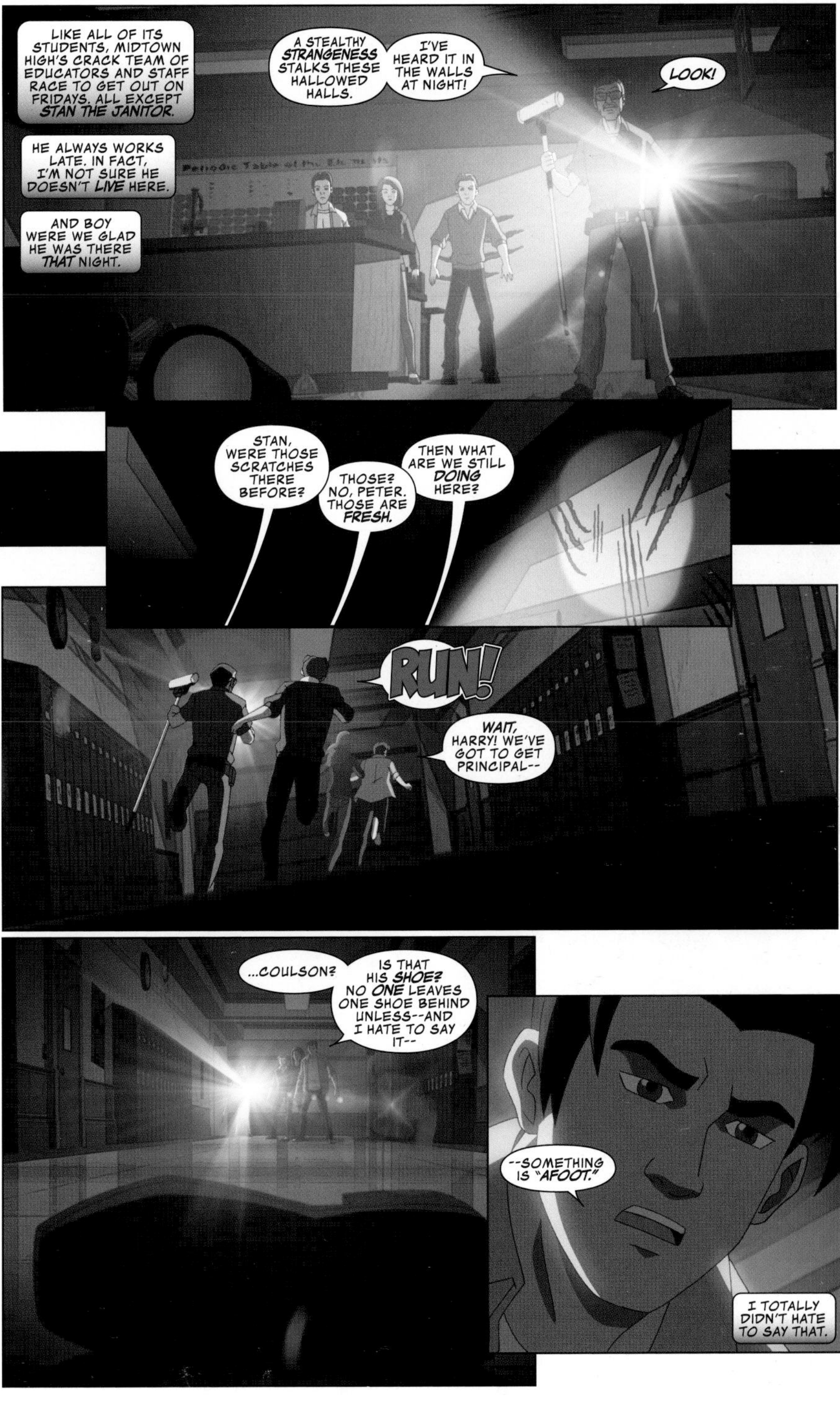
LIKE ALL OF ITS STUDENTS, MIDTOWN HIGH'S CRACK TEAM OF EDUCATORS AND STAFF RACE TO GET OUT ON FRIDAYS, ALL EXCEPT STAN THE JANITOR.
HE ALWAYS WORKS LATE. IN FACT, I'M NOT SURE HE DOESN'T LIVE HERE.
AND BOY WERE WE GLAD HE WAS THERE THAT NIGHT.
A STEALTHY STRANGENESS STALKS THESE HALLOWED HALLS.
I'VE HEARD IT IN THE WALLS AT NIGHT!
LOOK!
STAN, WERE THOSE SCRATCHES THERE BEFORE?
THOSE? NO, PETER. THOSE ARE FRESH.
THEN WHAT ARE WE STILL DOING HERE?
RUN!
WAIT, HARRY! WE'VE GOT TO GET PRINCIPAL--
...COULSON?
IS THAT HIS SHOE? NO ONE LEAVES ONE SHOE BEHIND UNLESS--AND I HATE TO SAY IT--
--SOMETHING IS "AFOOT."
I TOTALLY DIDN'T HATE TO SAY THAT.

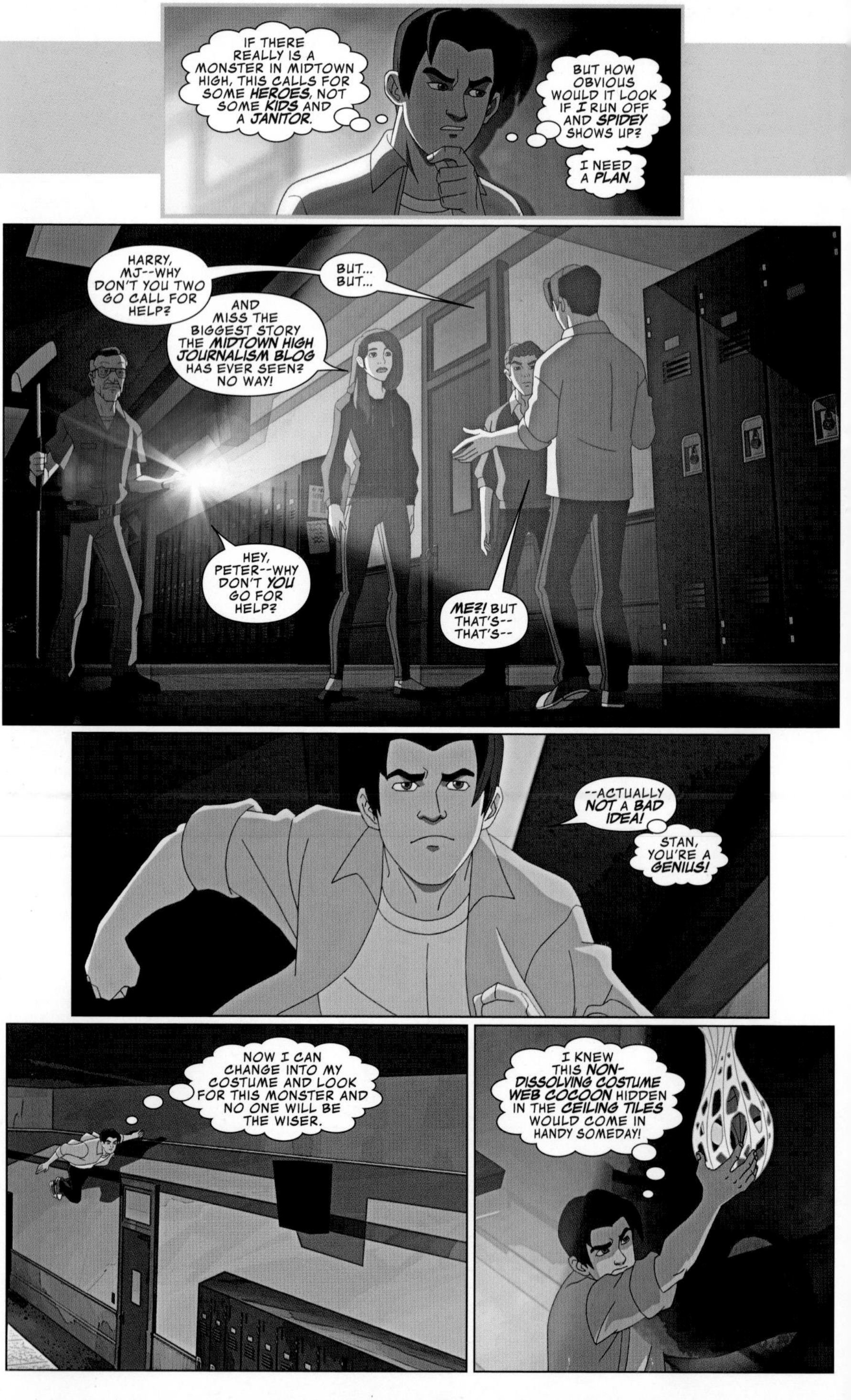

IF THERE REALLY IS A MONSTER IN MIDTOWN HIGH, THIS CALLS FOR SOME HEROES, NOT SOME KIDS AND A JANITOR.
BUT HOW OBVIOUS WOULD IT LOOK IF I RUN OFF AND SPIDEY SHOWS UP?
I NEED A PLAN.
HARRY, MJ--WHY DON'T YOU TWO GO CALL FOR HELP?
BUT... BUT...
AND MISS THE BIGGEST STORY THE MIDTOWN HIGH JOURNALISM BLOG HAS EVER SEEN? NO WAY!
HEY, PETER--WHY DON'T YOU GO FOR HELP?
ME?! BUT THAT'S--THAT'S--
--ACTUALLY NOT A BAD IDEA!
STAN, YOU'RE A GENIUS!
NOW I CAN CHANGE INTO MY COSTUME AND LOOK FOR THIS MONSTER AND NO ONE WILL BE THE WISER.
I KNEW THIS NON-DISSOLVING COSTUME WEB COCOON HIDDEN IN THE CEILING TILES WOULD COME IN HANDY SOMEDAY!

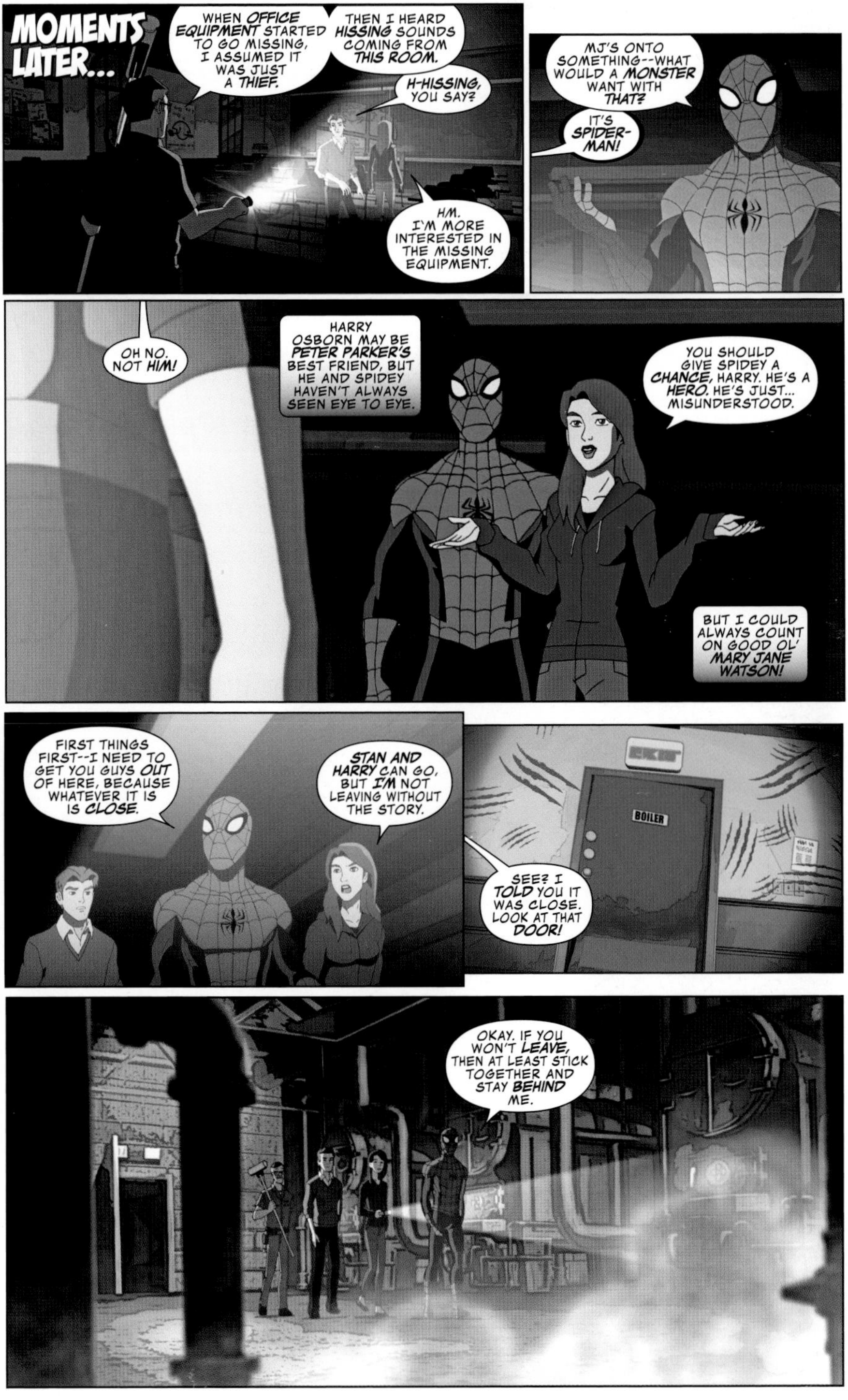
MOMENTS LATER...
WHEN OFFICE EQUIPMENT STARTED TO GO MISSING, I ASSUMED IT WAS JUST A THIEF.
THEN I HEARD HISSING SOUNDS COMING FROM THIS ROOM.
H-HISSING, YOU SAY?
HM. I'M MORE INTERESTED IN THE MISSING EQUIPMENT.
MJ'S ONTO SOMETHING--WHAT WOULD A MONSTER WANT WITH THAT?
IT'S SPIDER-MAN!
OH NO. NOT HIM!
HARRY OSBORN MAY BE PETER PARKER'S BEST FRIEND, BUT HE AND SPIDEY HAVEN'T ALWAYS SEEN EYE TO EYE.
YOU SHOULD GIVE SPIDEY A CHANCE, HARRY. HE'S A HERO. HE'S JUST... MISUNDERSTOOD.
BUT I COULD ALWAYS COUNT ON GOOD OL' MARY JANE WATSON!
FIRST THINGS FIRST--I NEED TO GET YOU GUYS OUT OF HERE, BECAUSE WHATEVER IT IS IS CLOSE.
STAN AND HARRY CAN GO, BUT I'M NOT LEAVING WITHOUT THE STORY.
BOILER
SEE? I TOLD YOU IT WAS CLOSE. LOOK AT THAT DOOR!
OKAY. IF YOU WON'T LEAVE, THEN AT LEAST STICK TOGETHER AND STAY BEHIND ME.

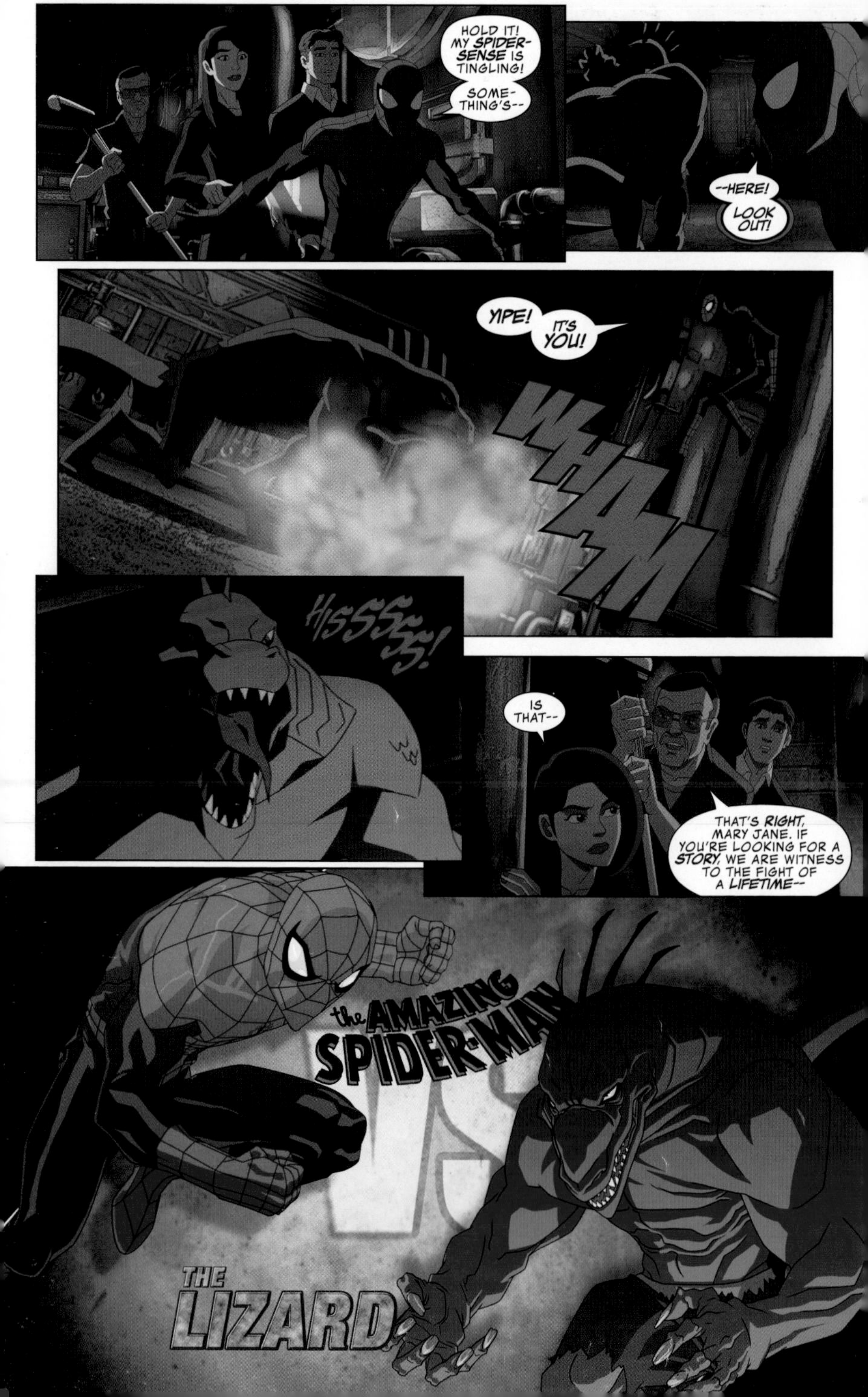
HOLD IT! MY SPIDER-SENSE IS TINGLING!
SOME-THING'S--
--HERE!
LOOK OUT!
YIPE!
IT'S YOU!
WHAM
HISSSSS!
IS THAT--
THAT'S RIGHT, MARY JANE. IF YOU'RE LOOKING FOR A STORY, WE ARE WITNESS TO THE FIGHT OF A LIFETIME--
the AMAZING SPIDER-MAN
VS
THE LIZARD

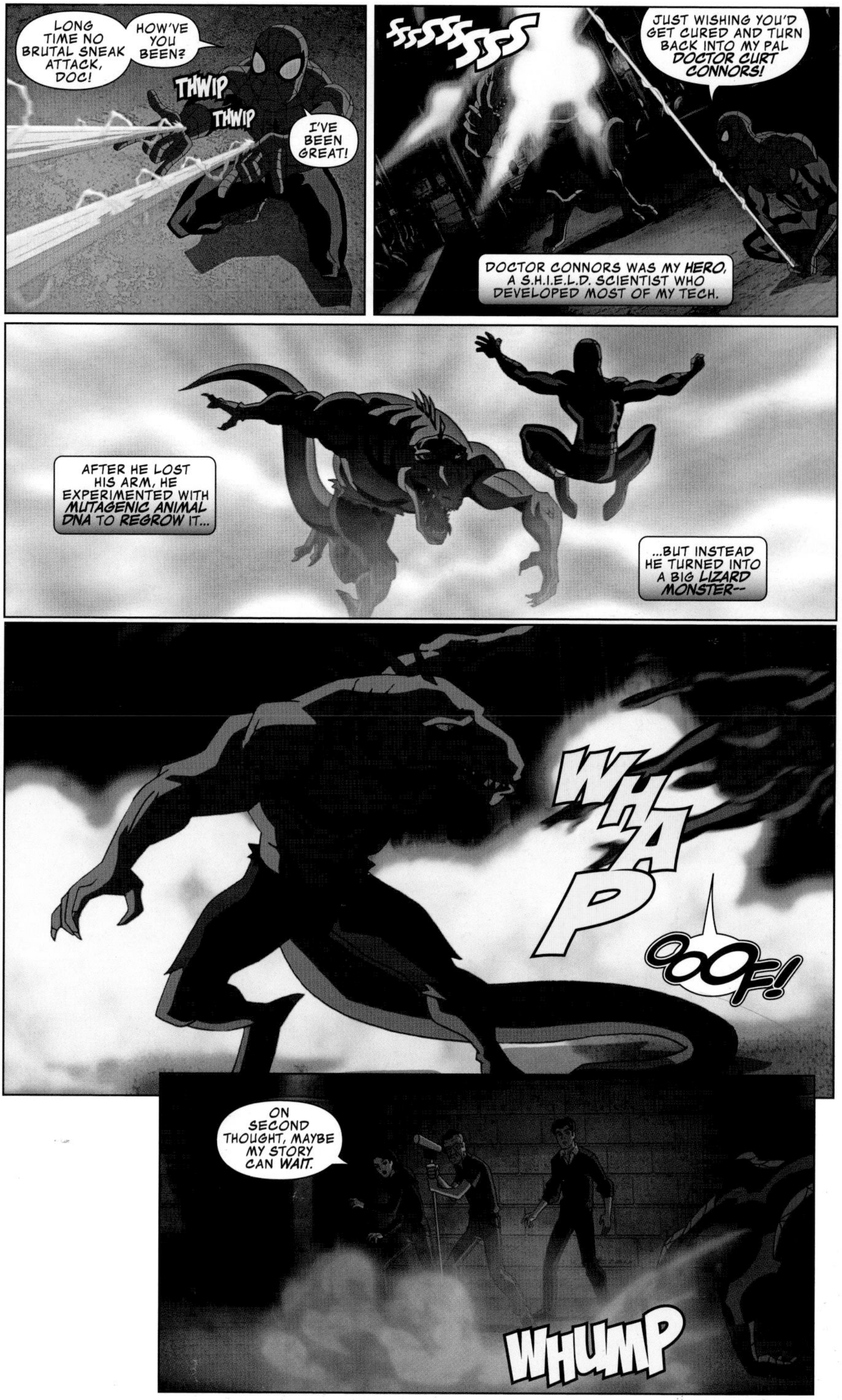
LONG TIME NO BRUTAL SNEAK ATTACK, DOC!
HOW'VE YOU BEEN?
THWIP
THWIP
I'VE BEEN GREAT!
FSSSSSSS
JUST WISHING YOU'D GET CURED AND TURN BACK INTO MY PAL DOCTOR CURT CONNORS!
DOCTOR CONNORS WAS MY HERO, A S.H.I.E.L.D. SCIENTIST WHO DEVELOPED MOST OF MY TECH.
AFTER HE LOST HIS ARM, HE EXPERIMENTED WITH MUTAGENIC ANIMAL DNA TO REGROW IT...
...BUT INSTEAD HE TURNED INTO A BIG LIZARD MONSTER--
WHAP
OOOF!
ON SECOND THOUGHT, MAYBE MY STORY CAN WAIT.
WHUMP

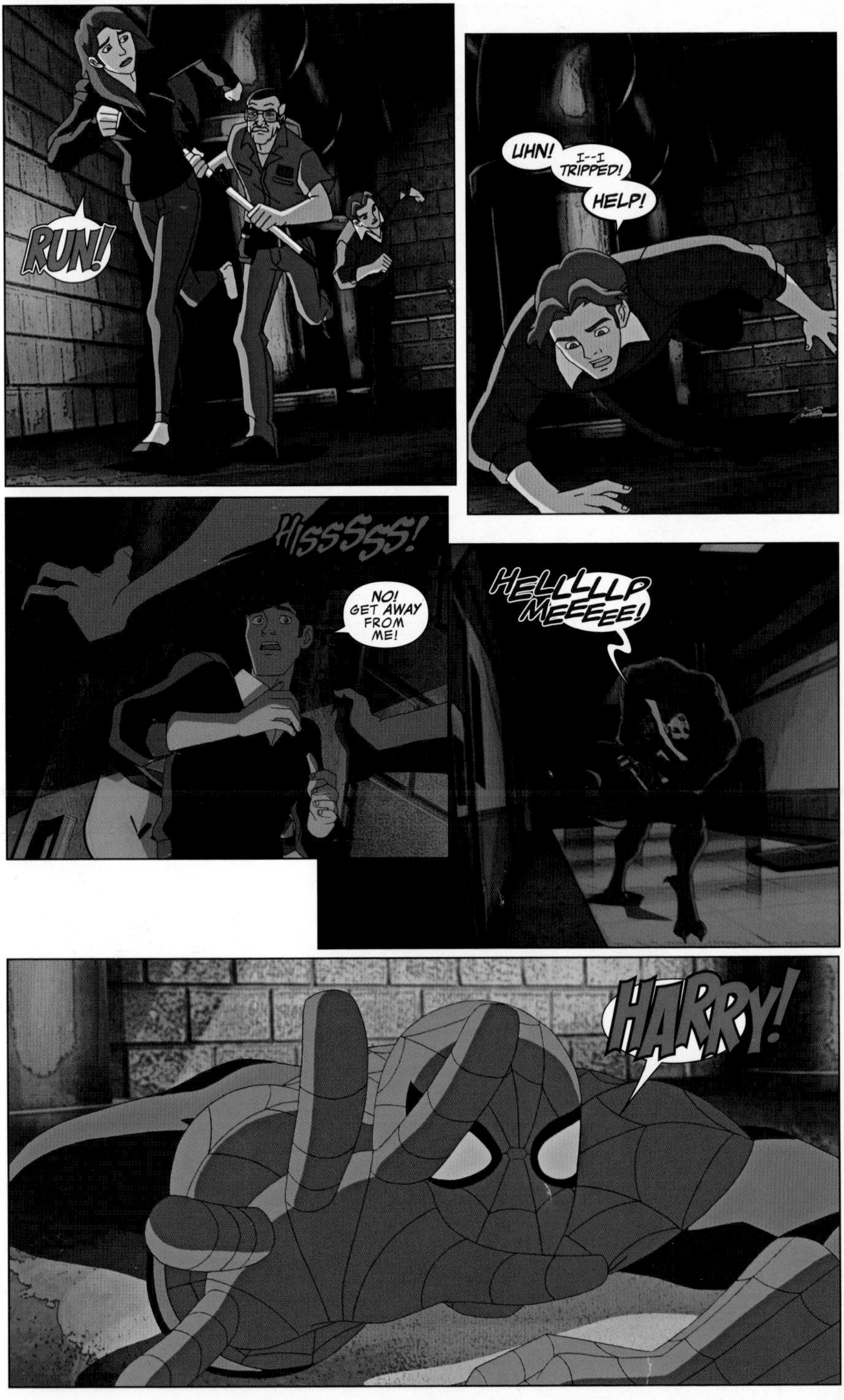
RUN!
UHN!
I--I TRIPPED!
HELP!
HISSSSS!
NO! GET AWAY FROM ME!
HELLLLLP MEEEEEE!
HARRY!

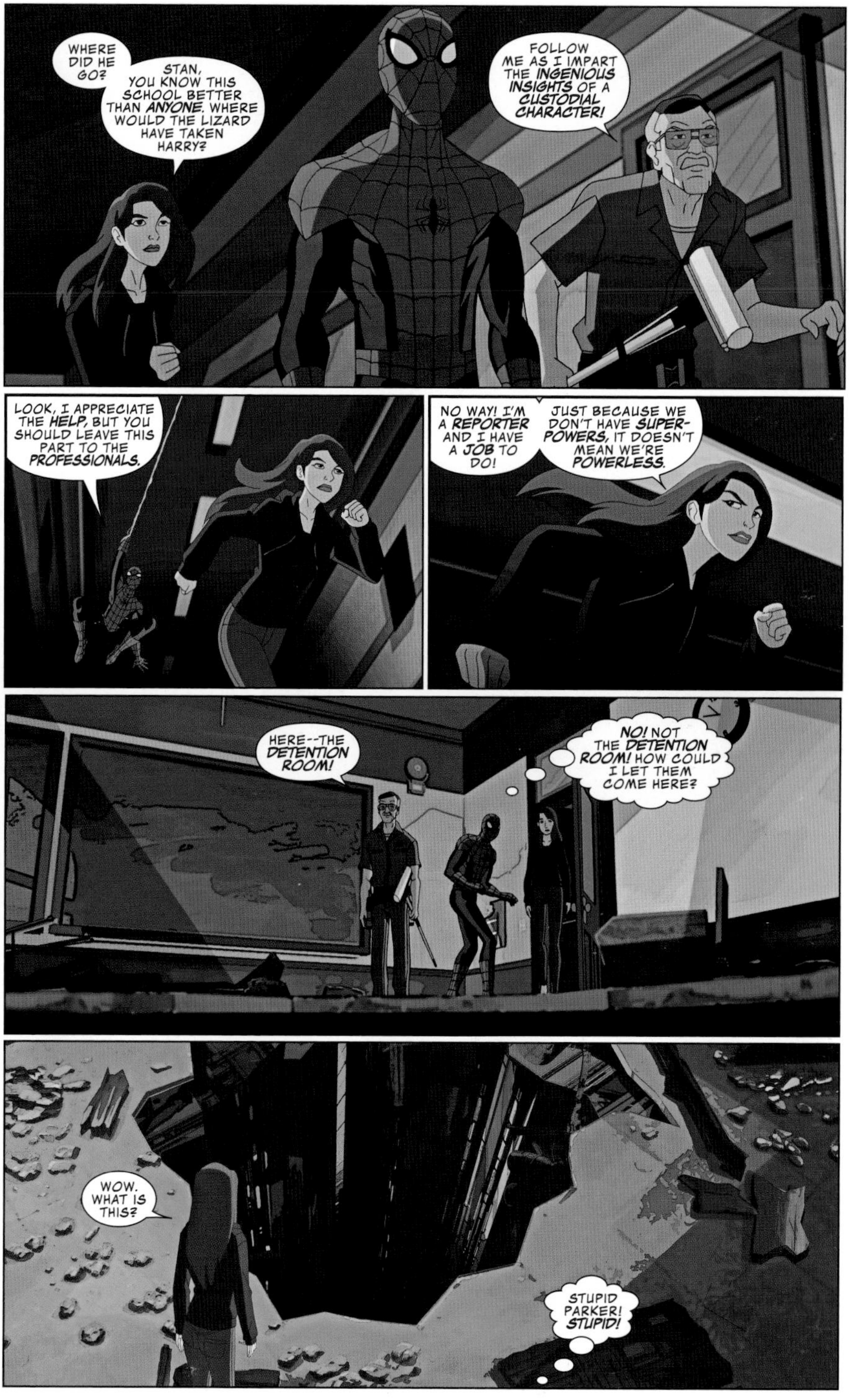
WHERE DID HE GO?
STAN, YOU KNOW THIS SCHOOL BETTER THAN ANYONE. WHERE WOULD THE LIZARD HAVE TAKEN HARRY?
FOLLOW ME AS I IMPART THE INGENIOUS INSIGHTS OF A CUSTODIAL CHARACTER!
LOOK, I APPRECIATE THE HELP, BUT YOU SHOULD LEAVE THIS PART TO THE PROFESSIONALS.
NO WAY! I'M A REPORTER AND I HAVE A JOB TO DO!
JUST BECAUSE WE DON'T HAVE SUPER-POWERS, IT DOESN'T MEAN WE'RE POWERLESS.
HERE--THE DETENTION ROOM!
NO! NOT THE DETENTION ROOM! HOW COULD I LET THEM COME HERE?
WOW. WHAT IS THIS?
STUPID PARKER! STUPID!

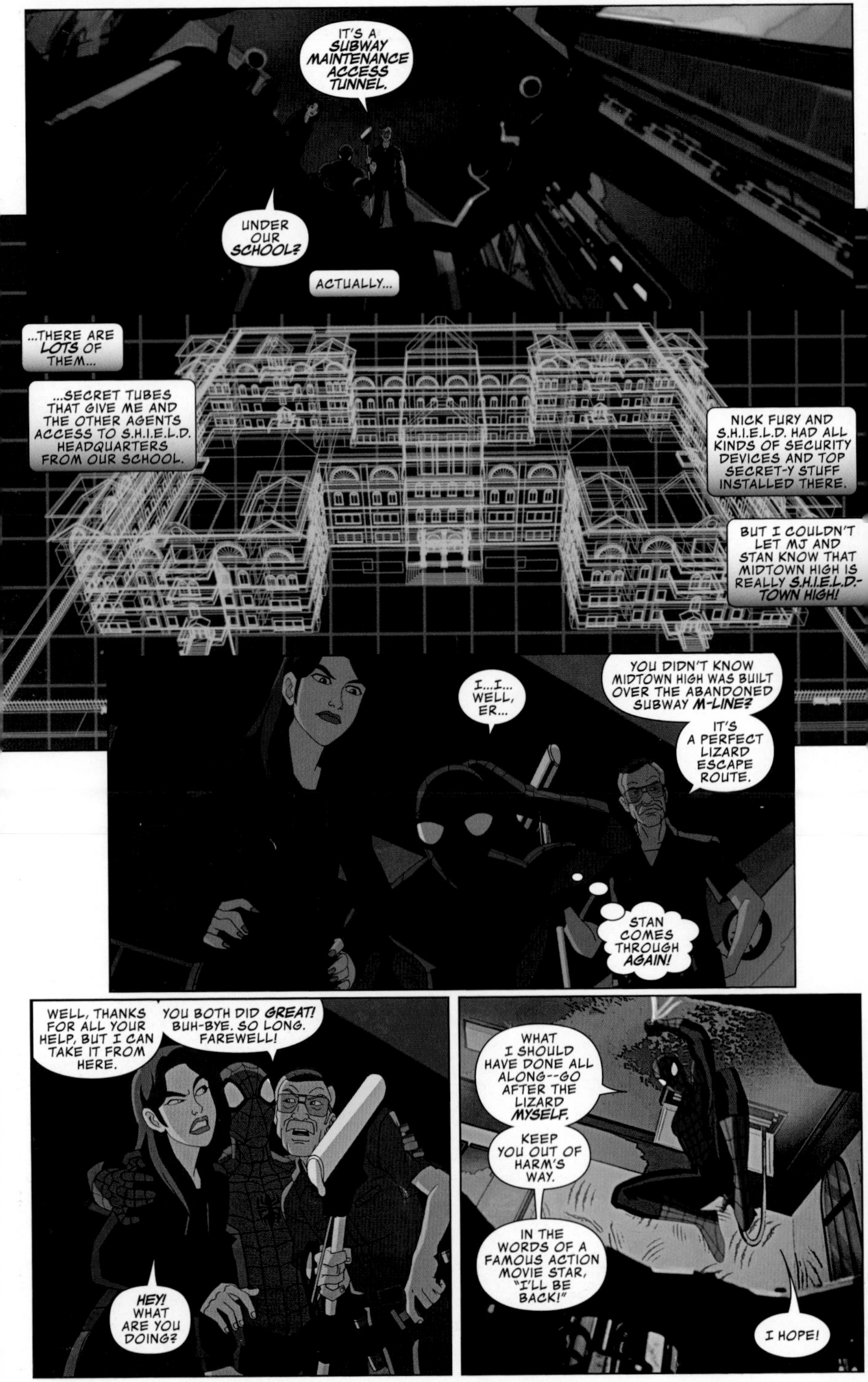
IT'S A SUBWAY MAINTENANCE ACCESS TUNNEL.
UNDER OUR SCHOOL?
ACTUALLY...
...THERE ARE LOTS OF THEM...
...SECRET TUBES THAT GIVE ME AND THE OTHER AGENTS ACCESS TO S.H.I.E.L.D. HEADQUARTERS FROM OUR SCHOOL.
NICK FURY AND S.H.I.E.L.D. HAD ALL KINDS OF SECURITY DEVICES AND TOP SECRET-Y STUFF INSTALLED THERE.
BUT I COULDN'T LET MJ AND STAN KNOW THAT MIDTOWN HIGH IS REALLY S.H.I.E.L.D.-TOWN HIGH!
I...I... WELL, ER...
YOU DIDN'T KNOW MIDTOWN HIGH WAS BUILT OVER THE ABANDONED SUBWAY M-LINE?
IT'S A PERFECT LIZARD ESCAPE ROUTE.
STAN COMES THROUGH AGAIN!
WELL, THANKS FOR ALL YOUR HELP, BUT I CAN TAKE IT FROM HERE.
YOU BOTH DID GREAT! BUH-BYE. SO LONG. FAREWELL!
HEY! WHAT ARE YOU DOING?
WHAT I SHOULD HAVE DONE ALL ALONG--GO AFTER THE LIZARD MYSELF.
KEEP YOU OUT OF HARM'S WAY.
IN THE WORDS OF A FAMOUS ACTION MOVIE STAR, "I'LL BE BACK!"
I HOPE!

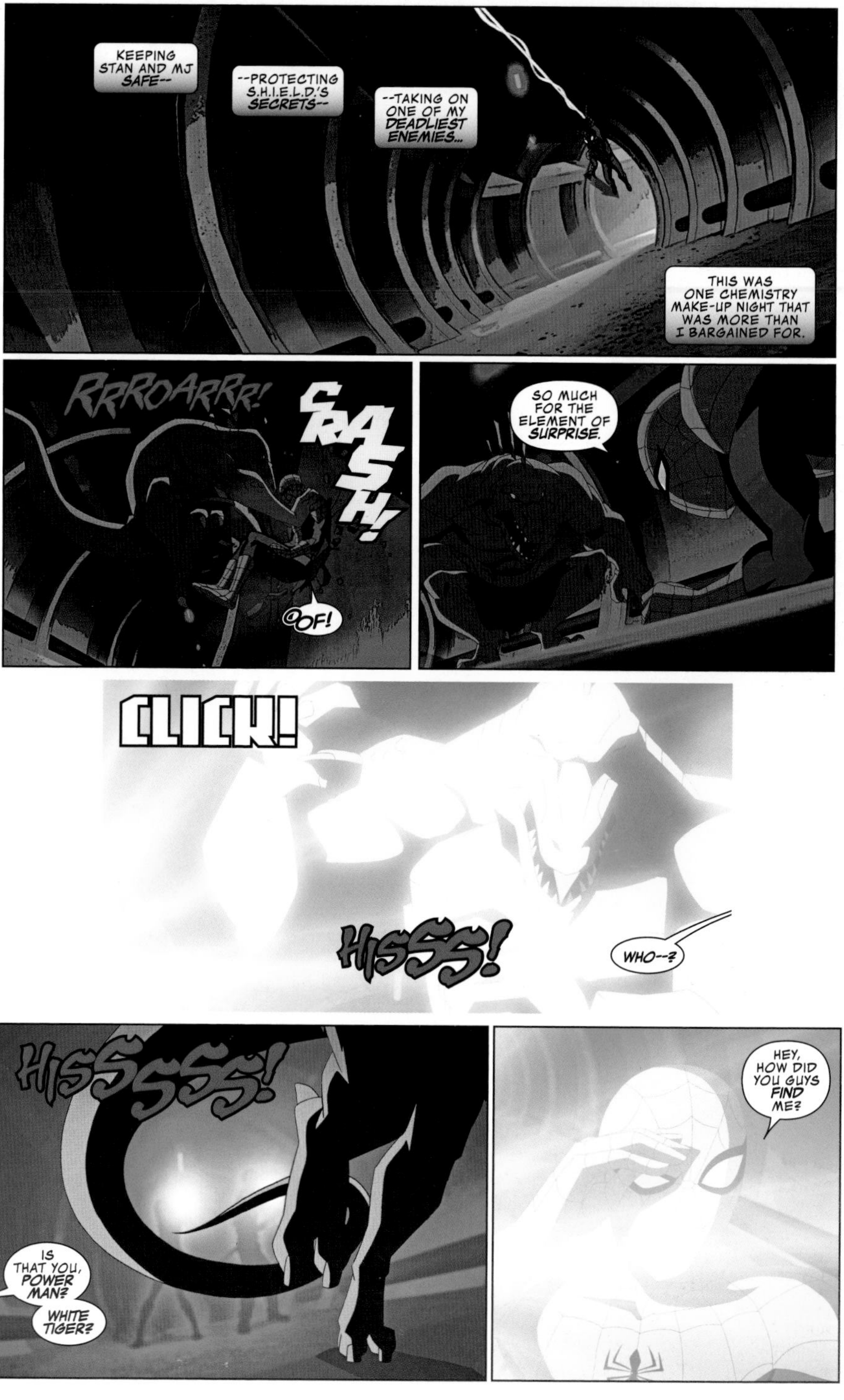
KEEPING STAN AND MJ SAFE--
--PROTECTING S.H.I.E.L.D.'S SECRETS--
--TAKING ON ONE OF MY DEADLIEST ENEMIES...
THIS WAS ONE CHEMISTRY MAKE-UP NIGHT THAT WAS MORE THAN I BARGAINED FOR.
RRROARRR!
CRASH!
OOF!
SO MUCH FOR THE ELEMENT OF SURPRISE.
CLICK!
HISSS!
WHO--?
HISSSSS!
IS THAT YOU, POWER MAN?
WHITE TIGER?
HEY, HOW DID YOU GUYS FIND ME?

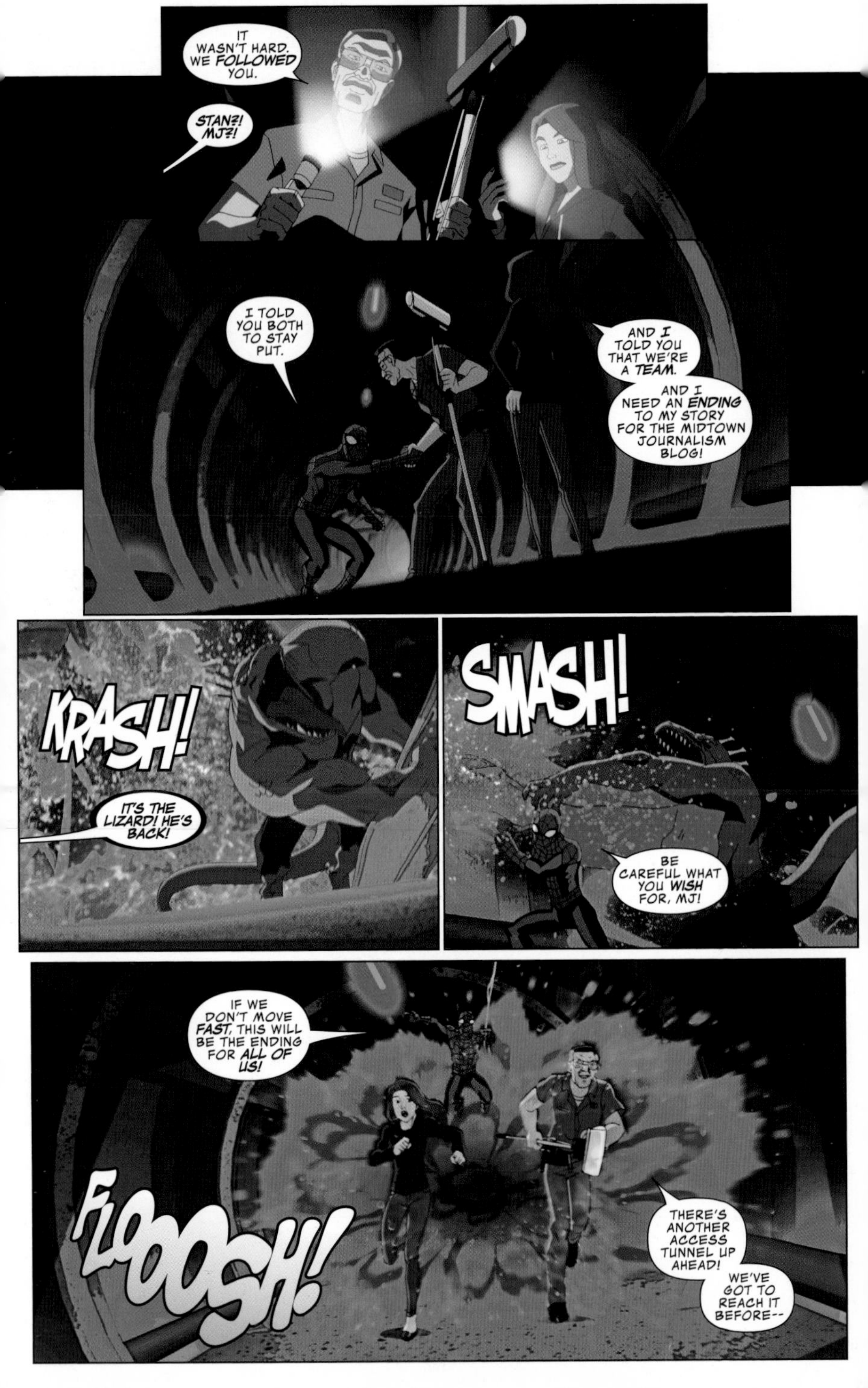
IT WASN'T HARD. WE FOLLOWED YOU.
STAN?! MJ?!
I TOLD YOU BOTH TO STAY PUT.
AND I TOLD YOU THAT WE'RE A TEAM.
AND I NEED AN ENDING TO MY STORY FOR THE MIDTOWN JOURNALISM BLOG!
KRASH!
IT'S THE LIZARD! HE'S BACK!
SMASH!
BE CAREFUL WHAT YOU WISH FOR, MJ!
IF WE DON'T MOVE FAST, THIS WILL BE THE ENDING FOR ALL OF US!
FLOOOSH!
THERE'S ANOTHER ACCESS TUNNEL UP AHEAD!
WE'VE GOT TO REACH IT BEFORE--

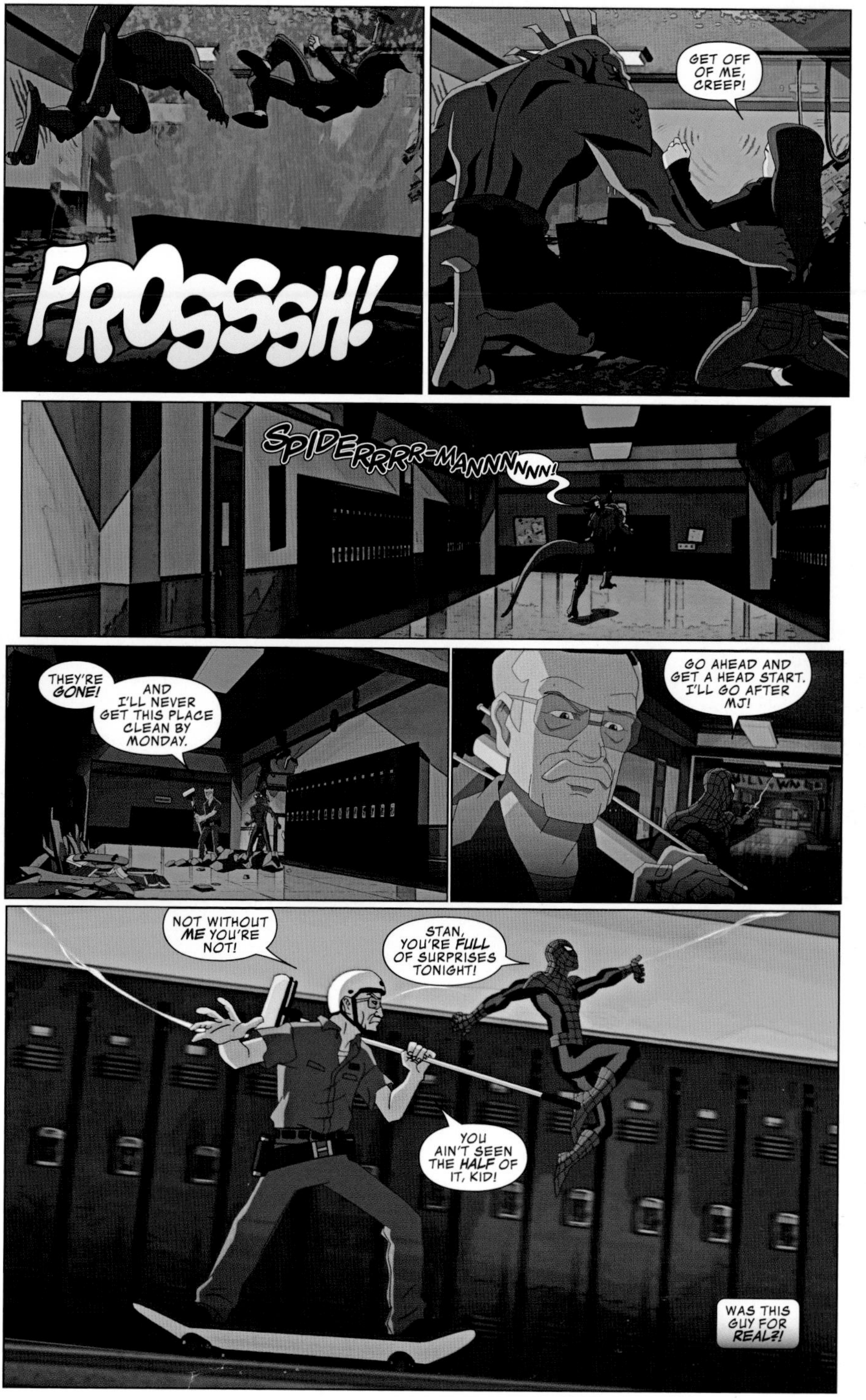
FROSSSH!
GET OFF OF ME, CREEP!
SPIDERRRR-MANNNNNN!
THEY'RE GONE!
AND I'LL NEVER GET THIS PLACE CLEAN BY MONDAY.
GO AHEAD AND GET A HEAD START. I'LL GO AFTER MJ!
NOT WITHOUT ME YOU'RE NOT!
STAN, YOU'RE FULL OF SURPRISES TONIGHT!
YOU AIN'T SEEN THE HALF OF IT, KID!
WAS THIS GUY FOR REAL?!

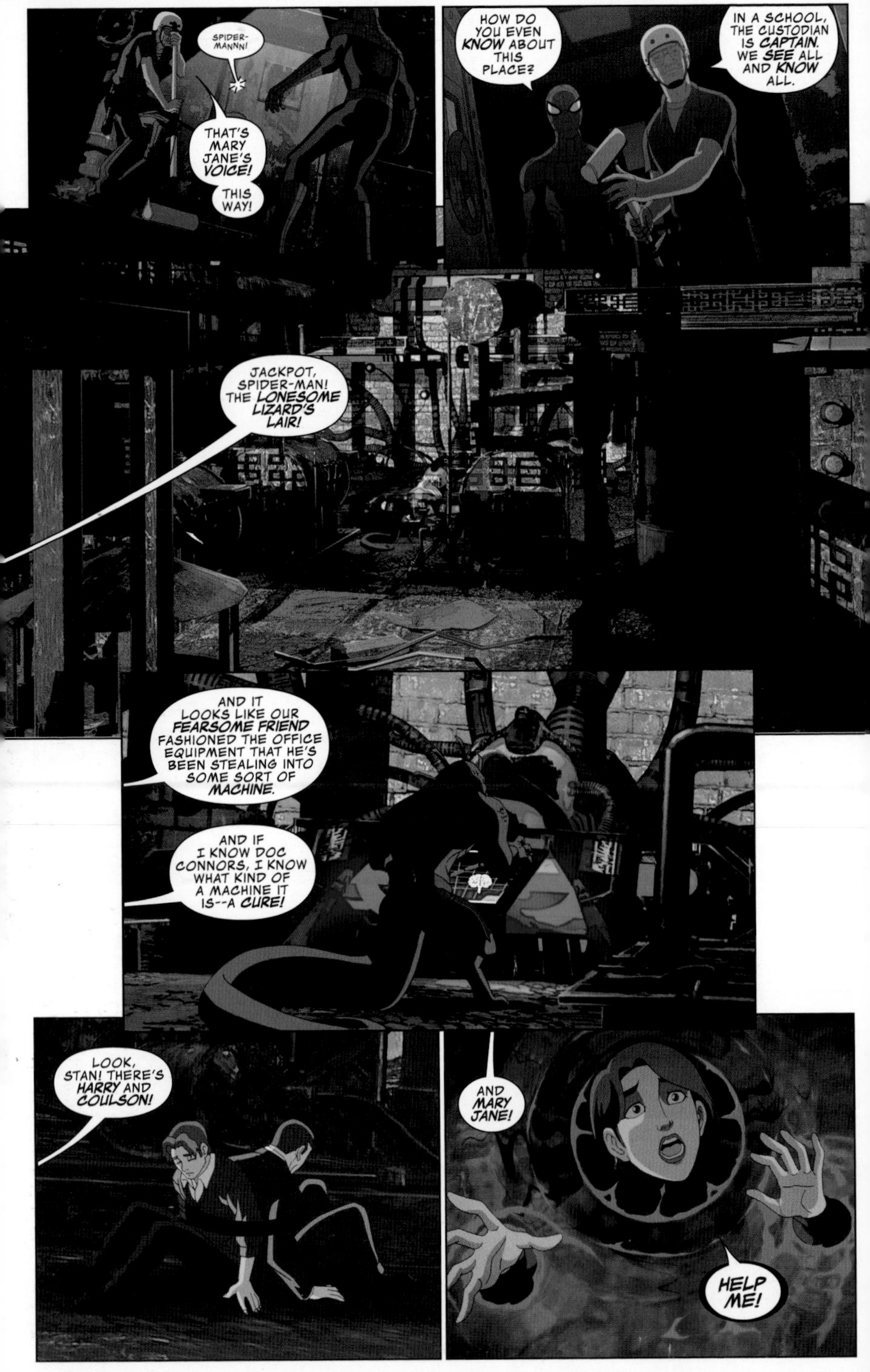
SPIDER-MANNN!
THAT'S MARY JANE'S VOICE!
THIS WAY!
HOW DO YOU EVEN KNOW ABOUT THIS PLACE?
IN A SCHOOL, THE CUSTODIAN IS CAPTAIN. WE SEE ALL AND KNOW ALL.
JACKPOT, SPIDER-MAN! THE LONESOME LIZARD'S LAIR!
AND IT LOOKS LIKE OUR FEARSOME FRIEND FASHIONED THE OFFICE EQUIPMENT THAT HE'S BEEN STEALING INTO SOME SORT OF MACHINE.
AND IF I KNOW DOC CONNORS, I KNOW WHAT KIND OF A MACHINE IT IS--A CURE!
LOOK, STAN! THERE'S HARRY AND COULSON!
AND MARY JANE!
HELP ME!

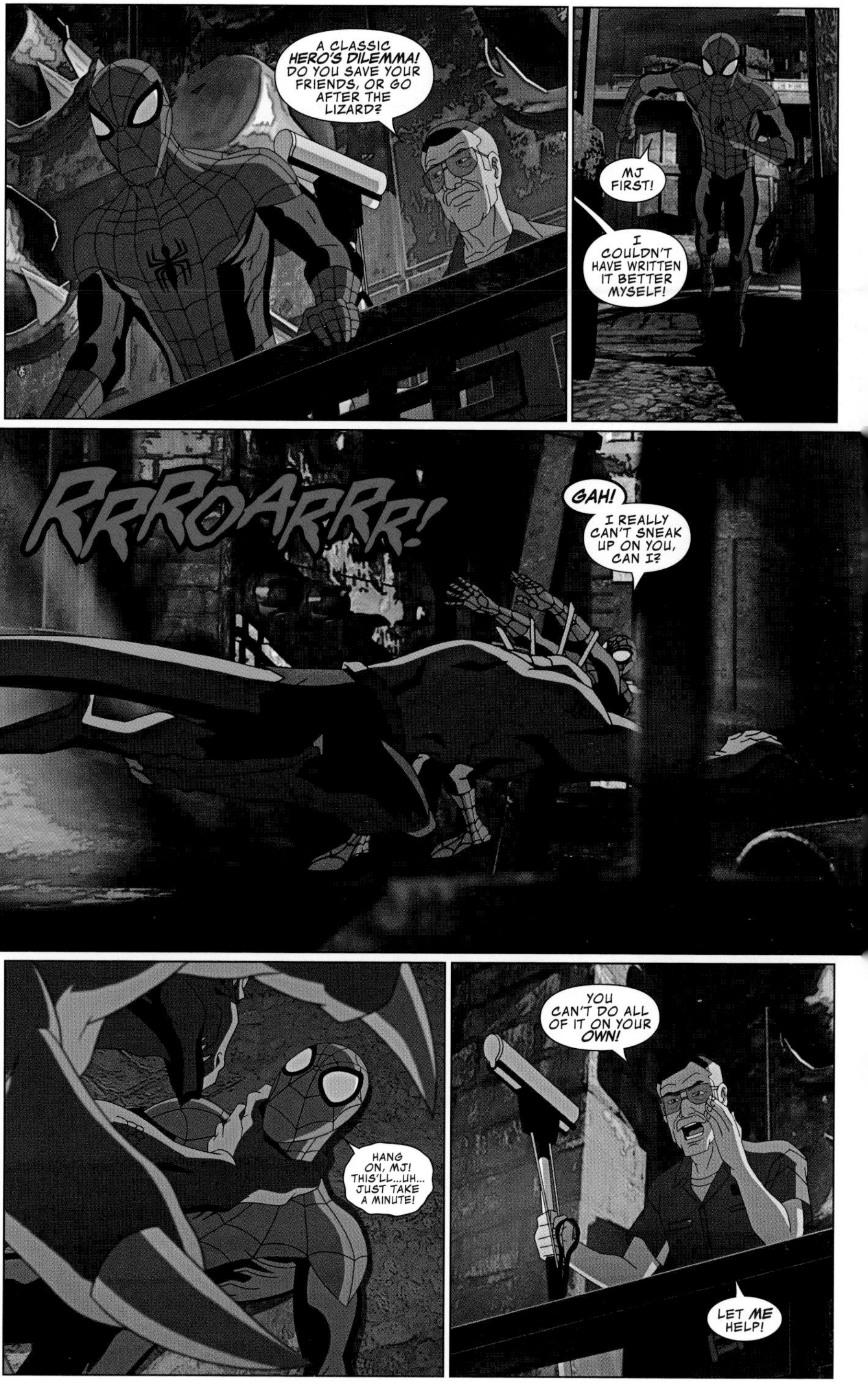
A CLASSIC HERO'S DILEMMA! DO YOU SAVE YOUR FRIENDS, OR GO AFTER THE LIZARD?
MJ FIRST!
I COULDN'T HAVE WRITTEN IT BETTER MYSELF!
RRROARRR!
GAH!
I REALLY CAN'T SNEAK UP ON YOU, CAN I?
HANG ON, MJ! THIS'LL...UH... JUST TAKE A MINUTE!
YOU CAN'T DO ALL OF IT ON YOUR OWN!
LET ME HELP!

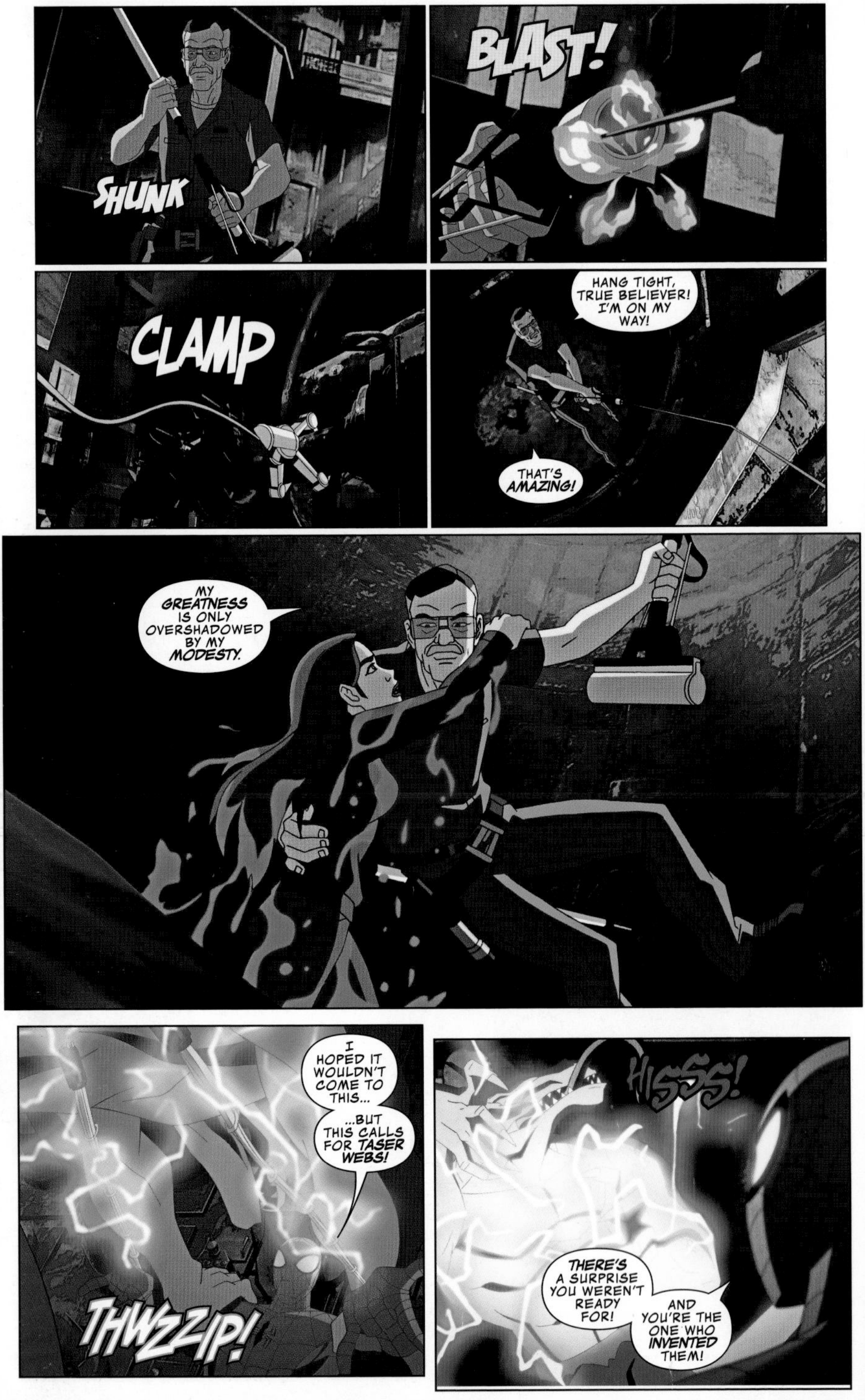
SHUNK
BLAST!
CLAMP
HANG TIGHT, TRUE BELIEVER! I'M ON MY WAY!
THAT'S AMAZING!
MY GREATNESS IS ONLY OVERSHADOWED BY MY MODESTY.
I HOPED IT WOULDN'T COME TO THIS...
...BUT THIS CALLS FOR TASER WEBS!
THWZZIP!
HISSS!
THERE'S A SURPRISE YOU WEREN'T READY FOR!
AND YOU'RE THE ONE WHO INVENTED THEM!

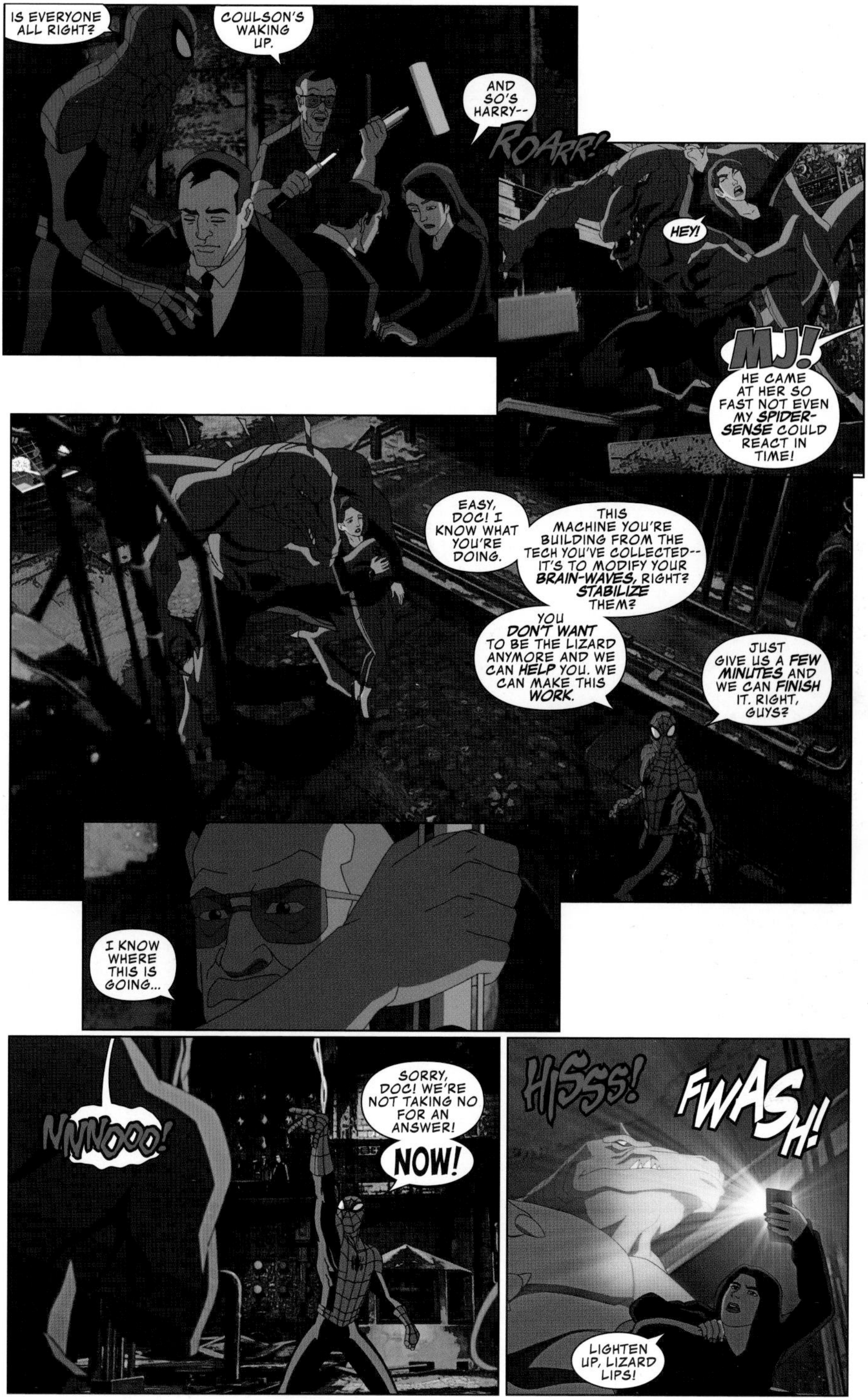
IS EVERYONE ALL RIGHT?
COULSON'S WAKING UP.
AND SO'S HARRY--
ROARR!
HEY!
MJ!
HE CAME AT HER SO FAST NOT EVEN MY SPIDER-SENSE COULD REACT IN TIME!
EASY, DOC! I KNOW WHAT YOU'RE DOING.
THIS MACHINE YOU'RE BUILDING FROM THE TECH YOU'VE COLLECTED-- IT'S TO MODIFY YOUR BRAIN-WAVES, RIGHT? STABILIZE THEM?
YOU DON'T WANT TO BE THE LIZARD ANYMORE AND WE CAN HELP YOU. WE CAN MAKE THIS WORK.
JUST GIVE US A FEW MINUTES AND WE CAN FINISH IT. RIGHT, GUYS?
I KNOW WHERE THIS IS GOING...
NNNOOO!
SORRY, DOC! WE'RE NOT TAKING NO FOR AN ANSWER!
NOW!
HISSS!
FWASH!
LIGHTEN UP, LIZARD LIPS!

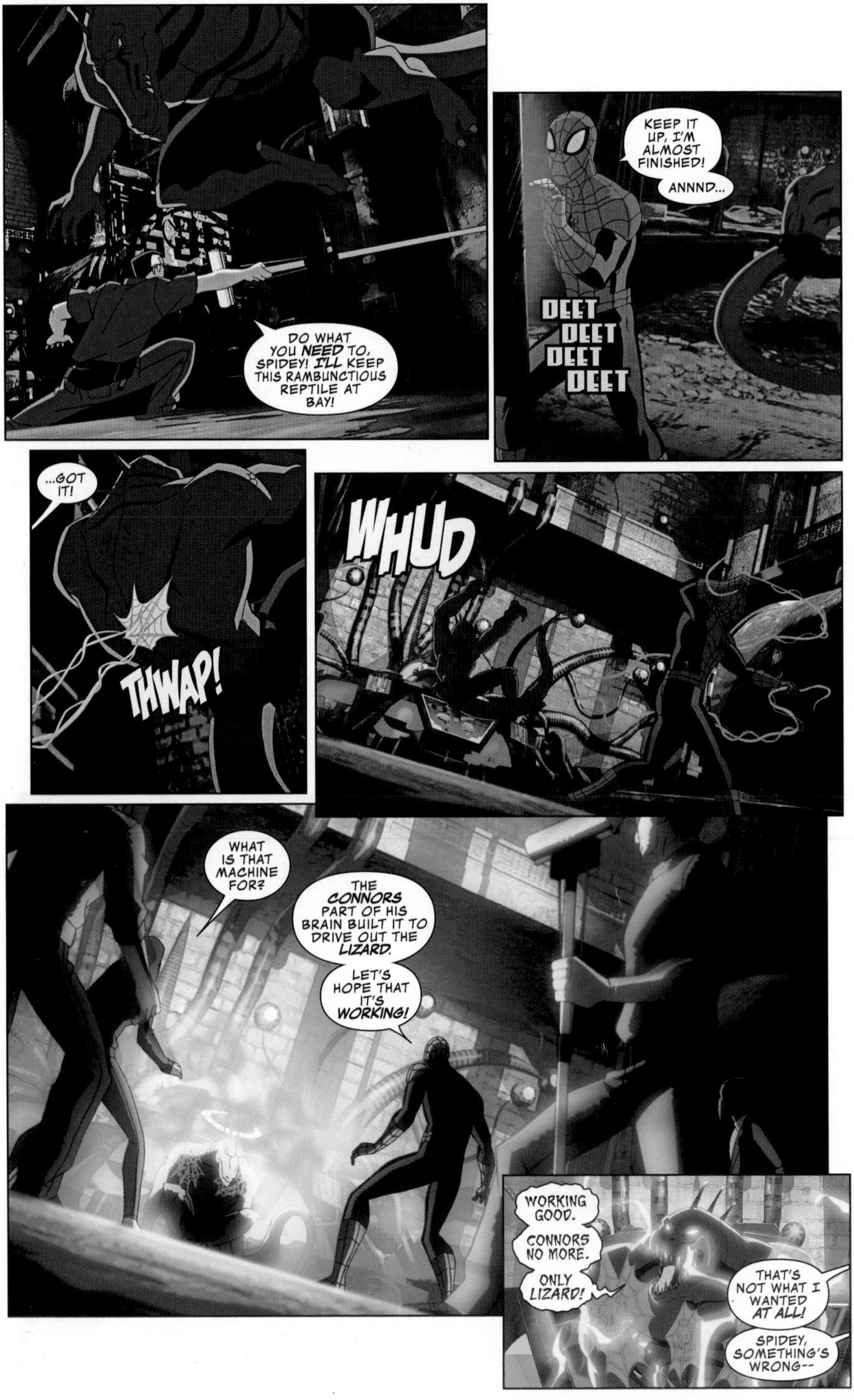
DO WHAT YOU NEED TO, SPIDEY! I'LL KEEP THIS RAMBUNCTIOUS REPTILE AT BAY!
KEEP IT UP, I'M ALMOST FINISHED!
ANNND...
DEET DEET DEET DEET
...GOT IT!
THWAP!
WHUD
WHAT IS THAT MACHINE FOR?
THE CONNORS PART OF HIS BRAIN BUILT IT TO DRIVE OUT THE LIZARD.
LET'S HOPE THAT IT'S WORKING!
WORKING GOOD.
CONNORS NO MORE.
ONLY LIZARD!
THAT'S NOT WHAT I WANTED AT ALL!
SPIDEY, SOMETHING'S WRONG--

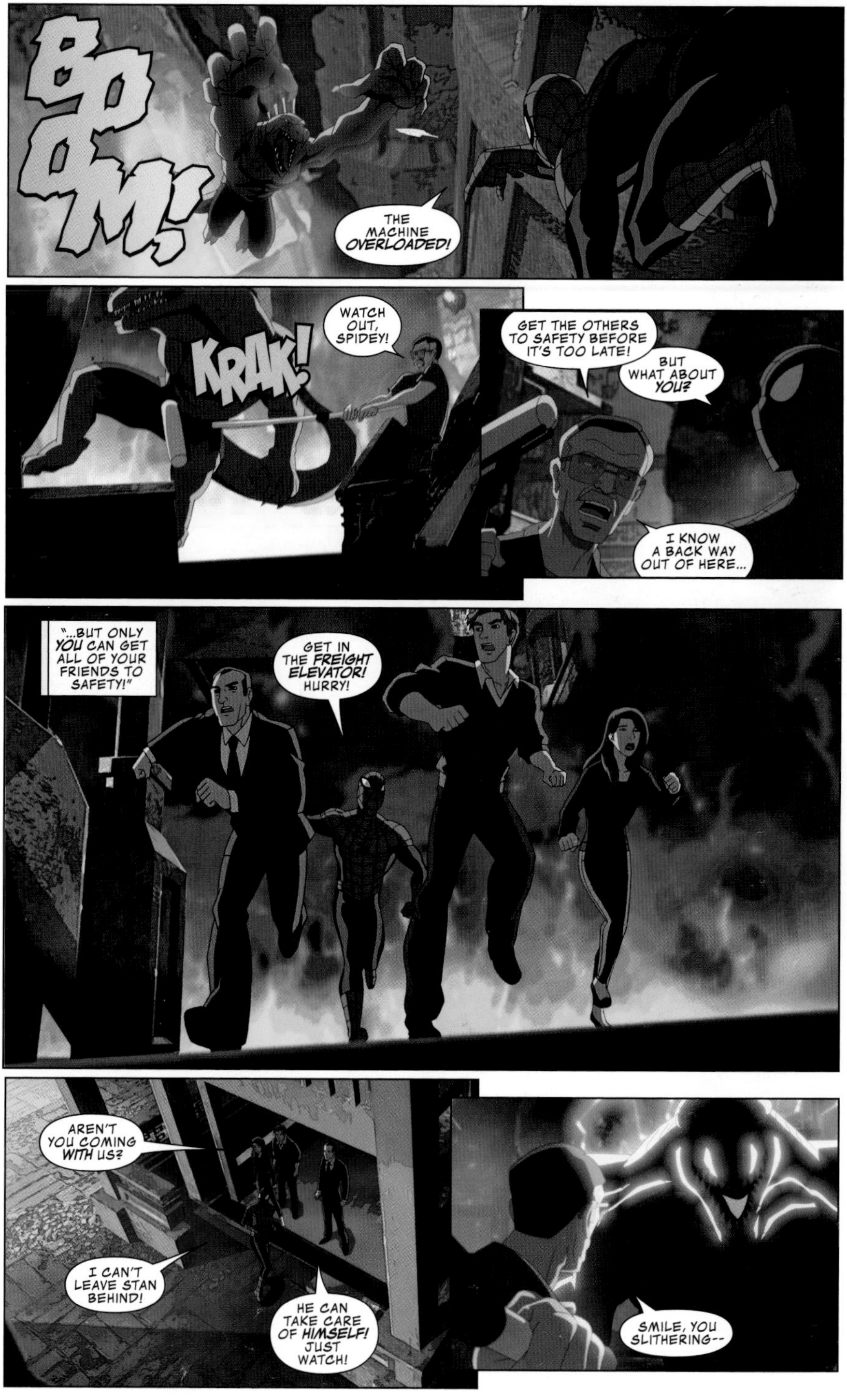
BOOM!
THE MACHINE OVERLOADED!
KRAK!
WATCH OUT, SPIDEY!
GET THE OTHERS TO SAFETY BEFORE IT'S TOO LATE!
BUT WHAT ABOUT YOU?
I KNOW A BACK WAY OUT OF HERE...
"...BUT ONLY YOU CAN GET ALL OF YOUR FRIENDS TO SAFETY!"
GET IN THE FREIGHT ELEVATOR! HURRY!
AREN'T YOU COMING WITH US?
I CAN'T LEAVE STAN BEHIND!
HE CAN TAKE CARE OF HIMSELF! JUST WATCH!
SMILE, YOU SLITHERING--

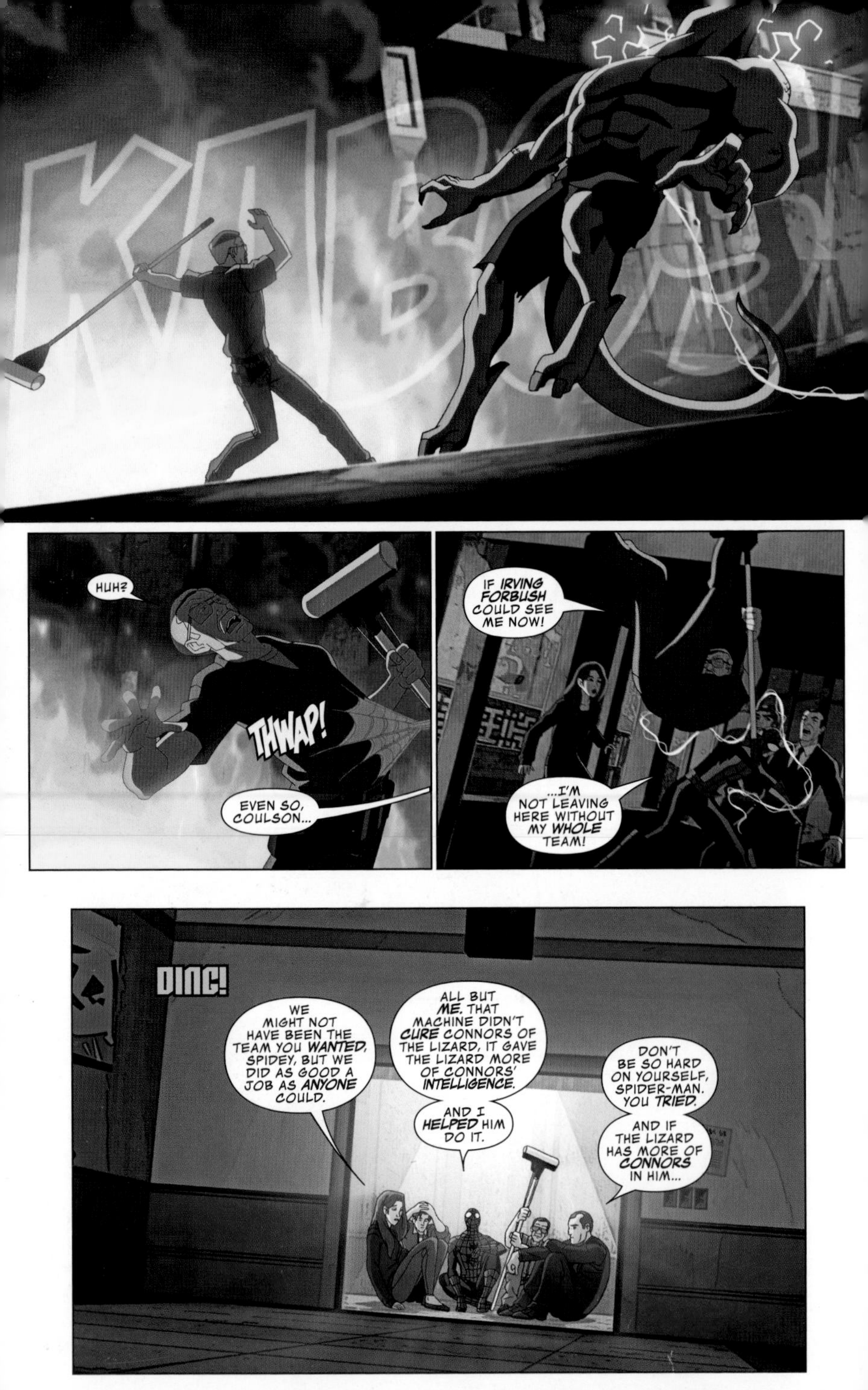
HUH?
THWAP!
EVEN SO, COULSON...
IF IRVING FORBUSH COULD SEE ME NOW!
...I'M NOT LEAVING HERE WITHOUT MY WHOLE TEAM!
DING!
WE MIGHT NOT HAVE BEEN THE TEAM YOU WANTED, SPIDEY, BUT WE DID AS GOOD A JOB AS ANYONE COULD.
ALL BUT ME. THAT MACHINE DIDN'T CURE CONNORS OF THE LIZARD, IT GAVE THE LIZARD MORE OF CONNORS' INTELLIGENCE.
AND I HELPED HIM DO IT.
DON'T BE SO HARD ON YOURSELF, SPIDER-MAN. YOU TRIED.
AND IF THE LIZARD HAS MORE OF CONNORS IN HIM...

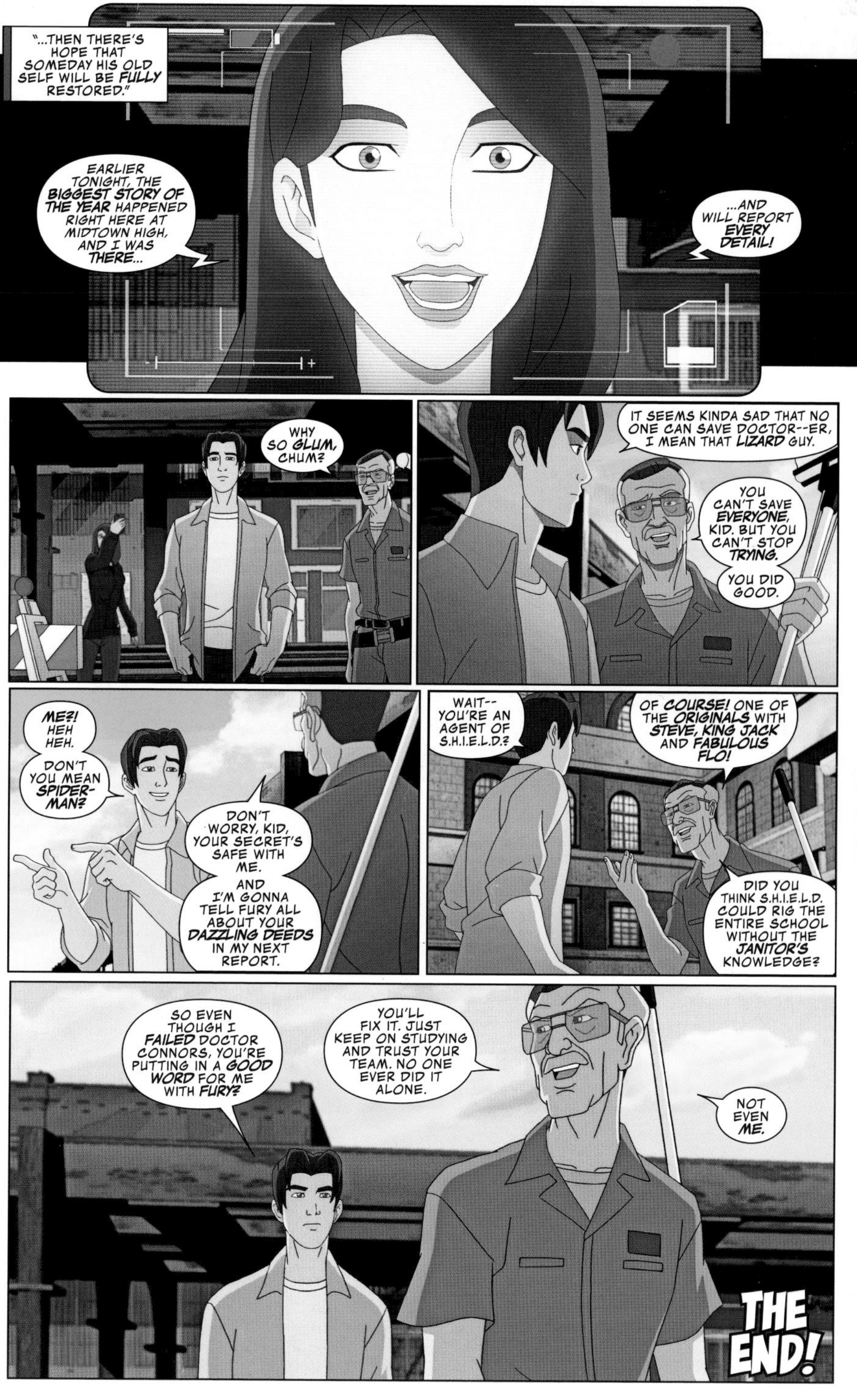
"...THEN THERE'S HOPE THAT SOMEDAY HIS OLD SELF WILL BE FULLY RESTORED."
EARLIER TONIGHT, THE BIGGEST STORY OF THE YEAR HAPPENED RIGHT HERE AT MIDTOWN HIGH, AND I WAS THERE...
...AND WILL REPORT EVERY DETAIL!
WHY SO GLUM, CHUM?
IT SEEMS KINDA SAD THAT NO ONE CAN SAVE DOCTOR--ER, I MEAN THAT LIZARD GUY.
YOU CAN'T SAVE EVERYONE, KID. BUT YOU CAN'T STOP TRYING.
YOU DID GOOD.
ME?! HEH HEH.
DON'T YOU MEAN SPIDER-MAN?
DON'T WORRY, KID, YOUR SECRET'S SAFE WITH ME.
AND I'M GONNA TELL FURY ALL ABOUT YOUR DAZZLING DEEDS IN MY NEXT REPORT.
WAIT--YOU'RE AN AGENT OF S.H.I.E.L.D.?
OF COURSE! ONE OF THE ORIGINALS WITH STEVE, KING JACK AND FABULOUS FLO!
DID YOU THINK S.H.I.E.L.D. COULD RIG THE ENTIRE SCHOOL WITHOUT THE JANITOR'S KNOWLEDGE?
SO EVEN THOUGH I FAILED DOCTOR CONNORS, YOU'RE PUTTING IN A GOOD WORD FOR ME WITH FURY?
YOU'LL FIX IT. JUST KEEP ON STUDYING AND TRUST YOUR TEAM. NO ONE EVER DID IT ALONE.
NOT EVEN ME.
THE END!

D-POOL RULES!! Spidey drools!!

8

Based on "Ultimate Deadpool"

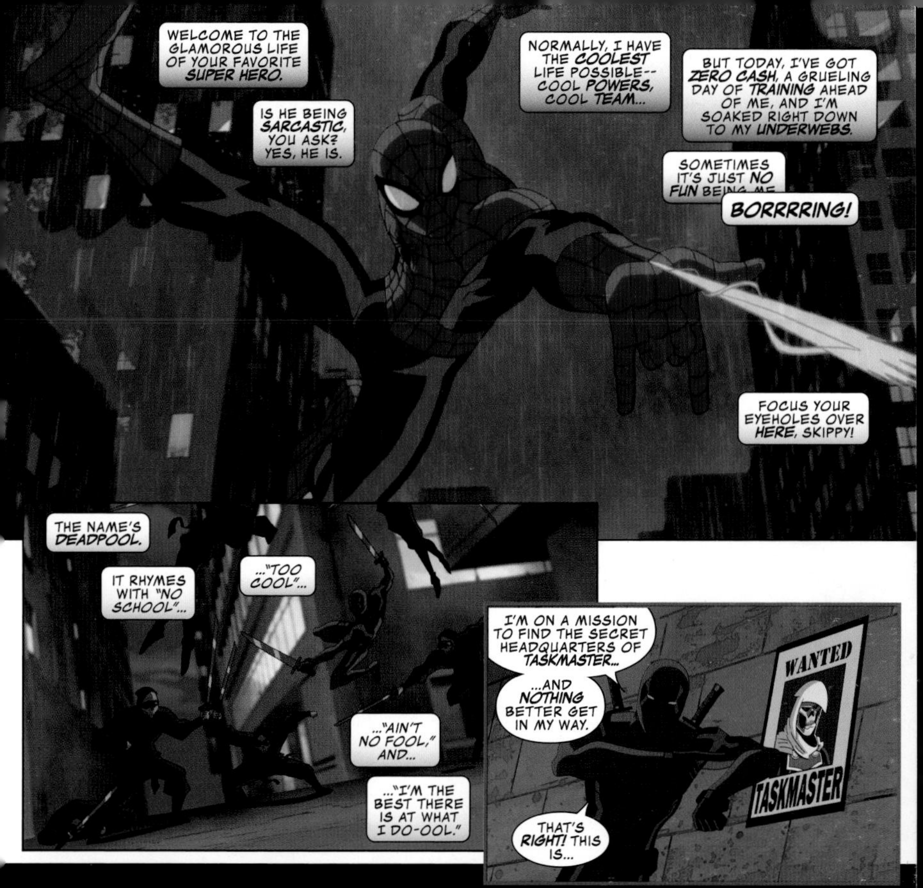
WELCOME TO THE GLAMOROUS LIFE OF YOUR FAVORITE SUPER HERO.
IS HE BEING SARCASTIC, YOU ASK? YES, HE IS.
NORMALLY, I HAVE THE COOLEST LIFE POSSIBLE-- COOL POWERS, COOL TEAM...
BUT TODAY, I'VE GOT ZERO CASH, A GRUELING DAY OF TRAINING AHEAD OF ME, AND I'M SOAKED RIGHT DOWN TO MY UNDERWEBS.
SOMETIMES IT'S JUST NO FUN BEING ME.
BORRRRING!
FOCUS YOUR EYEHOLES OVER HERE, SKIPPY!
THE NAME'S DEADPOOL.
IT RHYMES WITH "NO SCHOOL"...
..."TOO COOL"...
..."AIN'T NO FOOL," AND...
..."I'M THE BEST THERE IS AT WHAT I DO-OOL."
I'M ON A MISSION TO FIND THE SECRET HEADQUARTERS OF TASKMASTER...
...AND NOTHING BETTER GET IN MY WAY.
WANTED
TASKMASTER
THAT'S RIGHT! THIS IS...

# "...THAT TIME I TOOK OVER SPIDER-MAN'S LAME COMIC BOOK AND MADE IT AWWWESSSOME!"

MARVEL

## ULTIMATE DEADPOOL

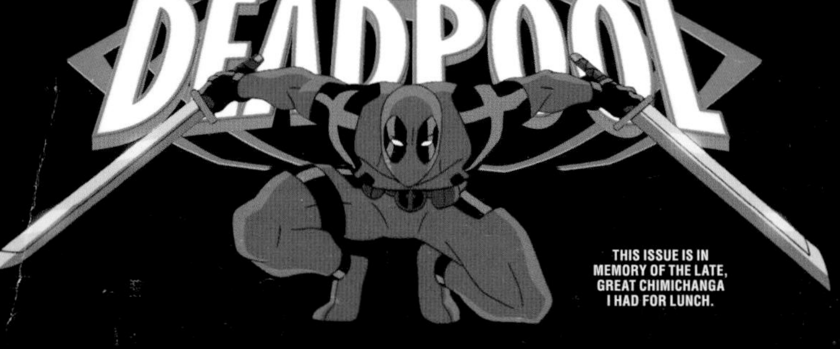

THIS ISSUE IS IN MEMORY OF THE LATE, GREAT CHIMICHANGA I HAD FOR LUNCH.

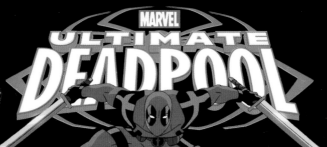

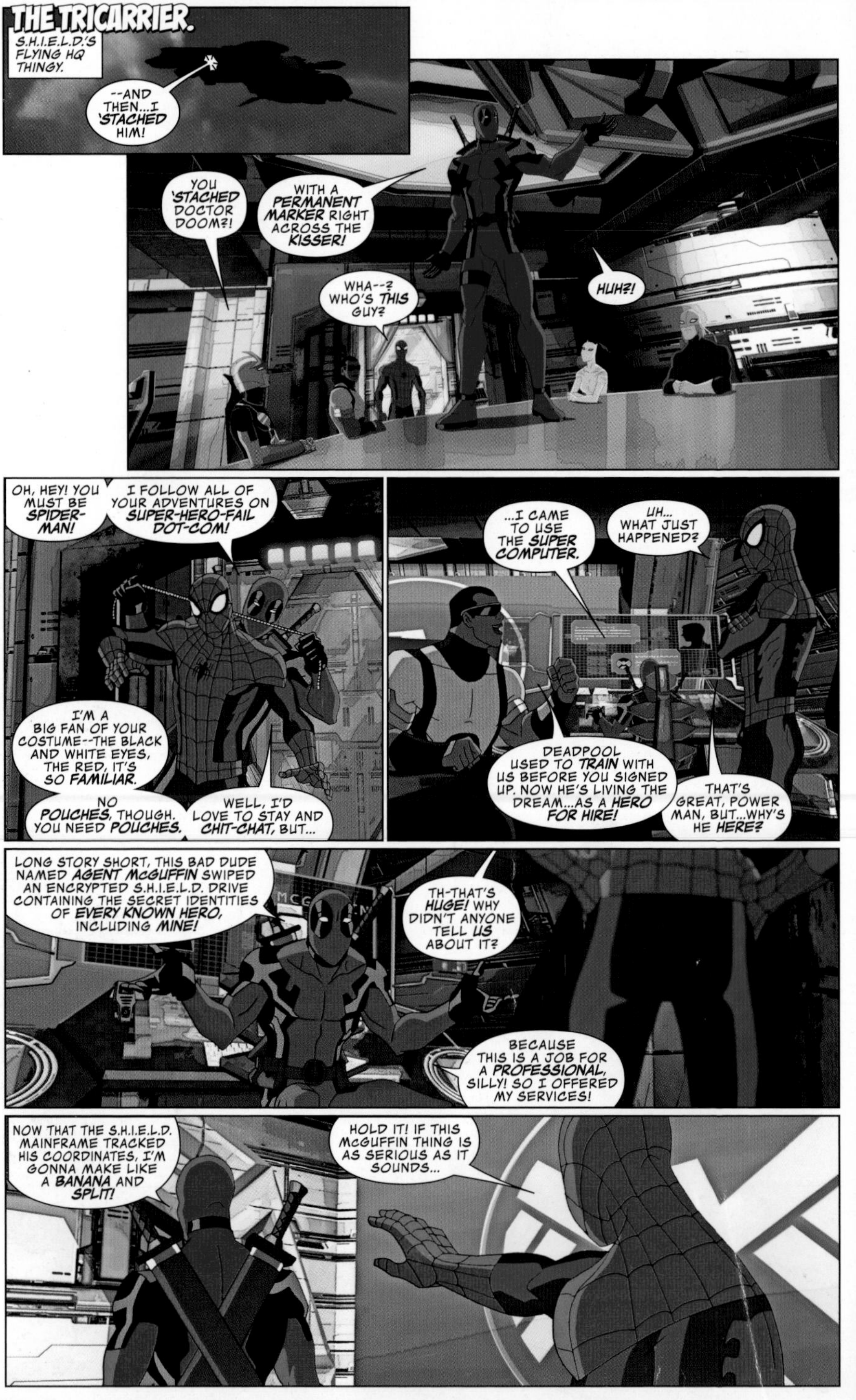
THE TRICARRIER.
S.H.I.E.L.D.'S FLYING HQ THINGY.
--AND THEN...I 'STACHED HIM!
YOU 'STACHED DOCTOR DOOM?!
WITH A PERMANENT MARKER RIGHT ACROSS THE KISSER!
WHA--? WHO'S THIS GUY?
HUH?!
OH, HEY! YOU MUST BE SPIDER-MAN!
I FOLLOW ALL OF YOUR ADVENTURES ON SUPER-HERO-FAIL DOT-COM!
I'M A BIG FAN OF YOUR COSTUME--THE BLACK AND WHITE EYES, THE RED, IT'S SO FAMILIAR.
NO POUCHES, THOUGH. YOU NEED POUCHES.
WELL, I'D LOVE TO STAY AND CHIT-CHAT, BUT...
...I CAME TO USE THE SUPER COMPUTER.
UH... WHAT JUST HAPPENED?
DEADPOOL USED TO TRAIN WITH US BEFORE YOU SIGNED UP. NOW HE'S LIVING THE DREAM...AS A HERO FOR HIRE!
THAT'S GREAT, POWER MAN, BUT...WHY'S HE HERE?
LONG STORY SHORT, THIS BAD DUDE NAMED AGENT McGUFFIN SWIPED AN ENCRYPTED S.H.I.E.L.D. DRIVE CONTAINING THE SECRET IDENTITIES OF EVERY KNOWN HERO, INCLUDING MINE!
TH-THAT'S HUGE! WHY DIDN'T ANYONE TELL US ABOUT IT?
BECAUSE THIS IS A JOB FOR A PROFESSIONAL, SILLY! SO I OFFERED MY SERVICES!
NOW THAT THE S.H.I.E.L.D. MAINFRAME TRACKED HIS COORDINATES, I'M GONNA MAKE LIKE A BANANA AND SPLIT!
HOLD IT! IF THIS McGUFFIN THING IS AS SERIOUS AS IT SOUNDS...

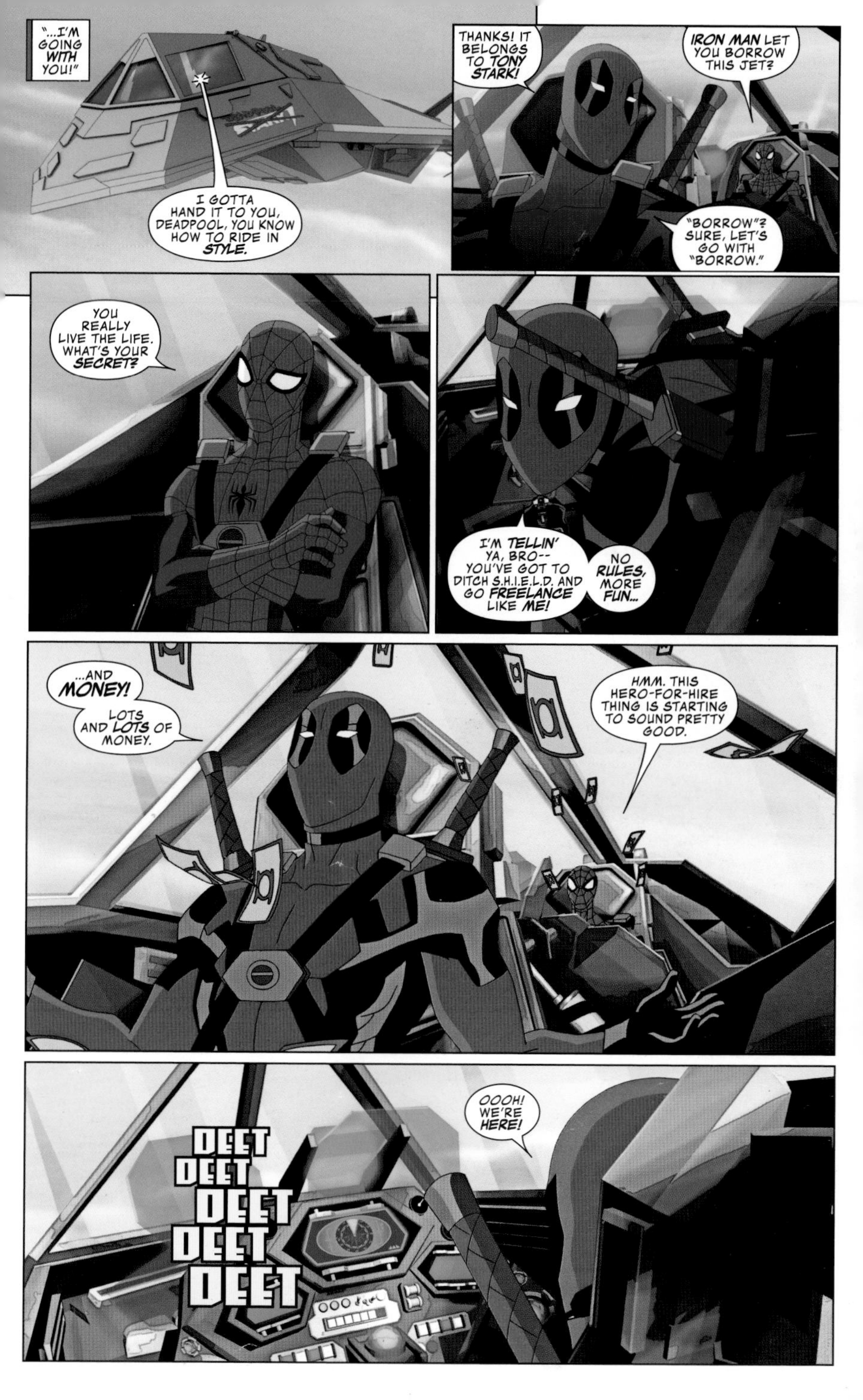
"...I'M GOING WITH YOU!"
I GOTTA HAND IT TO YOU, DEADPOOL, YOU KNOW HOW TO RIDE IN STYLE.
THANKS! IT BELONGS TO TONY STARK!
IRON MAN LET YOU BORROW THIS JET?
"BORROW"? SURE, LET'S GO WITH "BORROW."
YOU REALLY LIVE THE LIFE. WHAT'S YOUR SECRET?
I'M TELLIN' YA, BRO-- YOU'VE GOT TO DITCH S.H.I.E.L.D. AND GO FREELANCE LIKE ME!
NO RULES, MORE FUN...
...AND MONEY!
LOTS AND LOTS OF MONEY.
HMM. THIS HERO-FOR-HIRE THING IS STARTING TO SOUND PRETTY GOOD.
DEET DEET DEET DEET DEET
OOOH! WE'RE HERE!

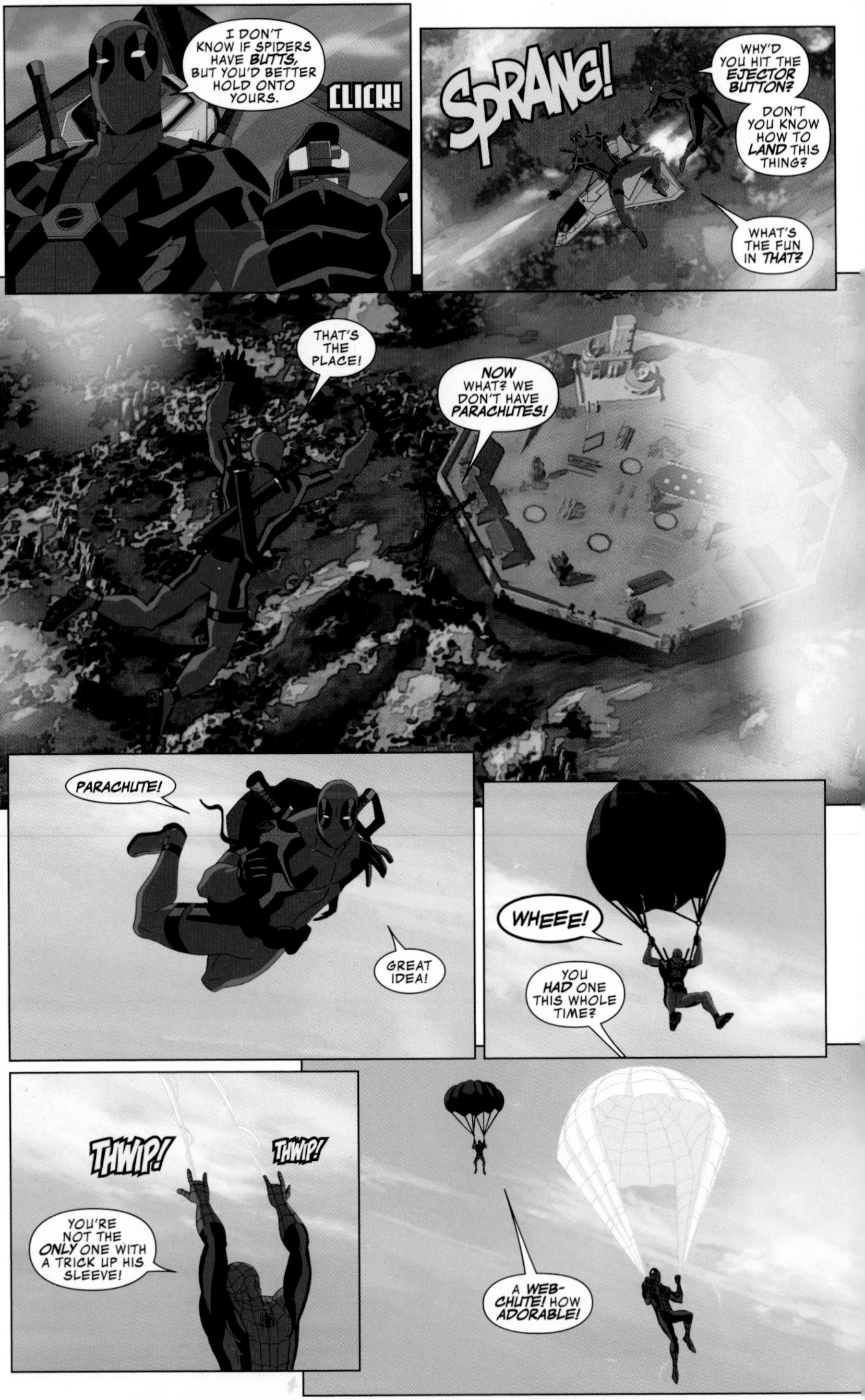
I DON'T KNOW IF SPIDERS HAVE BUTTS, BUT YOU'D BETTER HOLD ONTO YOURS.
CLICK!
SPRANG!
WHY'D YOU HIT THE EJECTOR BUTTON?
DON'T YOU KNOW HOW TO LAND THIS THING?
WHAT'S THE FUN IN THAT?
THAT'S THE PLACE!
NOW WHAT? WE DON'T HAVE PARACHUTES!
PARACHUTE!
GREAT IDEA!
WHEEE!
YOU HAD ONE THIS WHOLE TIME?
THWIP!
THWIP!
YOU'RE NOT THE ONLY ONE WITH A TRICK UP HIS SLEEVE!
A WEB-CHUTE! HOW ADORABLE!

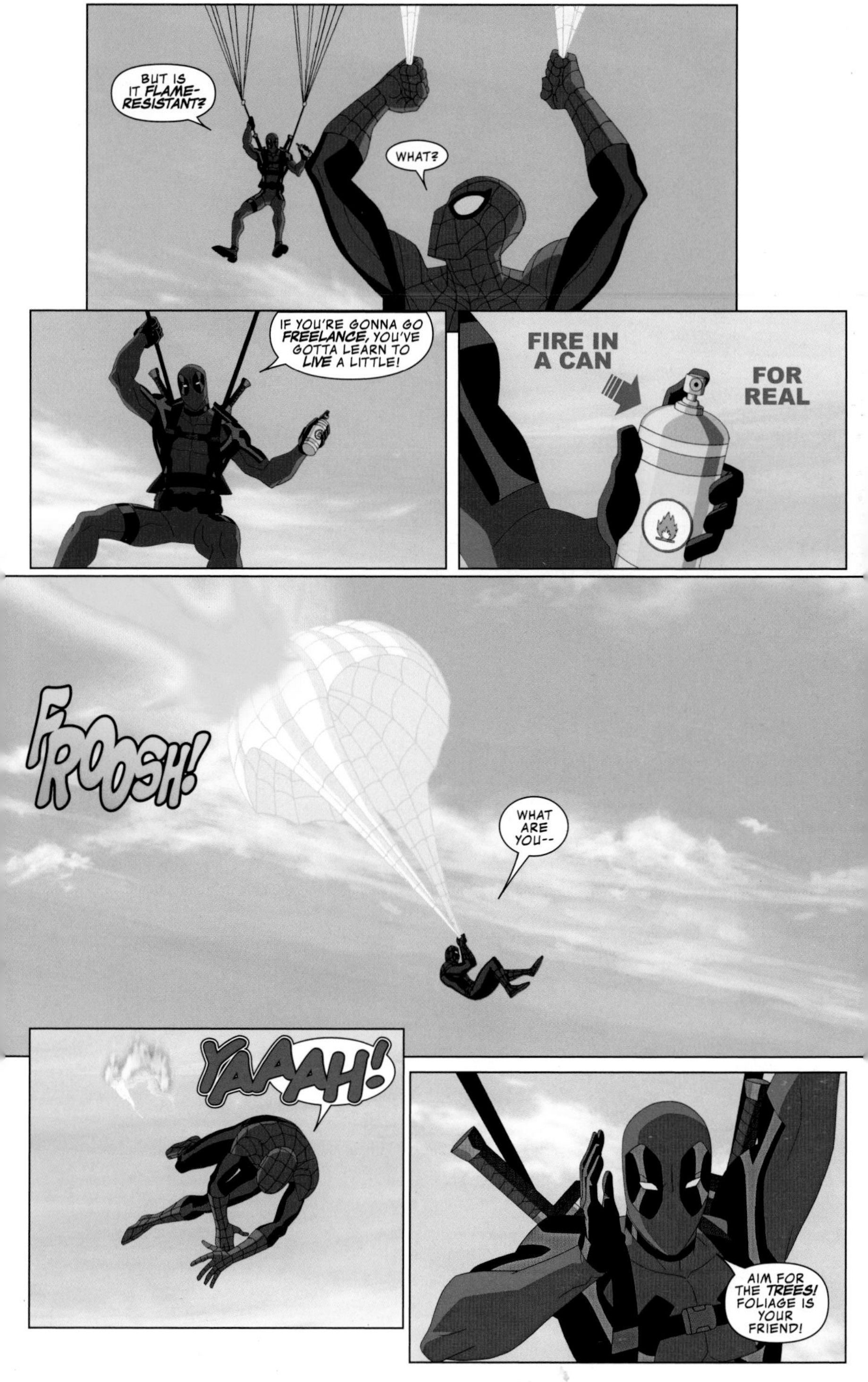
BUT IS IT FLAME-RESISTANT?
WHAT?
IF YOU'RE GONNA GO FREELANCE, YOU'VE GOTTA LEARN TO LIVE A LITTLE!
FIRE IN A CAN
FOR REAL
FROOSH!
WHAT ARE YOU--
YAAAH!
AIM FOR THE TREES! FOLIAGE IS YOUR FRIEND!

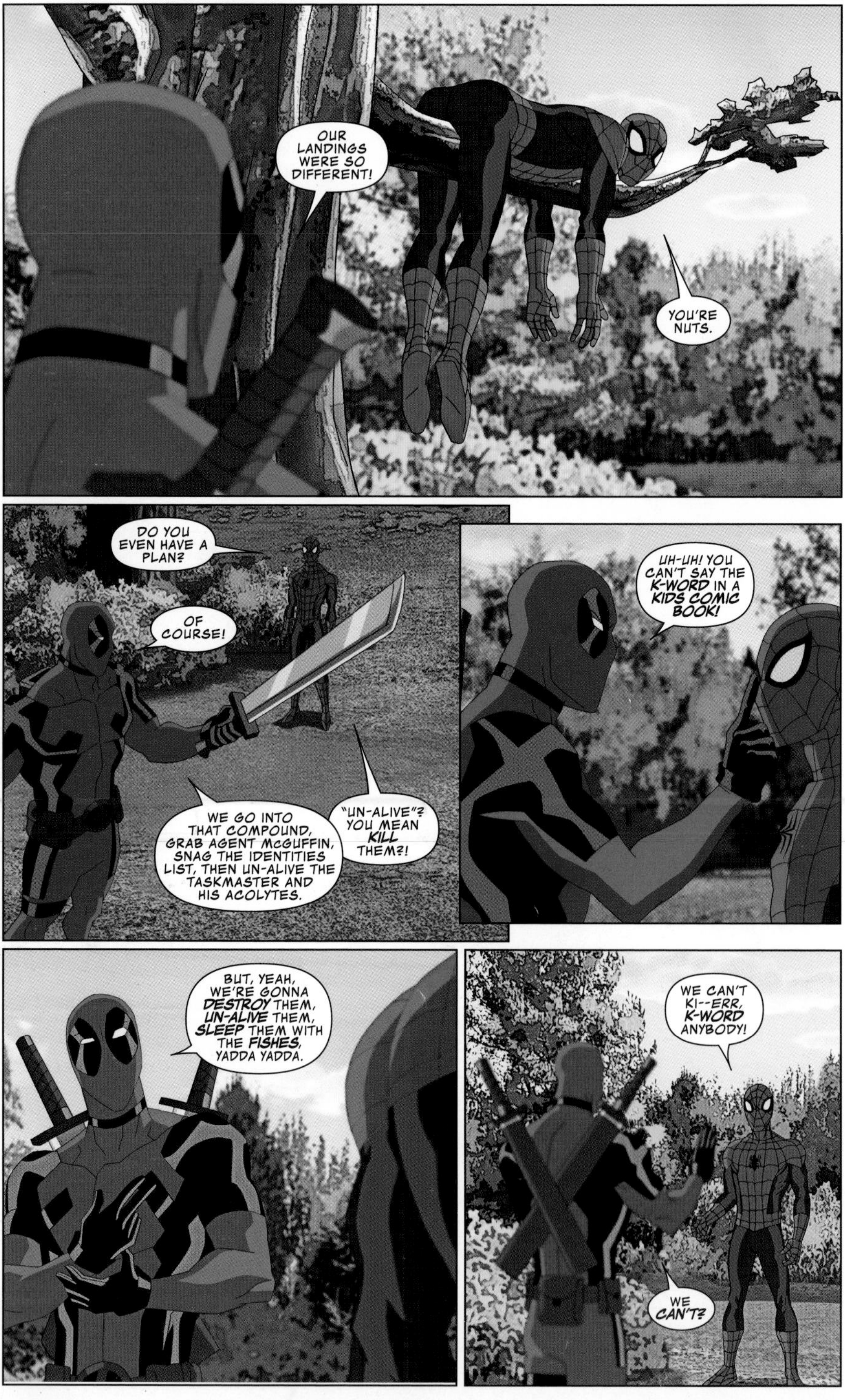
OUR LANDINGS WERE SO DIFFERENT!
YOU'RE NUTS.
DO YOU EVEN HAVE A PLAN?
OF COURSE!
WE GO INTO THAT COMPOUND, GRAB AGENT McGUFFIN, SNAG THE IDENTITIES LIST, THEN UN-ALIVE THE TASKMASTER AND HIS ACOLYTES.
"UN-ALIVE"? YOU MEAN KILL THEM?!
UH-UH! YOU CAN'T SAY THE K-WORD IN A KIDS COMIC BOOK!
BUT, YEAH, WE'RE GONNA DESTROY THEM, UN-ALIVE THEM, SLEEP THEM WITH THE FISHES, YADDA YADDA.
WE CAN'T KI--ERR, K-WORD ANYBODY!
WE CAN'T?

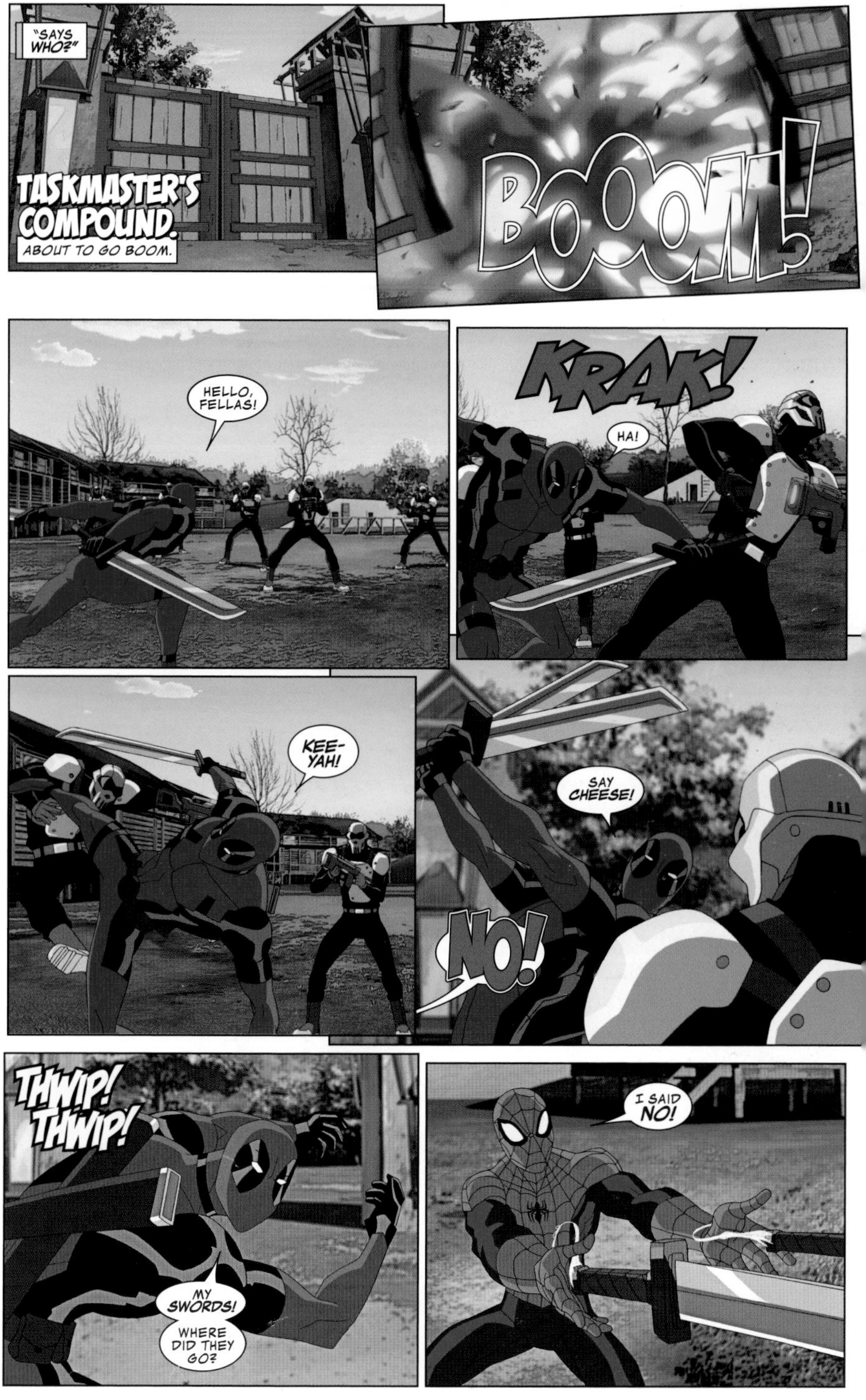
"SAYS WHO?"
TASKMASTER'S COMPOUND.
ABOUT TO GO BOOM.
BOOOM!
HELLO, FELLAS!
KRAK!
HA!
KEE-YAH!
SAY CHEESE!
NO!
THWIP! THWIP!
MY SWORDS!
WHERE DID THEY GO?
I SAID NO!

POW!

HRNN...

NGH...

SEE? SITUATION'S UNDER CONTROL AND NOBODY GOT *K-WORDED!*

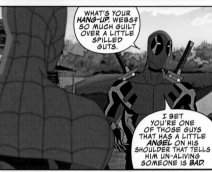

WHAT'S YOUR *HANG-UP,* WEBS? SO MUCH GUILT OVER A LITTLE SPILLED GUTS.

I BET YOU'RE ONE OF THOSE GUYS THAT HAS A LITTLE *ANGEL* ON HIS SHOULDER THAT TELLS HIM UN-ALIVING SOMEONE IS *BAD.*

DON'T LISTEN TO HIM.

FLOOSH!

OH, BUG OFF!

YOU'RE NOT A FREELANCE HERO, YOU'RE A *MERCENARY!*

WHAT'S THE *BIG DEAL?* IF YOU WANNA MAKE THE *BIG BUCKS,* YOU'VE GOTTA BREAK SOME RULES.

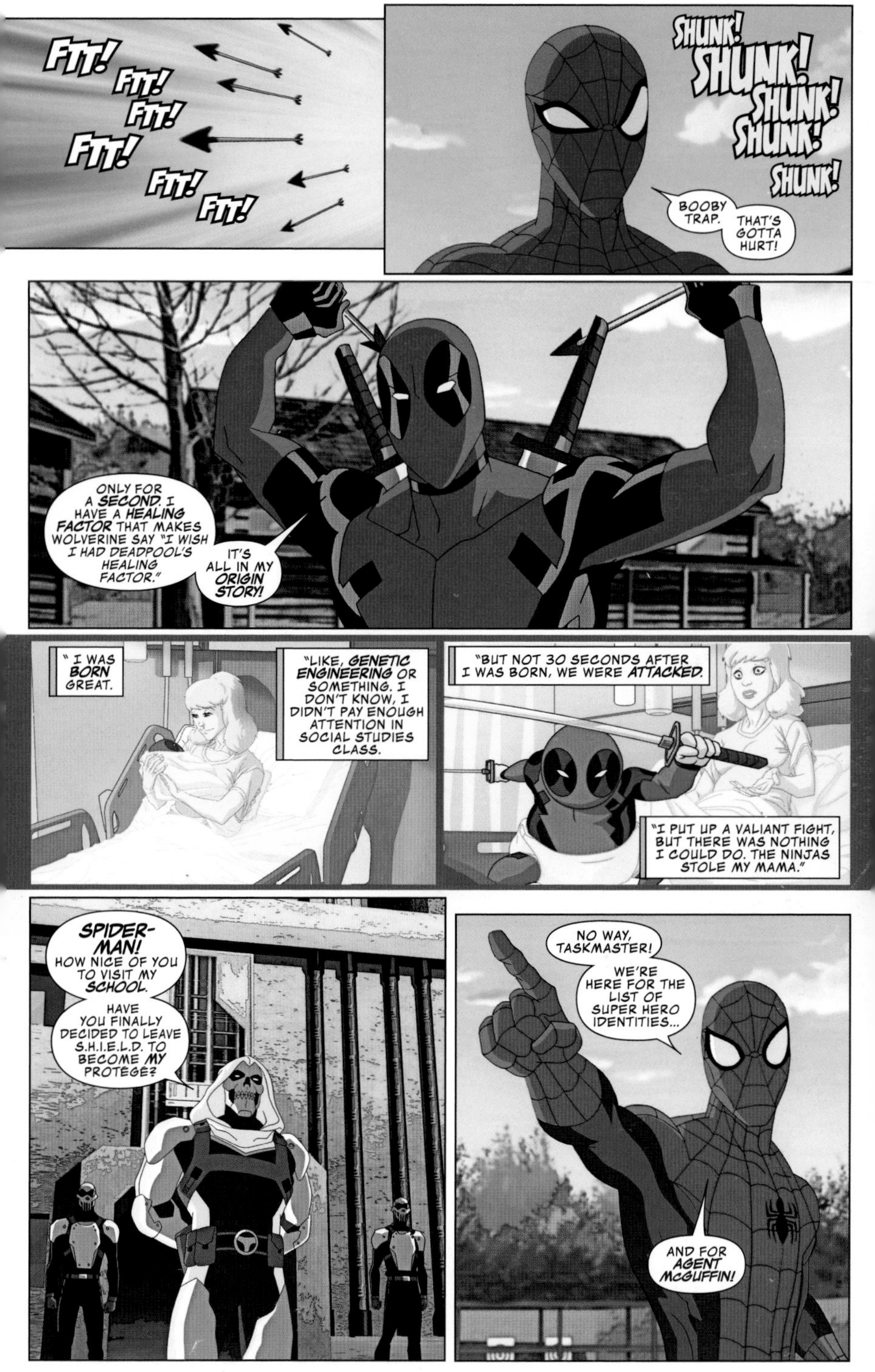

FTT!
FTT!
FTT!
FTT!
FTT!
FTT!
SHUNK!
SHUNK!
SHUNK!
SHUNK!
SHUNK!
BOOBY TRAP.
THAT'S GOTTA HURT!
ONLY FOR A SECOND. I HAVE A HEALING FACTOR THAT MAKES WOLVERINE SAY "I WISH I HAD DEADPOOL'S HEALING FACTOR."
IT'S ALL IN MY ORIGIN STORY!
"I WAS BORN GREAT.
"LIKE, GENETIC ENGINEERING OR SOMETHING. I DON'T KNOW, I DIDN'T PAY ENOUGH ATTENTION IN SOCIAL STUDIES CLASS.
"BUT NOT 30 SECONDS AFTER I WAS BORN, WE WERE ATTACKED.
"I PUT UP A VALIANT FIGHT, BUT THERE WAS NOTHING I COULD DO. THE NINJAS STOLE MY MAMA."
SPIDER-MAN! HOW NICE OF YOU TO VISIT MY SCHOOL.
HAVE YOU FINALLY DECIDED TO LEAVE S.H.I.E.L.D. TO BECOME MY PROTÉGÉ?
NO WAY, TASKMASTER!
WE'RE HERE FOR THE LIST OF SUPER HERO IDENTITIES...
AND FOR AGENT McGUFFIN!

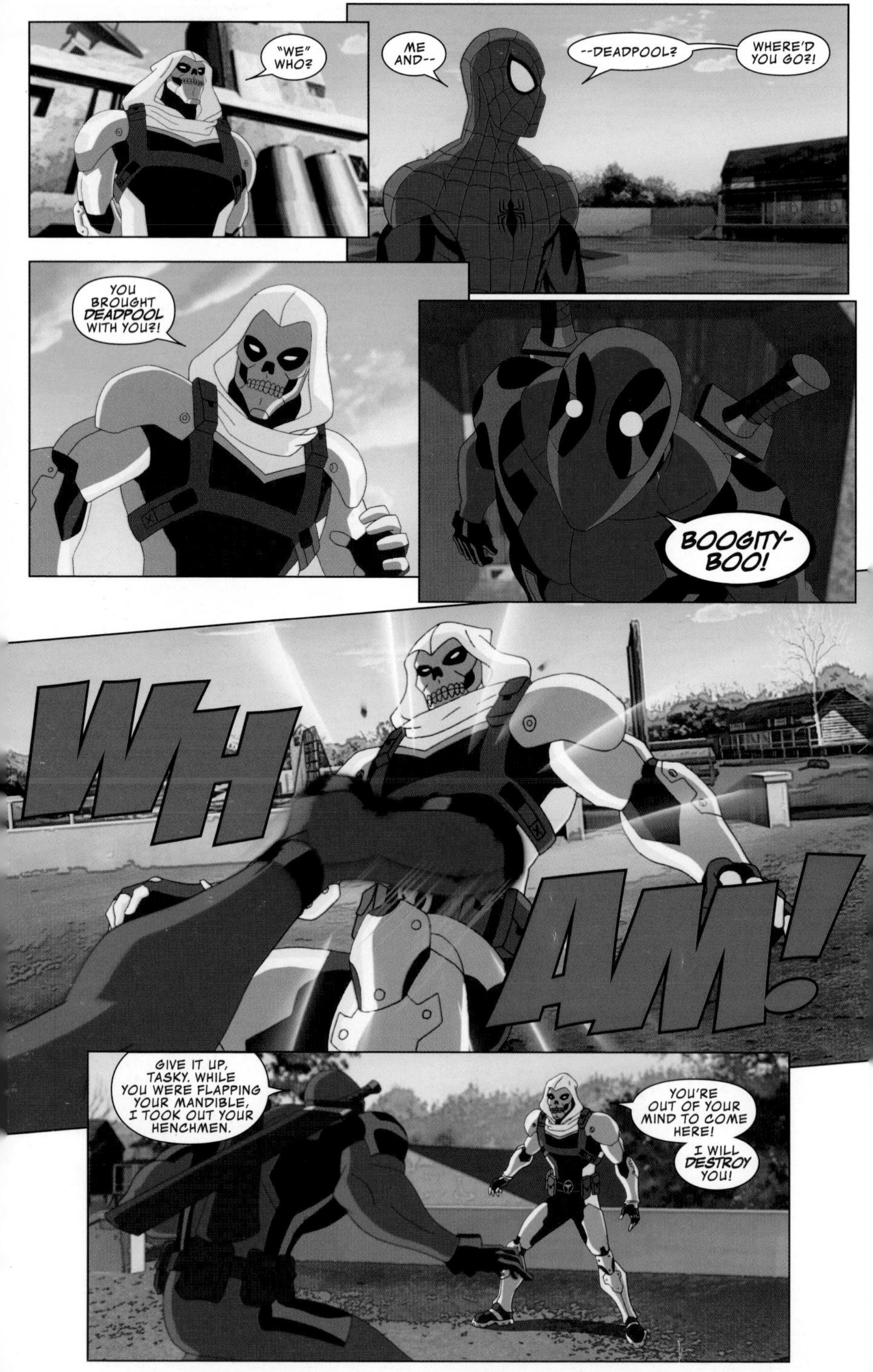
"WE" WHO?
ME AND--
--DEADPOOL?
WHERE'D YOU GO?!
YOU BROUGHT **DEADPOOL** WITH YOU?!
BOOGITY-BOO!
WHAM!
GIVE IT UP, TASKY. WHILE YOU WERE FLAPPING YOUR MANDIBLE, I TOOK OUT YOUR HENCHMEN.
YOU'RE OUT OF YOUR MIND TO COME HERE!
I WILL **DESTROY** YOU!

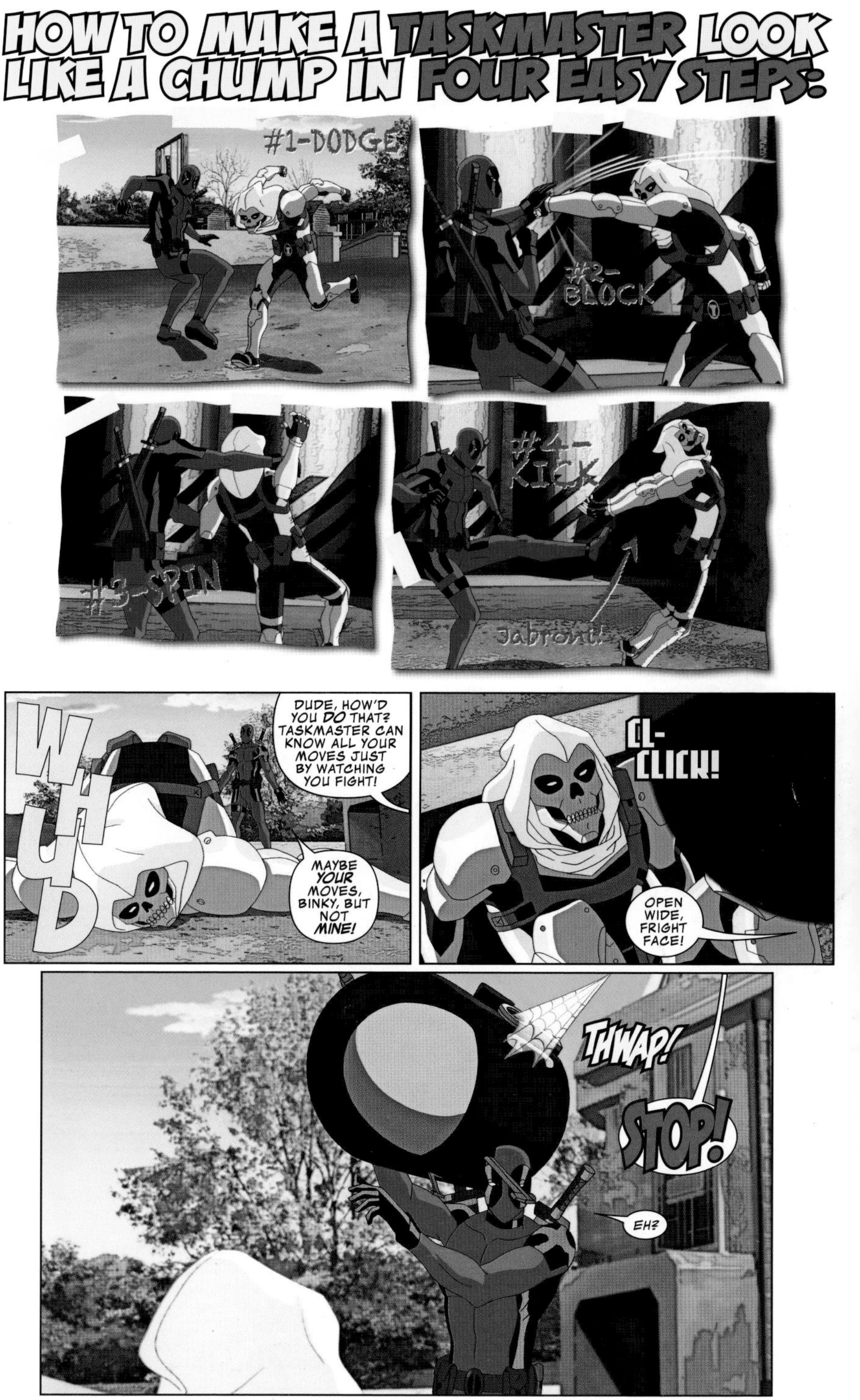
HOW TO MAKE A TASKMASTER LOOK LIKE A CHUMP IN FOUR EASY STEPS:
#1-DODGE
#2-BLOCK
#3-SPIN
#4-KICK
Jabroni!
WHUD
DUDE, HOW'D YOU DO THAT? TASKMASTER CAN KNOW ALL YOUR MOVES JUST BY WATCHING YOU FIGHT!
MAYBE YOUR MOVES, BINKY, BUT NOT MINE!
CL-CLICK!
OPEN WIDE, FRIGHT FACE!
THWAP!
STOP!
EH?

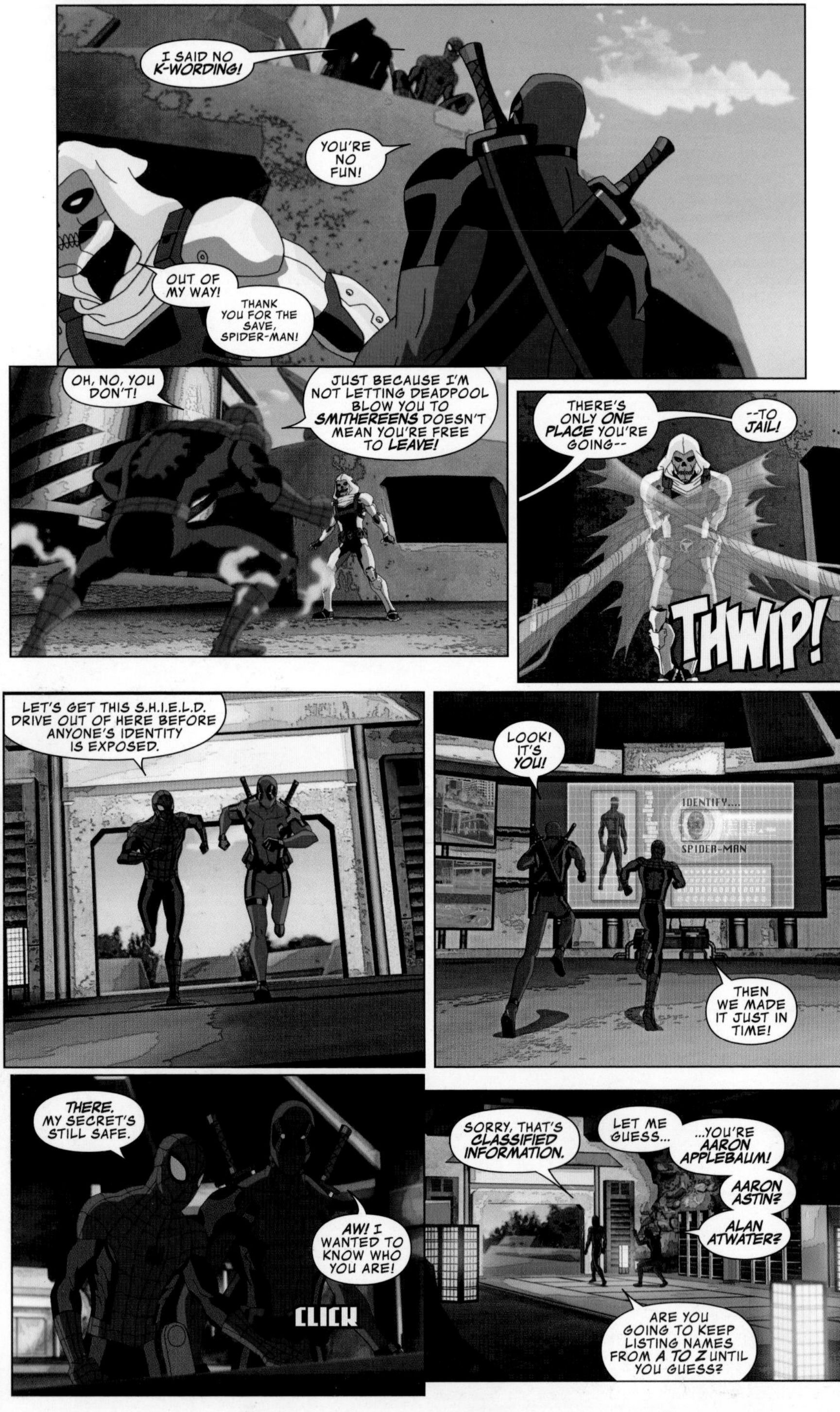
I SAID NO K-WORDING!
YOU'RE NO FUN!
OUT OF MY WAY!
THANK YOU FOR THE SAVE, SPIDER-MAN!
OH, NO, YOU DON'T!
JUST BECAUSE I'M NOT LETTING DEADPOOL BLOW YOU TO SMITHEREENS DOESN'T MEAN YOU'RE FREE TO LEAVE!
THERE'S ONLY ONE PLACE YOU'RE GOING--
--TO JAIL!
THWIP!
LET'S GET THIS S.H.I.E.L.D. DRIVE OUT OF HERE BEFORE ANYONE'S IDENTITY IS EXPOSED.
LOOK! IT'S YOU!
IDENTIFY.....
SPIDER-MAN
THEN WE MADE IT JUST IN TIME!
THERE. MY SECRET'S STILL SAFE.
AW! I WANTED TO KNOW WHO YOU ARE!
CLICK
SORRY, THAT'S CLASSIFIED INFORMATION.
LET ME GUESS...
...YOU'RE AARON APPLEBAUM!
AARON ASTIN?
ALAN ATWATER?
ARE YOU GOING TO KEEP LISTING NAMES FROM A TO Z UNTIL YOU GUESS?

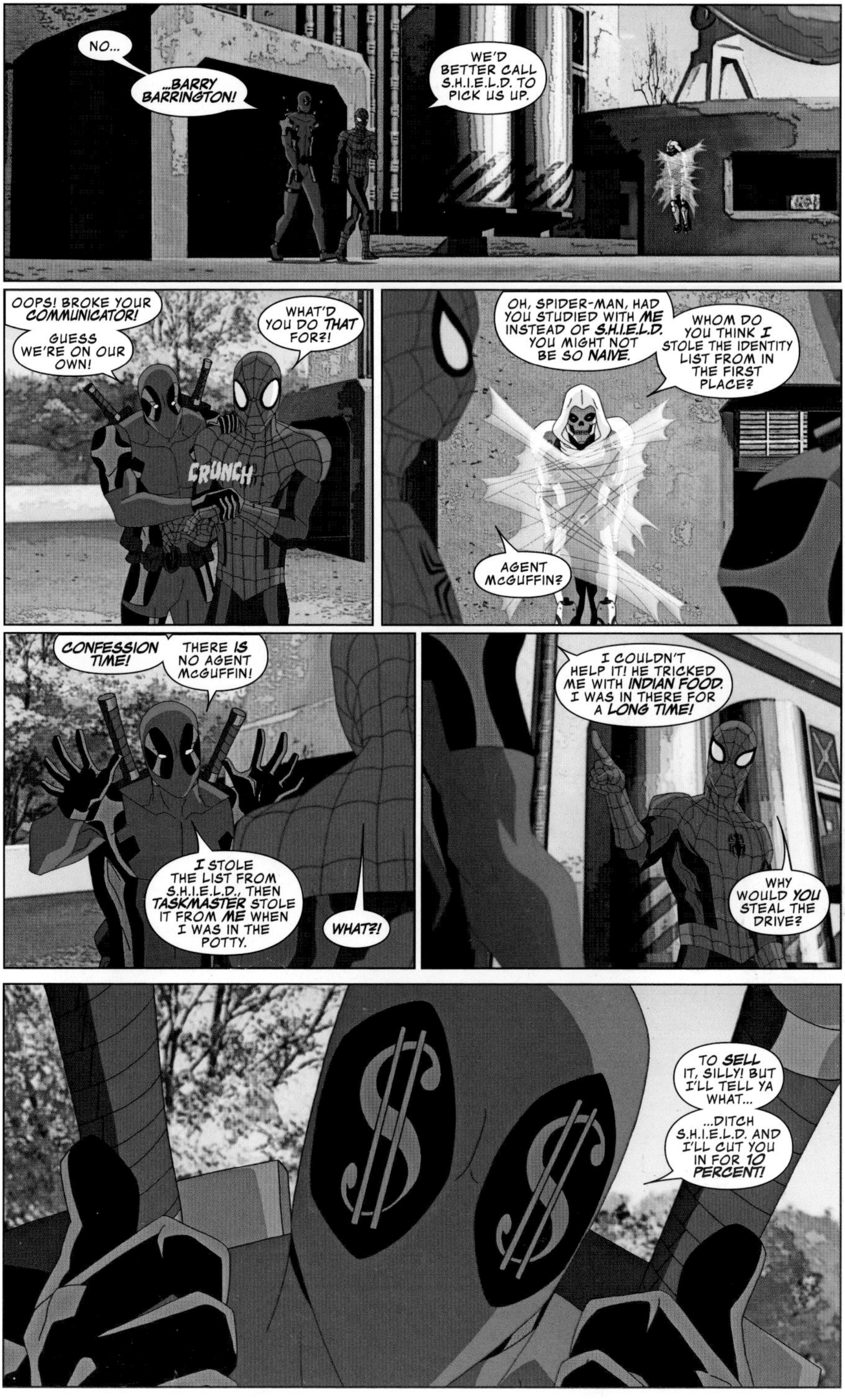
NO...
...BARRY BARRINGTON!
WE'D BETTER CALL S.H.I.E.L.D. TO PICK US UP.
OOPS! BROKE YOUR COMMUNICATOR!
GUESS WE'RE ON OUR OWN!
WHAT'D YOU DO THAT FOR?!
CRUNCH
OH, SPIDER-MAN, HAD YOU STUDIED WITH ME INSTEAD OF S.H.I.E.L.D. YOU MIGHT NOT BE SO NAIVE.
WHOM DO YOU THINK I STOLE THE IDENTITY LIST FROM IN THE FIRST PLACE?
AGENT McGUFFIN?
CONFESSION TIME!
THERE IS NO AGENT McGUFFIN!
I STOLE THE LIST FROM S.H.I.E.L.D., THEN TASKMASTER STOLE IT FROM ME WHEN I WAS IN THE POTTY.
WHAT?!
I COULDN'T HELP IT! HE TRICKED ME WITH INDIAN FOOD. I WAS IN THERE FOR A LONG TIME!
WHY WOULD YOU STEAL THE DRIVE?
TO SELL IT, SILLY! BUT I'LL TELL YA WHAT...
...DITCH S.H.I.E.L.D. AND I'LL CUT YOU IN FOR 10 PERCENT!

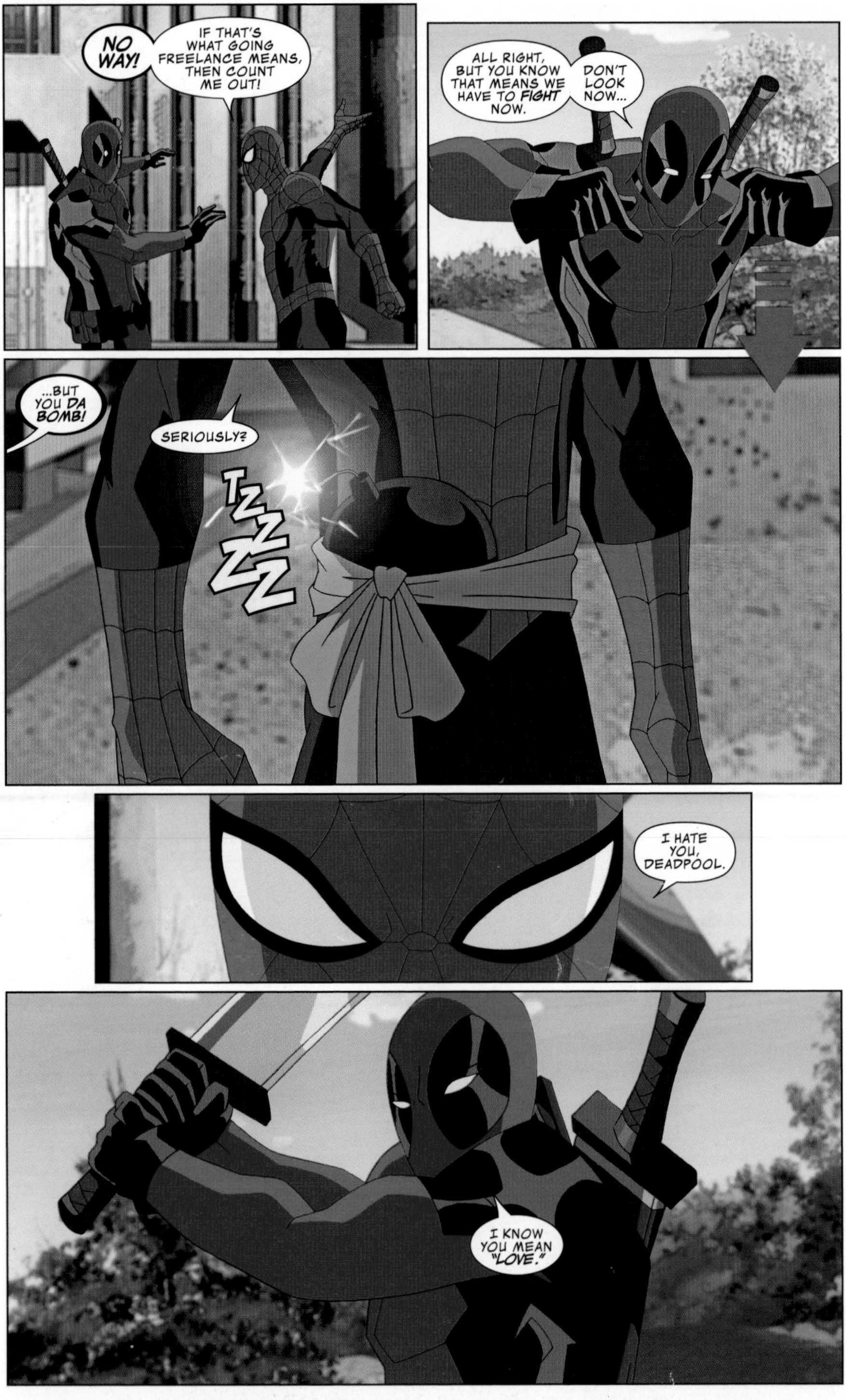
NO WAY!
IF THAT'S WHAT GOING FREELANCE MEANS, THEN COUNT ME OUT!
ALL RIGHT, BUT YOU KNOW THAT MEANS WE HAVE TO FIGHT NOW.
DON'T LOOK NOW...
...BUT YOU DA BOMB!
SERIOUSLY?
TZZZZ
I HATE YOU, DEADPOOL.
I KNOW YOU MEAN "LOVE."

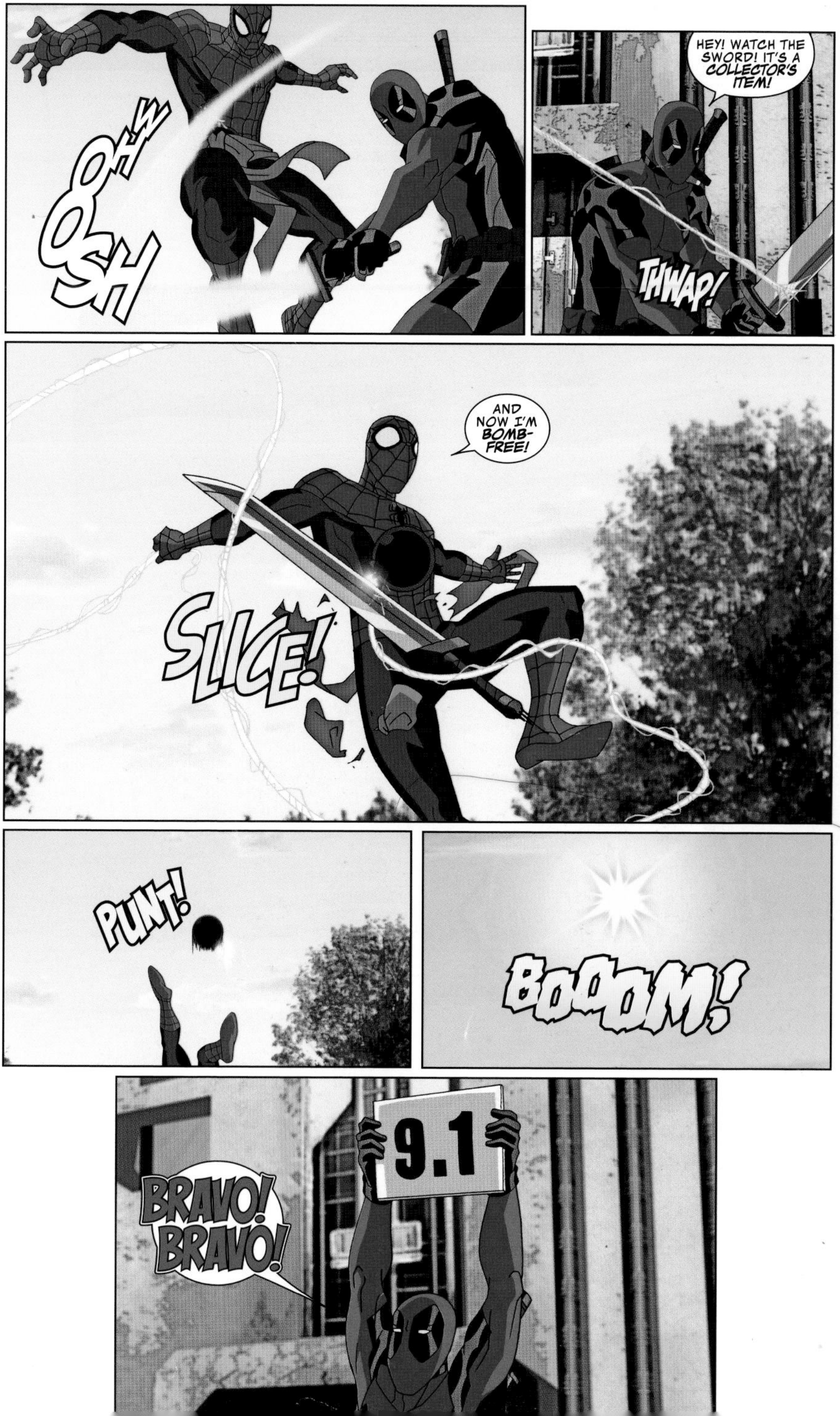
WHOOSH
HEY! WATCH THE SWORD! IT'S A COLLECTOR'S ITEM!
THWAP!
AND NOW I'M BOMB-FREE!
SLICE!
PUNT!
BOOOM!
9.1
BRAVO! BRAVO!

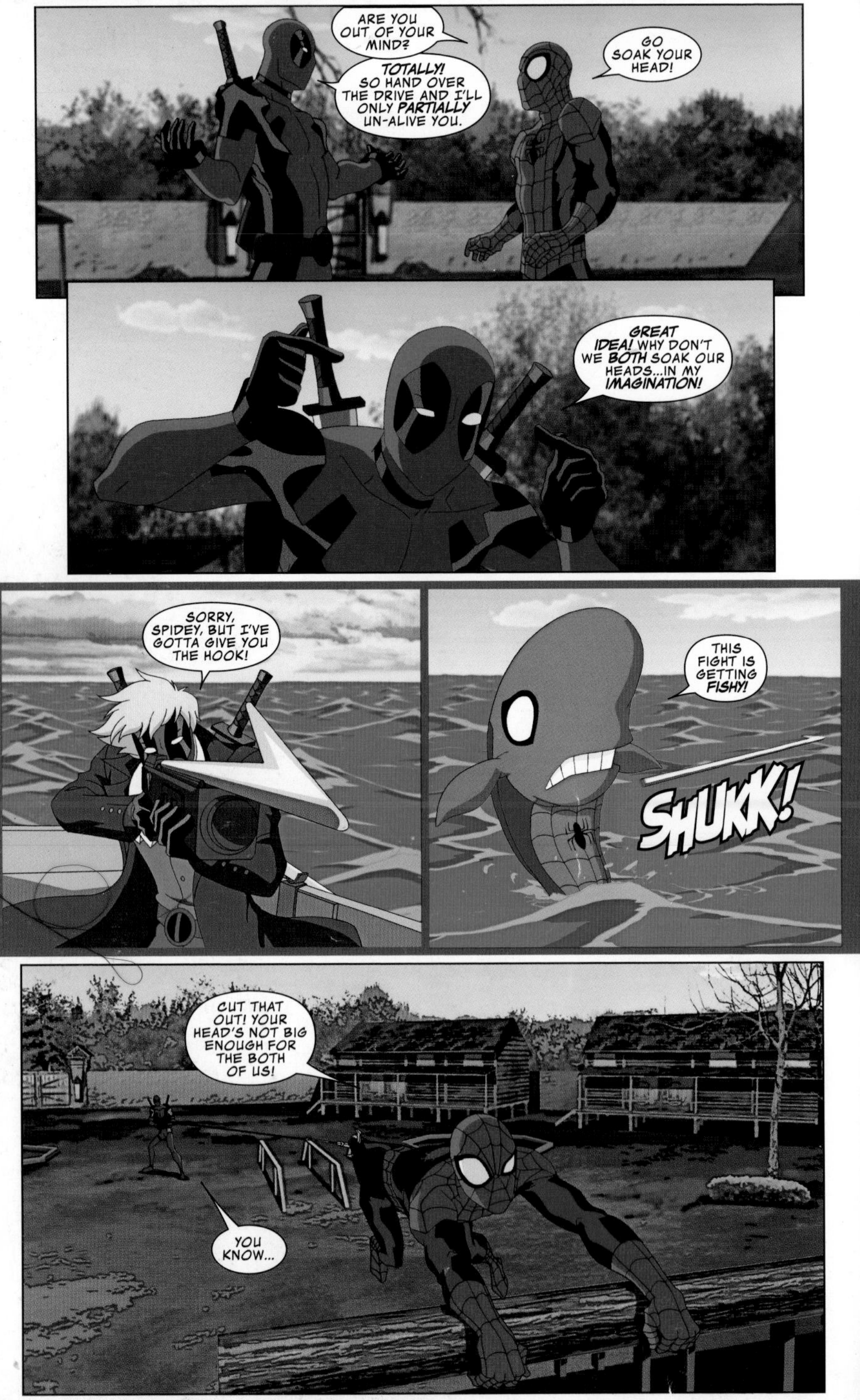

ARE YOU OUT OF YOUR MIND?
TOTALLY! SO HAND OVER THE DRIVE AND I'LL ONLY PARTIALLY UN-ALIVE YOU.
GO SOAK YOUR HEAD!
GREAT IDEA! WHY DON'T WE BOTH SOAK OUR HEADS...IN MY IMAGINATION!
SORRY, SPIDEY, BUT I'VE GOTTA GIVE YOU THE HOOK!
THIS FIGHT IS GETTING FISHY!
SHUKK!
CUT THAT OUT! YOUR HEAD'S NOT BIG ENOUGH FOR THE BOTH OF US!
YOU KNOW...

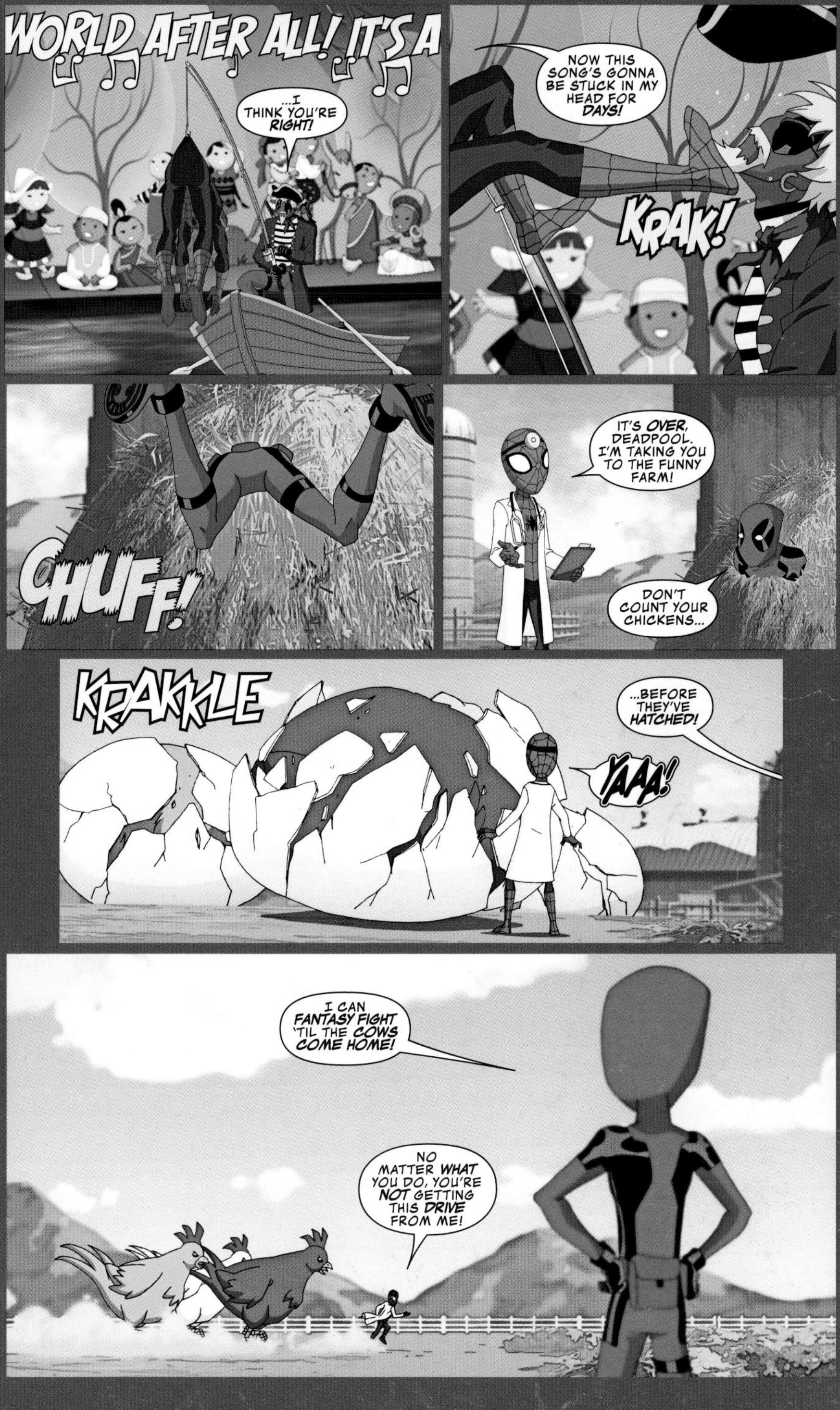
WORLD AFTER ALL! IT'S A
...I THINK YOU'RE RIGHT!
NOW THIS SONG'S GONNA BE STUCK IN MY HEAD FOR DAYS!
KRAK!
CHUFF!
IT'S OVER, DEADPOOL. I'M TAKING YOU TO THE FUNNY FARM!
DON'T COUNT YOUR CHICKENS...
KRAKKLE
...BEFORE THEY'VE HATCHED!
YAAA!
I CAN FANTASY FIGHT 'TIL THE COWS COME HOME!
NO MATTER WHAT YOU DO, YOU'RE NOT GETTING THIS DRIVE FROM ME!

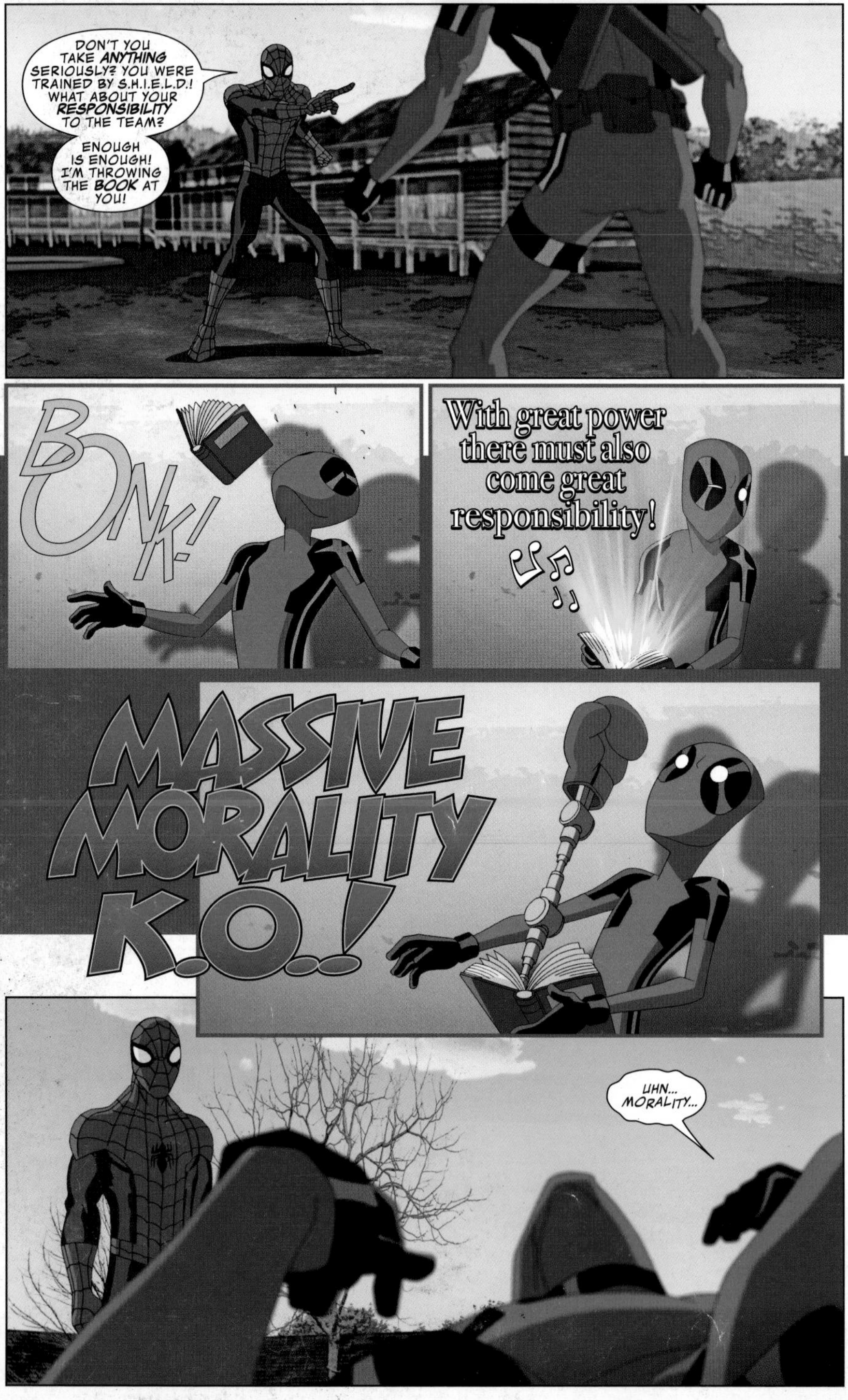
DON'T YOU TAKE ANYTHING SERIOUSLY? YOU WERE TRAINED BY S.H.I.E.L.D.! WHAT ABOUT YOUR RESPONSIBILITY TO THE TEAM?
ENOUGH IS ENOUGH! I'M THROWING THE BOOK AT YOU!
BONK!
With great power there must also come great responsibility!
MASSIVE MORALITY K.O.!
UHN... MORALITY...

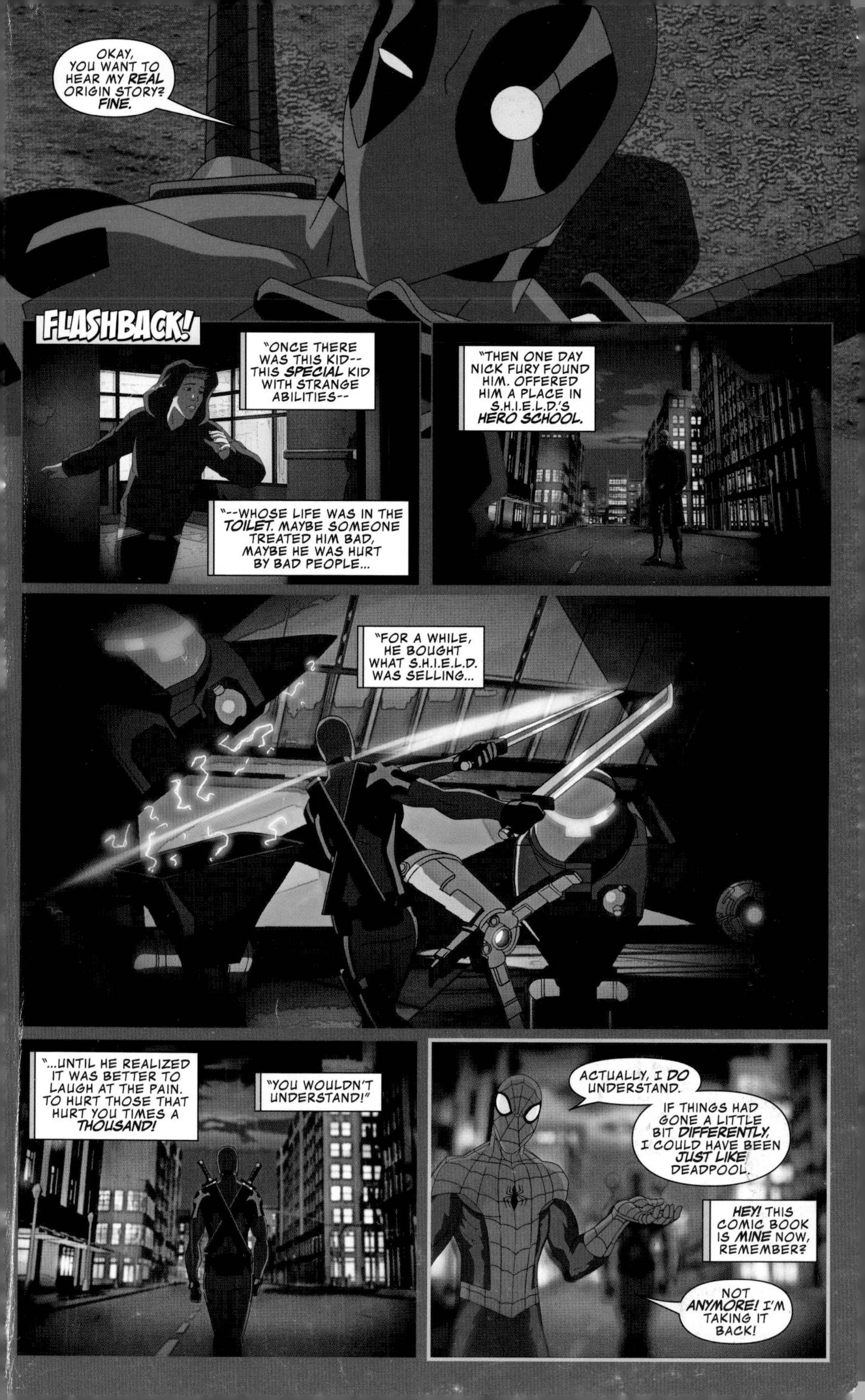
OKAY, YOU WANT TO HEAR MY REAL ORIGIN STORY? FINE.
FLASHBACK!
"ONCE THERE WAS THIS KID-- THIS SPECIAL KID WITH STRANGE ABILITIES--
"--WHOSE LIFE WAS IN THE TOILET. MAYBE SOMEONE TREATED HIM BAD, MAYBE HE WAS HURT BY BAD PEOPLE...
"THEN ONE DAY NICK FURY FOUND HIM. OFFERED HIM A PLACE IN S.H.I.E.L.D.'S HERO SCHOOL.
"FOR A WHILE, HE BOUGHT WHAT S.H.I.E.L.D. WAS SELLING...
"...UNTIL HE REALIZED IT WAS BETTER TO LAUGH AT THE PAIN. TO HURT THOSE THAT HURT YOU TIMES A THOUSAND!
"YOU WOULDN'T UNDERSTAND!"
ACTUALLY, I DO UNDERSTAND.
IF THINGS HAD GONE A LITTLE BIT DIFFERENTLY, I COULD HAVE BEEN JUST LIKE DEADPOOL.
HEY! THIS COMIC BOOK IS MINE NOW, REMEMBER?
NOT ANYMORE! I'M TAKING IT BACK!

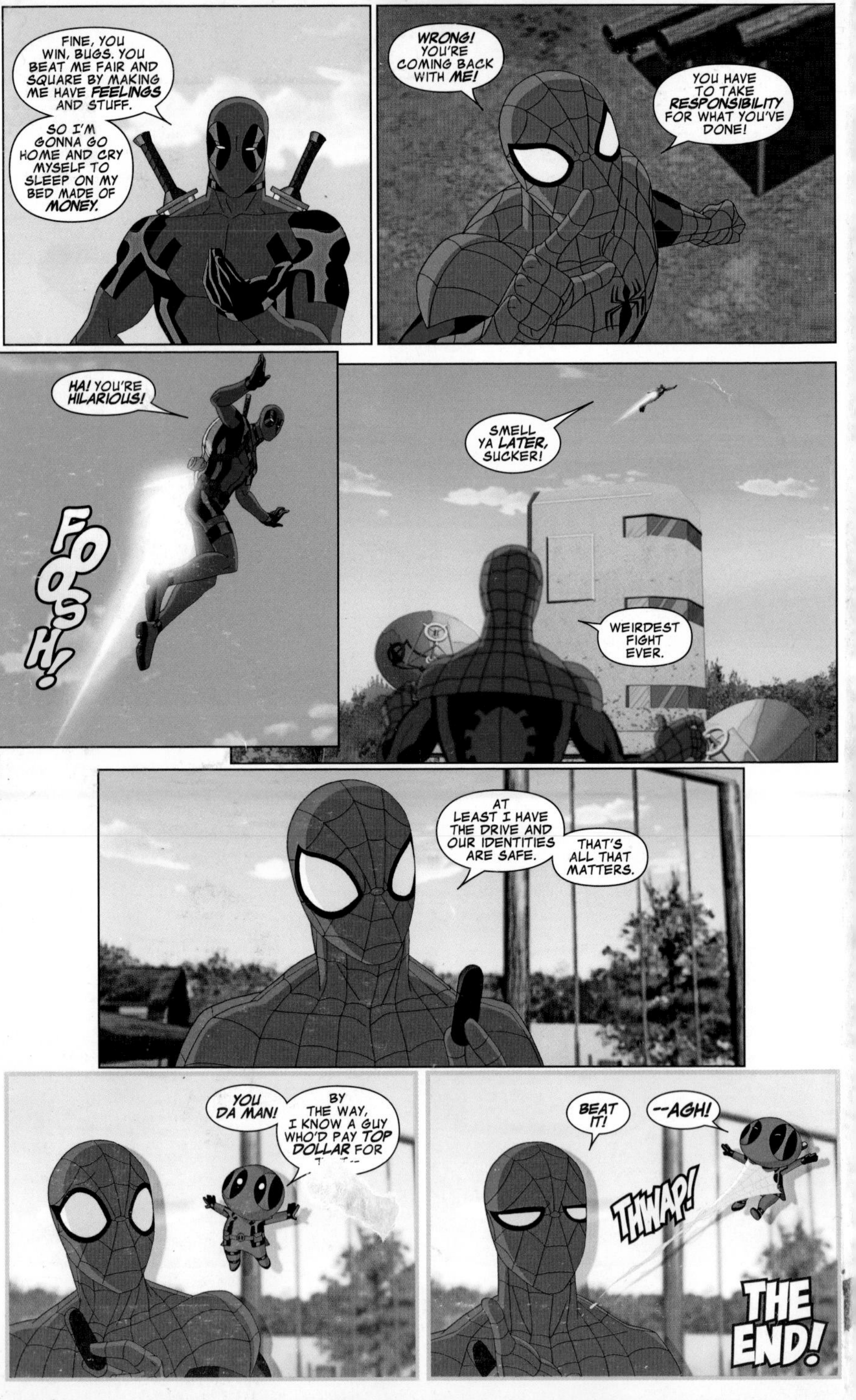

FINE, YOU WIN, BUGS. YOU BEAT ME FAIR AND SQUARE BY MAKING ME HAVE FEELINGS AND STUFF.
SO I'M GONNA GO HOME AND CRY MYSELF TO SLEEP ON MY BED MADE OF MONEY.
WRONG! YOU'RE COMING BACK WITH ME!
YOU HAVE TO TAKE RESPONSIBILITY FOR WHAT YOU'VE DONE!
HA! YOU'RE HILARIOUS!
FOOSH!
SMELL YA LATER, SUCKER!
WEIRDEST FIGHT EVER.
AT LEAST I HAVE THE DRIVE AND OUR IDENTITIES ARE SAFE.
THAT'S ALL THAT MATTERS.
YOU DA MAN!
BY THE WAY, I KNOW A GUY WHO'D PAY TOP DOLLAR FOR
BEAT IT!
--AGH!
THWAP!
THE END!